MW01146977

THE FIRE CHIEF'S DESIRE

A LAKE CHELAN NOVEL

SHIRLEY PENICK

THE FIRE CHIEF'S DESIRE

Photography by Jean Woodfin

Cover Models: Madison Howard and Kyle English

❀ Created with Vellum

CONTACT

Contact me:
www.shirleypenick.com
www.facebook.com/ShirleyPenickAuthor

To sign up for Shirley's New Release Newsletter, send email to shirleypenick@outlook.com, subject newsletter.

ALSO BY SHIRLEY PENICK

LAKE CHELAN SERIES

The Rancher's Lady: A Lake Chelan novella

Hank and Ellen's story

Sawdust and Satin: Lake Chelan #1

Chris and Barbara's story

Designs on Her: Lake Chelan #2

Nolan and Kristen's story

Smokin': Lake Chelan #3

Jeremy and Amber's story

Fire on the Mountain: Lake Chelan #4

Trey and Mary Ann's story

The Fire Chief's Desire: Lake Chelan #5

Greg and Sandy's story

BURLAP AND BARBED WIRE SERIES

A Cowboy for Alyssa: Burlap and Barbed Wire #1

Beau and Alyssa's story

Taming Adam: Burlap and Barbed Wire #2

Adam and Rachel's story

Tempting Chase: Burlap and Barbed Wire #3

Chase and Katie's story

Roping Cade: Burlap and Barbed Wire #4

Cade and Summer's story

To my dear sister Judy,
who passed away during the writing of this book. You were my greatest fan and I will miss your enthusiasm.

You are finally out of the chronic pain
you suffered with for over forty years,
and I know I will see you again on the other side.

Until then, I love you and will miss you every day. Say hi to mom
and dad for me and have fun
with all those dogs and cats!

CHAPTER 1

Greg Jones sat across the table from his best friend Terry Anderson, who was shoveling in fish and chips faster than anyone Greg had ever seen. Even though fish and chips were one of Greg's best sellers at the tavern, he mostly sold food to help dilute the alcohol and hopefully keep people from getting too drunk. He had a deep fryer, so he had lots of choices for the bar's customers as long as they liked deep-fried foods, or pretzels and nuts.

"Did you forget to eat today?" Greg asked and took a drink of his beer. It was late and almost all the patrons had left. The staff was throwing away the empty beer bottles and cleaning up. They had turned on all the lights, so they could wash the tables and scrub the floors after stacking the chairs on the tables.

Terry nodded. "As a matter of fact, yes, I did forget. I had breakfast at mom's B&B this morning and helped with feeding the tourists. Thank God mom has only a couple of people. Then I spent the rest of the day taking my furniture to Chelan to load on the semi."

Now, this was news. Terry had been postponing his trip

since his mother had fallen and had surgery. Greg just lifted one eyebrow in question, they'd been friends for so long they hardly needed words.

"Sandy will be here tomorrow. She just got back from New York tonight. Thankfully, she's going to be able to spend the whole summer here, so I can make my delivery run after all. It would have cost me a fortune to ship all that work."

Terry kept talking but Greg didn't hear another word. His heart had leapt at the idea of Terry's sister, Sandy, coming back for the whole summer. Was he finally going to have the chance to convince Sandy that he wasn't too young for her—now that they were adults? With Terry on the road the whole time he wouldn't be around to provide the ick factor about her dating her younger brother's best friend.

Greg honestly could not think of a better scenario to finally have a chance with Sandy. He'd loved her since middle school, but she'd left town the day she graduated high school and hadn't been back in over fifteen years, except for a rare weekend here and there.

Greg looked up as Terry stopped talking. "Did you want something else to eat?"

Terry finished his beer. "No. I gotta go home to get some sleep. I need to take another load on the barge to Chelan again tomorrow. Oh, and don't forget to assign someone to manage my squad while I'm gone."

"Of course, who do you think would be best?" Greg was the assistant fire chief of their all-volunteer fire department and Terry was one of the squad captains. Greg would need to select someone to take Terry's place. They'd been trying out a couple of guys to see who was ready for the responsibility.

"I think you should give Jennifer a try at it. She's got a good head on her shoulders. The men respect her and she's a quick thinker."

Greg thought about that for a minute. Jennifer was the mayor's admin and was everything Terry had just said. She might be an excellent squad captain. "That's a great idea, I'll call her on her lunch hour tomorrow and see if she's open to it. Want me to come help you load up in the morning? We could do those big hutches."

"Yeah, that would be great. Then we can go by the B&B and see if they need any help." Terry sighed. "I hate to ask, but Janet's dirt-bag husband rolled into town today, so if she wants to stay safe, she can't go be with mom tomorrow."

Greg frowned, everyone assumed Janet's husband knocked her around. But Terry's younger sister would never say a word about that possibility. "Say no more. I'll be happy to sit with your mom until Sandy gets into town. She'll be here early afternoon—if she's bringing her car—and then you can take her place on the barge's return trip."

"Yeah. I really appreciate you helping, Greg."

"Don't you worry about that. I plan to keep an eye on your mom while you're gone."

"Great. I'm going home, got a couple of things I need to do before hitting the hay. See you in the morning."

Greg sat there thinking for a moment, recounting the half-dozen times he'd seen Sandy since she'd left for college fifteen years before. She'd come back six years ago when the town had wanted to use the game she'd developed—and was creating—to draw tourists. It had worked, too. Their town was doing well as the birthplace and setting for the *Adventures with Tsilly* game. They'd been going under fast before Sandy's mom, Carol—who'd been the mayor—had called the town meeting. He'd almost told Sandy how he felt back then, he'd kind of hinted at it, but it had gone completely over her head, so he'd chickened out.

Greg had danced with Sandy at a wedding a couple of years ago. He'd escorted Mabel Erickson—everyone's third grade teacher, who was well into her eighties—to the wedding in Colorado. She'd been determined to attend so he'd flown with her into Denver and then rented a car for the two-hour drive to Spirit Lake.

He was lost in memories when his dishwasher came out to get Terry's dishes. "We're about finished here, boss."

Greg looked up—and sure enough—nearly everything was done. How long had he been sitting there thinking, remembering, planning? Standing, Greg got out of the way, so the staff could finish cleaning his table and the floor underneath. "Thanks guys, go ahead and leave. I'll close up."

Once everyone was out, Greg locked the door and turned off all the lights except for the one behind the bar. He took out a clean shot glass and poured himself a shot of Jameson's. He chuckled. "Only one, don't want to do anything stupid."

He ran a finger down his forearm. "Like get her name tattooed on my arm. In big-ass letters." Greg's laugh was a mirthless one. "Had a hell of a time covering it up too. Dumbass."

He washed out his glass and put the bottle back in the liquor rack. Staring sightlessly into his bar he ran his hand over the tat again. "Damn, but it will be good to see her again. Come on home, Sandy darlin'."

SANDY ANDERSON DROVE off the ferry with a sigh. Ah, home sweet home. Or at least it would be for the next few months. She hadn't lived in this little town since she'd gone off to college in Seattle, other than short holiday breaks or a long weekend.

But this would be different, her mom needed help, and she would be able to run her mom's B&B while at the same time trying to keep her mother from doing too much, so she could heal. Keeping her mom occupied—but off her feet—was probably the hardest part of the equation. Her mother, Carol Anderson, the former mayor of their town, did not like sitting. She was a go-getter, and letting someone else run her B&B was going to be a hard pill for her to swallow. Even if it was her daughter—maybe especially since it was her daughter.

Sandy parked on the street in front of the house and noted how pretty it was. Her mom had made their old house—a Queen Anne Victorian—look new, so people enjoyed staying there. It was a nice alternative to the big new resort on the lake, and also the remodeled motel closer to the pier. The B&B was painted a medium dusty blue with white window trim, white gingerbread, and a darker blue on the shutters, accents, steps, and front door. With the many windows and wraparound porch, it was very homey.

Sandy grabbed her purse and laptop case and started for the front door; she would move her car and bring in the luggage later. For now, she wanted to see how her mom was. Since she had been in New York during the surgery, she still felt uneasy. Terry and Janet had done an excellent job of texting her, so she knew what was happening every minute. But she'd been distracted and worried. Finally, right before she had to go on the talk show, she'd gotten the word that her mother was out of surgery and it had gone well. If the talk show hadn't specifically asked for the inventor of the game to appear, Sandy would have left the interview in the hands of one of her team members.

Even though Janet and Terry had continued to call and text her with reassurances that their mom was doing fine, Sandy needed to see that with her own two eyes. She strode up the sidewalk where tulips bordered both sides and up the steps to the porch with all the flower boxes. Such a lovely and welcoming walk on a pretty day.

As she neared the door her mother's voice cried out from the parlor window, "No, no I can't take anymore!"

A man's voice rumbled, low and mocking, but Sandy couldn't hear the words. She hurried up to the door her hand automatically reaching in her purse for the pepper spray. She snuck in the door as she heard her mom say, "No more. Have mercy, I'm an old lady."

Damn, she couldn't use pepper spray near her mom. Sandy quietly dropped her purse and laptop and looked around for another weapon. Ah, the fireplace poker, she moved to it and clutched it. Lifting it high above her head she charged into the parlor.

And practically skidded to a halt when she saw her mom propped up with pillows on the chaise, a cold glass of lemonade in her hand and Greg Jones—her brother's best friend—sitting opposite gathering up the cards, from what looked like a game of rummy.

"Going to whack me for beating your mom at rummy?" Greg asked lifting an eyebrow with a grin slowly sliding over his face. "You look like Kalar, the warrior woman."

Lowering her weapon, Sandy could feel her face turning red, while she tried to get her brain to engage her mouth to say something. Anything would do, but something witty would be a miracle. Coming face to face with Greg when thinking she was saving her mom from an attacker was enough to make any woman lose their train of thought. Greg was quite a hunk with his dark hair and piercing blue eyes; his body was pure muscle.

Finally, she said, "You play my game, Greg?"

"Of course. All of us do, so we can interact with the tourists. And Kalar, is hot."

The game did depict Kalar as a strong, sexy, warrior woman. Sandy flushed thinking he'd just compared her to the Kalar character. Did Greg think she was strong and sexy?

With nothing to say about that, Sandy rushed over to give her mom a kiss. "Mom, how are you? I'm so sorry I couldn't get here sooner."

Carol Anderson patted her daughter's arm. "Nonsense, you were mid-release and in New York. I had Joann record the interview. You looked great and very professional. And you did well deflecting the questions away from the real release problems."

Sandy knew her smile was weak, but it's all she could muster. "Yeah, we don't want the world to know about the sabotage."

"Sabotage? Is that why you didn't launch before Christmas like normal?" Greg asked.

Dammit she shouldn't go around spouting out that information, her company didn't want anyone to know what had happened. "Oh, um, this has to stay in this room, Greg."

"Of course, do I need to sign a non-disclosure agreement for this conversation? I could write one up."

"No. Sorry, Greg. I didn't mean to imply you would blab. No, an NDA is not needed. It's just with the game being sabotaged we're all a little on edge." She slumped into a chair and kicked off her shoes.

Sandy sighed. "One of our supposed interns snuck pornography into the game. Lots of porn, which was very well hidden and never showed in debug mode, so it was hard to find. As it turns out he wasn't the college kid we thought he was."

Sandy shook her head at the way the guy had played them. "He found a student we were talking to, that needed to go back home—right before the semester ended—for a family emergency. The hacker compromised the kid's school records, so we sent communication about the internship to him. We still aren't sure who he really is. The police and private investigators are continuing to track him, eight months later."

Greg's eyebrows shot nearly to his hairline. "Wow, that's crazy! I didn't realize your game would warrant that kind of attention."

"Yeah we were pretty surprised ourselves. It took us months to find all the places he hid the pictures and what commands invoked them. Then we had to test the crap out of it to make sure we missed nothing. But it's finally clean and released, so I could make it home. I can easily telecommute for the summer, since we are only brainstorming the next version."

Carol spoke up, "Well, you didn't need to rush here, anyway. I'll be just fine in a day or two."

"Mom! Terry and Janet both said the doctor told you a *minimum* of four weeks off the leg, and then easing back into it."

Carol grimaced. "Oh, Sandy that's just silly. That young doctor is simply a worry wart, and your brother and sister are no better." She waved a hand at the man watching. "Even Greg was assigned to babysit me until you got here, since Terry is in Chelan and Janet is home with Brett."

Her mother's attitude was exactly as Sandy suspected it to be, which is why she knew the hard part of this job would be convincing her mom to take it easy. She said exasperatedly, "Mom…"

Carol didn't back down and said in the exact tone of voice, "Sandy…"

CHAPTER 2

Greg cringed as the two strong women readied for a battle of wills. He stood and said, "I think this is my cue to leave. Good to have you back in town, Sandy."

"Chicken?" Sandy challenged.

Greg let out a chuckle. "Hell, yes. I'm not getting between you two. My mama didn't raise no fool. Miz Carol, it was a pleasure beating you at Rummy."

"Oh, you stinker!" Carol said as Greg leaned down to kiss her cheek.

He turned to Sandy and said, "Do you want me to bring in your suitcases?"

"No need, I only brought one suitcase. I leave lots of clothes in my room for quick visits, so I didn't bring many of my 'city' clothes."

Greg was surprised by that. She didn't come home very often. More so since the town had started using her game to promote tourism a few years ago, but still. "Come into the bar some night and tell us all about this newest release. We need to have the scoop before the tourists get here. Knowing which of your stories are in this version gives us a head start on playing the game, too. Don't wait too long, though. I think my copy will be here in a week."

"Sandy," her mom said, "You could go on Wednesday. That's my book club night and I'll have plenty of company."

"I will, if you're feeling good enough. Thanks for looking in on mama, Greg."

"My pleasure, see you lovely ladies later. I'll let myself out."

As Greg ambled through town he thought about Sandy, she was still so beautiful to him, with her long blond hair, blue eyes, and killer body. But today? Wow, just wow! With fire in her eyes and weapon raised to protect her mom, she had knocked his socks off and taken the breath right out of his lungs.

Fortunately, she had been too shocked that nothing bad was happening, to notice his reaction to her appearance and he'd recovered quickly. He sure hoped he would be able to spend some time with her this summer. With Terry out of the way maybe he could convince her to look at him as someone other than her younger brother's best friend.

He wondered if there was something he could do to help with the sabotage issue. He had some connections from back when he was in law school. But the game company she worked for was huge and probably had plenty of fire power. He shrugged, he was only a lowly bartender now, so any help he could give was probably minimal.

He hoped Sandy would come in on Wednesday. Terry would be out of town by then, so maybe, just maybe, he could start his 'Win Sandy' campaign. The last time they'd spent any significant time in the same town, he'd been in high school. Back then the three-year age gap had been insurmountable, but now that they were both adults it was nothing. At least that's the way he saw it. He hoped Sandy would see it that way, too.

Greg was going to give it his best shot, and not let her get away again, without her knowing exactly how he felt about her. Sandy might not feel the same way he did—in the end—but she wouldn't be in the dark any longer.

He thought back to the conversation they'd had six years ago. She'd been in town to work on the amusement park and had come into his bar. After they'd been there for a while, they'd all started dancing.

Greg had cut in on Terry who was dancing with Sandy. "My turn, she's probably tired of you stepping on her feet."

"Hey, I do not..." Terry started to say, but Greg deftly swung Sandy away from her brother.

"Ah, now I have you all alone," he'd said with a mocking sinister tone of voice.

Sandy rolled her eyes, "Right. On a crowded dance floor, in a crowded bar."

"Well, as alone as we can get in this place. Damn, it's good to have you back in town, Sandy."

"Thanks, Greg, I have to admit I've missed it. I didn't know how much I missed it, until I got here."

He twirled her around. "Yeah. So, how are you? Do you have a boyfriend back in Seattle?"

"There's a guy named Peter I go out with sometimes. He's one of the developers on the game. Nothing serious. I have to admit, I'm a bit of a workaholic."

"Not driven Sandy. Of course you are. You always have been, but you should take more time off and enjoy life. Come back here more often, so we can see you," he said spinning them past another couple.

She nodded. "I think I'll do that a bit more than I have been. At least until they get the amusement park finished."

"I hope you'll stop in to see your friendly neighborhood bartender." He grinned.

"I'll try to do that. What about you, Greg, any sweethearts in your life?"

Greg shook his head. "Just one I'd like to have as a sweetheart, but she lives in Seattle."

"That's not too far away."

"No, but she's not interested in me," he said with a shrug.

"Oh, I find that hard to believe, Greg, you are a fine specimen." She patted his arm.

"Yeah, well, I'll let you know when she figures it out."

"I'm sure she will. Now I'm thinking it's time for bed. Chris and mom have kept me hopping this week."

Greg kissed her cheek. "Okay but come back soon."

As she left his bar, Greg watched the love of his life walk out the door, with no clue, whatsoever, that he'd been talking about her.

He'd chickened out back then. When he'd tried to hint at the love he felt for her and it had gone right over her head. Well, not this time. He planned to spell it out in no uncertain terms. He might end up looking like a fool but that didn't matter. What mattered was that he gave this his best shot, he had three, maybe four months at most. Carol would be back on her feet by then and Terry's deliveries would be completed, so Sandy would be free to resume her life in Seattle.

SANDY GAVE her mother the pain medication and sat in a nearby chair. "So, mom, give me a rundown on what's going on here. How many guests do you have now?"

Carol set the water glass on the table. "Just a couple of ladies who are here for the week. Coming in this weekend are a family and an engaged couple. The family is coming for the amusement park and the lovebirds are looking for a wedding venue."

"I have a high school student, Judy Daniels, who's been going by the bakery to pick up a coffee cake or sweet rolls every morning before school, and she helps get breakfast on. She can cook and prepare the easy stuff, but not the baking, so we've been buying that from Samantha since my accident. If you're ready to do the baking. I can cancel the order."

Sandy felt like the baking for the breakfast was going to be the best part of being home. She hadn't done much baking in Seattle. What was she—a single person—going to do with a whole batch of anything? When the baking bug bit her hard, she would make something and take it into the office to let her co-workers devour it. "Sure, mom, you know I love to bake."

"Good. Judy's done a fine job keeping up, but I think she's been a little overwhelmed with the few spring guests we've had. You being here during the summer rush will help a lot. Karen Smith, I mean Karen Willis, now that she's married again, comes in to help with cleaning after she gets her kids in school. Greg or Terry come by mid-morning to see what needs to be done 'by a man' as they say. I think their major motivation is to see what's left over from breakfast."

Sandy laughed. "That wouldn't surprise me a bit, but I suppose they can both be handy if you do need something done. Karen Willis was a couple of years behind me in school and Judy Daniels was just a toddler when I left. I think I babysat her a few times. Time sure does get away from a person." Karen had been married twice and Sandy had never even come close. She supposed that was because she was married to her career, but it still felt very odd.

Carol nodded. "Yes, it can, if you don't pay attention. All my friends in town have been coming by to help out when they are able, and your sister has dropped by as often as she can, without attracting negative attention from that jerk she married."

Anger sparked through Sandy's veins. She'd never liked her sister's husband. Ever since she married the man, nothing she heard about him was ever good. "I wish she would just divorce him and move on. I really think he smacks her around more than she admits. But I don't think he's physically abusive to the kids; verbally I'm sure, but not physically. Thank God she only has to put up with him one week a month since he's gone the other three for work."

"I think she's afraid to leave him, but I don't know if it's fear of him retaliating or if she's worried she can't make it on her own."

"We would all help her. While I'm here, I am going to try to find out what's going on and see what can be done."

"Good luck. Janet's pretty closed mouthed about it."

She didn't want to discuss her plans to find out about Janet's marriage, so she changed the subject. "Matt mentioned during the ferry ride that Terry wants to leave on Monday. What's he got on this load? Did you see some of it?"

Carol's eyes sparkled with pride. "Yes, he's got three beautiful hutches; a cherry wood for someone in Denver, an oak for a family in St Louis and a mahogany for an older couple in Dallas. And at least five blanket chests, some commissioned, some going to retail stores. A dozen or more cradles, lots of babies are going to have a beautiful place to sleep for their first few weeks of life. Not quite half of those are going to stores. He has an arched arbor with benches built in, for a wedding. It's rather unique. Lots of his regular furniture too, tables, rocking chairs, clocks, cribs, you name it. His business sky-rocketed once he got his website up. I think he's got a bin full of toys that he and Greg made, too. You know Terry, he's got enough to fill the semi. How he gets so much done in nine months, I have no idea."

"Strategic planning. I saw his spreadsheet once and almost fainted, it was way more complicated than my project management for the game. Of course, you were no slouch in the scheduling department when you were the mayor. I imagine you still have your fingers in a few pies, even though Mayor MacGregor is in charge."

Her mom laughed. "James is doing a very good job, he's been mayor almost five years now. He does consult with me from time to time. Anyway, Terry told me he'll be gone until late July or early August, he said he wants to be back for the fundraiser and fire department picnic."

"Umm hmm. I guess he will come back with a bunch of new orders and more wood to keep him going for the next nine months. He does such beautiful work. All my friends have commented on the pieces I have in my apartment."

"He's gotten a lot of business from your friends." Carol yawned.

Her mother was starting to droop, it was probably the pain meds kicking in. "Mama, you're looking tired. Why don't you take a little nap while I get all my stuff in and unpacked? I'll check on everything, too."

"That does sound good, I hate getting tired so quickly, but I don't really have any choice."

"Let me help you get comfortable." It was just as difficult for Sandy to see her mom in this condition as it was for Carol to be in it. Her mom had been the mayor in town for most of Sandy's life and had recently retired from that, to open the Bed and Breakfast in their home. She was always busy and had no tolerance for sitting and doing nothing. Sandy had never seen her mom take a nap during the day, that she could recall anyway. So, it was hard to see her strong go-getter mother totally exhausted in the middle of the afternoon. Sandy was certain it was normal after surgery however, so she forced herself not to worry as she closed the door on the darkened room.

Now that her mom was settled, Sandy ran her purse and laptop, which were where she'd left them by the front door, up to her room. She was still mortified about storming into the parlor and seeing Greg playing cards with her mom. The good-looking boy had grown into a gorgeous man. But she had always kept her distance and never gotten too close, the age difference and her brother made her stay away.

Checking that everything around the top two floors was in order, she went down to bring in her suitcase and put her car in the garage. While she helped her mom, she could ponder on the ideas for the next release and talk to her team back in Seattle every afternoon. She knew everything would work out fine.

GREG NODDED to his buddy as Terry walked into the bar. He grabbed his best friend a beer and went over to the table Terry had plopped his laptop on. It was early, and Greg could take a few minutes to shoot the shit.

Terry took the beer and had a large swig of it. "Ah, just what the doctor ordered. Thought I'd come soak up a little atmosphere before I head out on Monday. Three months in the truck is a long time to be alone."

Greg chuckled. Looking at the epitome of the Greek god across from him. Terry's blond hair and blue-eyed good looks, coupled with the man's laid back and friendly personality, meant he was never alone, unless he wanted to be. "Except for all those customers you have to talk to when you deliver their stuff, and store managers, and lumber yards. Not counting hotel clerks and waitresses. I'm guessing you could even find a bar or two, driving all over the US of A."

"Yes, but those aren't *my* people. Only a bunch of strangers." Terry whined while his eyes laughed.

"I'm pretty sure you've never met a stranger in your life. You're always instant friends with every person on the planet." Greg envied Terry at times. Greg was not nearly as friendly, in fact some people had called him intense, bordering on rude. He didn't have Terry's fair hair either, his was darker, not quite black but a dark brown. People generally liked him once they got to know him, but it took them a long time to become comfortable around him. His fault, since he was pretty closed mouth about himself, but sometimes it would be nice to be more like Terry.

Terry laughed and took another long pull from his beer. Pointing the bottle at Greg he said, "You still know me the best."

"Yeah, since diapers. Have you seen Sandy yet?"

"Nope, trying to get all my inventory ready for the trip. It takes forever to get it all into Chelan. I thought I might see her at the barge landing, since she was coming, and I was going, but I got there late."

"I was playing cards with your mom when she got to the house."

"I can tell by your expression there's a story about that."

Terry could hardly breathe when Greg got finished telling him the story of Sandy charging in with the fireplace poker ready to knock someone's brains out.

"That's my sister for you. You'll be on point with her."

Greg startled and tensed, wondering if Terry could read his mind and his intentions to woo Sandy.

"I'll be on the road, so you'll have to do all the maintenance at the B&B. Sandy's got a good mind for how things work as an engineer, but her handy-man skills suck. So, for God's sake, don't let her fix anything or you'll have to redo it, and that will be a lot harder than simply doing it in the first place. And then Sandy will get her back up and be bitchy. Tell her you have to earn your breakfast or some BS, so she saves the chores for you."

Greg relaxed. "Of course, I'll take care of your girls. Do you want me to come over in the morning to help you with another load? We got the hutches this morning, anything else big?"

"No mostly smaller stuff, but if you don't mind, it goes a lot quicker with two. Then we'll go over and mooch breakfast."

CHAPTER 3

The next morning Sandy got up early to help with breakfast and have a chat with Judy. Since there were only a few guests, they didn't need to make too much food, so there was plenty of time to catch up with Judy while the cinnamon rolls were rising. Sandy decided to make half cinnamon rolls and half pecan sticky buns while Judy cut up fruit. When the rolls were in the oven, they made the scrambled eggs and bacon. Coffee, tea, and fresh squeezed orange juice rounded out the menu.

Later in the morning, not only did Terry come by for breakfast, but Greg walked in with him. Such good-looking men, both of them, one Nordic blond and the other dark. They were both large men with wide shoulders and blue eyes, but Greg's eyes had an intensity about them as he zeroed in on her. She felt caught in a snare of some kind that left her breathless and dried out her throat. Enough of that. She swallowed and fought to drag her gaze from his. "Oh, we get two moochers for the price of one this morning, do we?"

"Moochers!" Terry said as he grabbed her in a bear hug, "We are not moochers. We are very handy, handy-men. Who come only to help around the place. We are in high demand, but if mom or someone, like say you, want to push your left-over—" he lifted the lid on the warmer and groaned, "—cinnamon rolls off on us, who are we to argue?"

Greg caught Sandy's eye and they both rolled their eyes at his malarkey, and then grinned at each other. Sandy broke the connection before Greg noticed that her cheeks had flushed.

"Oh, you. Just help yourself," Sandy said as she waved her hand toward the breakfast buffet, still being kept warm, even though the guests had left over an hour ago. "So why do we have the pleasure of both of you this morning?"

"Greg was helping me load the truck for today's run to Chelan. I think after today I should only have two loads left, and then I'm leaving on Monday. As long as you are settled in, Sis, and able to help mom."

"Yeah, I've got it. Can we get together this weekend for a barbeque before you go? Do you think Janet will be able to come?"

"Sure, I'll simply send a joint text to both Janet and Brett. Inviting them, and then he'll have to let her come, because otherwise he'll look like a rat."

"Aren't you the sneaky one?" Sandy wagged her finger at him.

Terry grabbed her finger and kissed the tip. "Nope, just clever."

"Excellent. We'll have it here, so mom can join in as much as she is able. You come too, Greg."

"Love to. I'll bring drinks and chips."

Terry said, "I'll bring the meat and cook. You'll make brownies, right?"

"Yes, Terry," she said with a sigh, "don't I always get stuck on brownie detail?"

"Because yours are the best."

She didn't mind making the brownies, but she had to give Terry a hard time. It was her job as the big sister. "I can give you the recipe."

Terry put his hands up and backed away. "No, they wouldn't be the same."

"Okay, you big baby. I'll make some salads too. I'll cut up some fruit and make a green salad. Janet can make her world-famous potato salad and whatever else she wants."

Just then her mother rolled in, with the home health nurse that came in the mornings to get her up, bathed and dressed. So, Sandy could concentrate on the B&B, making sure breakfast was ready and doing anything else the guests needed.

"We seem to be having a party," her mom said.

Sandy answered, "Not yet, but we are planning a barbeque on Sunday before Terry starts on his road trip."

"Well that's a nice surprise, who all are *we* having?" Carol asked.

"Only the family and Greg. Unless you want to invite some friends."

"I'll think about it. I don't want to get too carried away, when I cannot do so much."

"We can take care of everything Miz Carol, you can sit back and enjoy," Greg said.

Carol smiled. "We'll have some guests for the weekend. Inviting them would be good."

Sandy nodded. "Of course, let us know if you want anyone else. We had a call earlier. A photographer is coming for the weekend, to scope out the area. Her publisher wants to create a picture and vacation book about Lake Chelan. So, she's checking out our town and the others on the lake with the intention to come back in for each of the four seasons for a couple of weeks each time. She's trying to get a handle on major events and what kinds of adventures people can take.

It sounds like it could be a beneficial book on the area for tourism."

Carol tapped one finger on the wheelchair. "Well, that sounds interesting, I hope she'll like us and stay here for each visit."

Terry harrumphed and said, "Well, as long as she shows us in a good light. I never trust the media. They can do as much harm as they do good."

"Oh, Terry," his mom said with a sigh.

"You know as well as I do, what happened before with the media, and I, for one, am going to make sure that never happens again."

"Yes Terry," Sandy and Carol said in unison.

Greg punched Terry in the arm. "Stop it, you're being an ass."

Terry punched Greg back. "Am not."

While Sandy watched the two men acting like grade schoolers, she wondered how she could possibly be attracted to Greg. She didn't normally like guys who reminded her of ten-year-olds.

Terry stopped clowning around with Greg. "Okay, well I better get a move on, if I'm going to catch the early barge and get back in a reasonable hour. Thanks for the breakfast, Sis. Your sticky buns are awesome."

Greg asked, "So do you need anything done this morning, Miz Carol?"

"Yes, Greg, could you mow the lawn? The lawn service cancelled this morning because one of the guys has the stomach flu."

"Yeah, I think maybe it's the brown bottle flu. They were in my bar last night tying one on, while one of the guys moaned about his girlfriend."

"Is that right? Well I might have to mention that next time they actually show up."

"Now, Miz Carol, don't go doing that. You might destroy my business if it gets out that the bartender rats people out."

"All right, Greg. For you, I'll refrain, but I hope this doesn't start happening often."

"I'm sure their dad will straighten them out. It is the family business after all, and he won't want a bad reputation. Anyway, I'll get started on the lawn before it gets too hot." Greg pushed his chair back and looked at Sandy, "Thanks for breakfast. Your buns are great."

She blushed at the double entendre and suddenly found something that needed cleaning in the sink.

After he had left the room her mom laughed and said, "That boy always could tie you in knots."

"Mom, he's Terry's best friend and three years younger than me!"

"So, three years is no big thing now that you're both grown. It was a show stopper in high school but now… not so much. And who cares if he's Terry's best friend! You could use a little romance. You've been doing nothing but your career for fifteen years. It's time for something else."

Sandy cringed inwardly at that. She was married to her career; did she want something else? With Greg of all people? The idea didn't sound nearly as bad as she thought it should. She could very easily imagine getting cozy with Greg, maybe a little too easily. Time to nip this conversation in the bud. "Something else? I love my life and I am not interested in Greg Jones. And I am certainly not discussing this with you."

Carol smirked. "Mmmh hmmm, you keep telling yourself that. You've been interested in that boy since he was twelve and pitching on your brother's baseball team."

"I need to go check in with my dev team. Do you need anything before I go?"

Carol chuckled. "Running away doesn't change the facts…. No, I'm fine."

Sandy hurried up to her room to escape her mother and to Skype into work, but before she did, she needed to shut the window to muffle the lawn mower sound. As she reached for the glass, movement caught her eye, there was Greg who had taken off his shirt, mowing. Dear God, the man was gorgeous. His back was tanned, and she could see the muscles working as he guided the mower. Then he turned to head back, and his chest was even better. Oh, how she would love to run her tongue over those beautiful muscles and follow that dark path of hair straight down to the Promised Land. Mmm, what a yummy idea that was.

He must have sensed her watching because he looked straight up to her window, smiled and winked.

She slammed the window shut.

Get ahold of yourself. You have work to do and you do not need to inflate Greg's ego by drooling over him. But he was definitely drool-worthy.

GREG GRINNED when Sandy slammed her window shut. He'd felt her ogling him. Maybe he should have let her watch without acknowledging it, but that wasn't the straightforward way he was planning to be with her, this time. Greg was going to let her know that he noticed her attraction to him. He'd felt it off and on over the years, but he'd never pushed her about it.

He wasn't quite sure how to go about trying to transform their relationship, but he was going to give it his best shot. After Terry left. Only because he didn't want to have to worry about what Terry thought, but also so *she* didn't have to. Terry was a laid-back guy, but Greg didn't know how he would react to his best friend dating his sister. Terry might be fine with it, angry about it, grossed out, or tease them mercilessly. But he would be gone for three months. If Greg could convince Sandy, and they were still together in three months, then they would get Terry's opinion. If not, no harm, no foul.

He had no idea what Sandy enjoyed doing. There was plenty of outdoors stuff to do in the Cascades, from hiking and camping, to water sports. Did she like activities like that? Not a clue and no one to ask, with her being gone nearly half her life, who would know? What about dates? Did she like going fancy, dressing up, dancing maybe? Again, no clue. Movies? Watching sports? Shit, he was batting blind here. But it still wasn't going to stop him, he was determined. This was his one and only shot and he was going to take it.

Greg *did* know that both the B&B and his bar were busy on the weekends, so he would have to see when she could swing some time off. Since he owned his bar, he could set his work hours. So whatever days she was free he would match them. He guessed Monday through Wednesday were his best shot. Surely, she wasn't going to be tied to the inn, seven days a week. At least he hoped not. Greg wondered what her mom would think about him dating Sandy. If Carol was on his side that would be awesome. If she wasn't… he'd have to convince both of them.

One step at a time. He had three months and Terry wasn't leaving for a few days, so he would simply be useful until then. He chuckled. Preferably, without his shirt.

CHAPTER 4

Sandy Skyped into work, knowing her team would be back in the office today, ready to get started thinking about the next release.

"Hi, guys."

"Hi, Sandy," they chorused together.

Mark McCarty, the technical lead she'd left in charge, said, "We need to wait a moment. We've got a new spring and summer intern in the lobby. Here he is now. Everyone, this is our summer intern, Vince Stanton. Vince, we have the head of our game team, Sandy Anderson, on Skype. She's going to be out of town for most of the time you'll be with us, but we will talk nearly every day."

When everyone was seated Sandy said, "Hi, Vince. Sorry I won't be there to work with you, but Mark is great, so I have no worries. How much do you know about the game?"

Vince blushed and stammered, "Not much really. I haven't played it, I have to work a lot to put myself through college."

"No problem. Let me tell you a bit about it. The game morphed out of bedtime stories I told the kids I babysat for, when I was a teenager. We have a lake monster on Lake Chelan where I lived, whose name is spelled T-S-I-L-L-Y which is pronounced like the word chilly. In my stories, the lake monster was magical and would take the children on adventures to other lands, times, and even outer space. I enjoyed telling the stories and always snuck in some education with them. The kids loved them and so did the parents, since I also added some rewards for good behavior. As a senior in high school, an artist friend and I wrote up the game for a competition. We won second place, and the rest, as they say, is history."

Vince squirmed in his chair, a look of boyish joy on his face. "Wow, that's so cool. I am honored you chose me to be your intern for the summer."

Sandy smiled at the excited young man. "You have great potential. We'll see how you like game development."

Mark folded his hands on the conference table in front of him. "So, let's get started, we all know we need to talk about concepts for the next release. Everyone has the list of the stories. We've done about a third of them in the last four versions. So, let's talk through the areas and get some ideas about what we might want. Let's start with the Bible stories since those are well defined by the Good Book. Which Bible stories sound good for this time?"

"Well, from the Old Testament we could do Moses and the Exodus, all those miracles to get Pharaoh to let the Israelites leave," one of the artists suggested.

"Let's do Abigail for the girls," another artist tapped her pencil on her ever-present sketch pad.

Mark nodded and scribbled down the ideas. "And I think for the Jesus story we're at Mary and Joseph looking for him at the temple."

"A maze might be fun for that. Okay, any objections?" Sandy asked, when no one said anything she continued.

"Start working on ideas for those suggestions. Then we can see how they might work in the game and what we'll need to tweak."

Vince raised his hand. "Question, how did Bible stories come into the game?"

Sandy felt a chuckle rise up in her at the young intern, but carefully pushed it down. She didn't want him to think she was laughing at him or his question. "You don't have to raise your hand, just butt in. Our town preacher asked me for some stories to use for Sunday school, flannel graph kind of things. In the first release of the video game, we put in a hodge-podge of adventures to see which one's people liked. They liked everything. So, we've continued with the variety of quests since the combination seems to hit every demographic, male, female, children, teens, and adults. For the Bible stories we include one Old Testament, one New Testament, one Female hero and one Male hero. Many of the Old Testament tales already include either a male or female hero so if it has one, we don't add another. Most of the Old Testament records have a male hero, like Moses for this plan, so we usually need to add a woman heroine adventure."

Vince nodded. So, they continued brainstorming.

"For outer space, we're at Jupiter. We could hop around the different moons and I was thinking maybe we could have a crystal monster, in the icy water on the moon Europa. It could be friends of Tsilly. It wouldn't be strictly factual, but fun." The lead developer, Peter, shrugged and grinned.

Sandy wasn't too sure about that idea, but she wasn't always right on her opinions. Sometimes something that sounded ridiculous turned out amazing. She also had to be careful not to let her emotions lead. Sandy had dated Peter off and on for the last few years, until the sabotage had happened. During the frantic and heated time of trying to find the pornography, he'd fallen in love with another member of the team he was paired with. It hadn't broken Sandy's heart by any means, but it did sting. That was the third time, she'd been dating a guy who'd left her, after working closely with someone else. It was getting to be a pattern and she didn't like it.

She shrugged. "Draw up a story-board for it and we can look it over and decide if we want to present it to the focus group."

"The American Revolution for American History," one of the animators interjected. "And I think we should do a fairy tale royalty, since we did real-life royalty last release, how about Snow White?"

Mark wrote quickly. "Okay, good. You've all been thinking about this. Let's do Europe for Geography. Our post-apocalyptic story is set already, I think that only leaves World History."

They all moaned.

Sandy said, "I know World History is everyone's least favorite subject, but let's all do some research on that one, to see where we can go. That's one area I didn't have a lot of knowledge or interest in as a teenager. We don't have ready-made stories, but we want to include history. So, everybody study up and we'll talk about it, next time. We've got a good start, so let's flesh out some ideas on these areas. For example, what will Kalar's role be in each adventure?"

"Who's Kalar?" asked Vince.

Sandy was very pleased with the intern. He was already asking good questions. Kalar had been her idea, she was kind of like the strong and forceful side of Sandy's personality. The part she didn't really show to the world. "Kalar was the female hero in the very first game Steve, my friend from high school, and I did. She was a warrior woman like Xena or Wonder Woman. Everyone loved her, so she has a part in each adventure, not always as a warrior woman."

"Is Steve part of the team?"

"No, he was more artist than programmer. After high school he stayed close to home and got a teaching degree, rather than interning and getting a degree that would put him on our team. But he was given a nice fat check when the rights were bought from us, and may still get a small royalty fee."

"Any other questions, Vince?"

"No. I'm good… but I kind of like world history."

Sandy grinned at the kid. "You do? Awesome, you can give that a shot. But first, you need to play the game. Mark, hook him up with the first four versions. Vince, I want to see sore thumbs by Monday, maybe calluses even."

Vince beamed. "Twist my arm, make me play games. By the way, thanks for indulging me and my many questions."

"Those were good queries. Never be afraid to ask, I would rather answer a question than assume you know something and have you fumbling in the dark. Mark, can you send out a summary about what we discussed today?"

Mark gave her a thumbs up. "You got it, boss."

"Good. I'm out of here, unless there is anything else, we want to go into."

"I think we're good. Talk to you Monday." Mark shut his notebook and put the top back on his pen.

When Sandy had signed off, she went downstairs to see what her mom might need, only to walk into the kitchen where Greg was getting a cold soda out of the fridge, still without his shirt on. He was sweaty and looked like sex on a stick.

She stumbled to a halt. "Oh, you're still here."

"Yeah, just cooling down some before I get going."

She forced her gaze toward the window and away from the sexy man. "It *is* getting hot out."

"Well yes, but I was thinking more about the beautiful

woman watching me work. Which made me hotter than the sun ever could."

Sandy's cheeks heated but she was determined to shut him down on this attraction issue. If only he wasn't such a great guy and was simply sexy. That she could deal with. But his deep caring nature, especially with the elderly, made the outside package even more intriguing. Now was not the time, however. She was going to be busy enough with her mom, running the B&B, and telecommuting to add in a distraction like Greg. "I wasn't watching you. I was shutting my window, you were making so much racket I couldn't hear myself think, let alone have a conference call."

He smirked and said, "Didn't know it took so long to shut a window."

"I was distracted, um, thinking about work." Her fingers were tapping her leg, so she made them still.

"Whatever you say, Sandy. Come over to the bar tonight and I'll buy you a drink."

The bar? Tonight? Oh no, no, no. She needed some distance from this man, he was dangerous. She was fidgeting again, and she never, ever, did that, so she forced herself to stop. But her brain had turned to mush, and she couldn't think. "Oh um, I don't know, ah, I might be… busy, or… I think mom will need me tonight."

"If you make it, I'll see you, if not, no harm, no foul." With that, he saluted her with his Pepsi and walked out.

She was such a coward. Him leaving made her sorry to end their conversation this way. "Hey," she called after him, "Thanks for mowing. I'll see you at the barbeque, if not before."

He kept going and waved a hand in acknowledgment.

~

Greg stormed across town, irritated by her rejection of him buying her a damn drink. He thought of her up there watching. She had been distracted all right, but not by work. He'd felt her gaze riveted on him from twenty-five feet away. Her watching him from her bedroom window had really gotten him hot under the collar—that he wasn't wearing—and he was pretty sure she felt it, too. Maybe that's why she was so jittery. Well, that made him feel better about the rejection.

He needed to calm down and keep the end game in mind. There was plenty of time to ease her into the idea of dating him. Slow and steady was the way to go. Maybe her skittishness was actually a good sign. Did he make her nervous because she was interested? He could see that.

He simply needed to be around her as much as possible, maybe tease her a little. Get her used to him. Greg knew he had an intense personality that made some people nervous. He used it at the bar when he needed to. It had also been a benefit when he'd thought to go into a law practice.

Time and patience are what was required, so she wouldn't feel intimidated by him.

Greg *would* see her at the barbeque, but he fully intended on stopping by her place long before Sunday. They might need some help, and with Terry busy getting his furniture down to the lake and into the semi, he probably wouldn't have any time, so it was up to Greg. And he didn't mind one little bit, nope not one bit.

CHAPTER 5

Sandy couldn't think of a way to avoid Greg, since she had to run the B&B, so she girded her loins so to speak and was ready for him mid-morning, but the only person that showed up was Terry. She felt relieved and at the same time miffed that she had worked herself up for no good reason.

She was not sitting around thinking about Greg, however. They had a busy weekend and people were all over the place, checking in, checking out, asking questions and for directions. She needed to help her mom with the B&B by making breakfast, shopping, helping with cleaning, dealing with the guests, and taking reservations for later. Between that and working with her team on the new release ideas she was swamped and had no time for Greg Jones. But she must admit she did occasionally wonder about where he was and why he hadn't come by.

She really enjoyed meeting the photographer, Deborah, who was going to be taking pictures along the Chelan valley for the travel book. She was a pretty woman with a lot of enthusiasm for her project. She'd asked Sandy all about her favorite places, what dates during each season would show the area off to its best, and if there were any special events coming up. Sandy gave her all kinds of hints and tips and then Deborah had asked Carol the same questions. Sandy wouldn't be at all surprised if she asked everyone else she came in contact with. It was a wise way to go about finding the best of the best.

The engaged couple were cute as could be, but were afraid the location was too remote. Sandy had given them the list of people to talk to about all areas of a wedding plan. Their town had become a full-fledged wedding destination and could handle nearly anything someone wanted to do. So, she talked about the services she and her mother could provide and sent them off to talk to the rest, starting with her best friend from high school who had a wedding boutique.

As it turned out Greg didn't make it over to the B&B until the barbeque. The senior center had called and needed him to help with their roof. So, he spent all his free time sweating on top of the building trying to get some temporary repairs done. In truth, the center needed an entirely new roof, but until he'd gone up there to look around, they didn't know that. Once he found out, they'd called a roofing company—but as was typical in their remote town—they couldn't make it for several weeks. So, he did what he could.

Greg always liked helping out at the senior center, and if it derailed his plans a bit, he could live with that. The people in town had always had his back and those seniors that used the center had helped mold him into the man he was today. Giving them a hand with repairs or hanging out to play chess or cards with them wasn't a chore in his mind, but a benefit.

However, it effectively kept him away from the inn. Fortunately, Terry was still in town and he could stop by to make sure they didn't need anything before heading to Chelan with the last couple loads of furniture, so Greg relaxed and plotted.

~

SUNDAY MORNING, Sandy took the brownies out of the oven. She would frost them later when they were still only slightly warm.

The front door slammed shut and footsteps echoed across the foyer. She tensed and then relaxed when Terry walked in.

"Hey Sis, is that brownies I smell?"

"Yes Terry, did you not command me to make them? I started the charcoal about fifteen minutes ago, so it should be perfect in a half hour for you to start cooking. Janet called, and she is on her way over with the kids. I'm so excited to see them, they grow so fast."

"Like weeds. Hey, Greg."

Sandy's heart skittered and she spun around so fast she caused a breeze. It was so good to see him again, it had only been a few days, but still. "Well hello, stranger."

"Stranger? Did you miss me? I was helping out at the senior center, their roof needed some repair, so I crawled around up there long enough to determine that they needed a new one, but since there isn't a roofing company that can get here quick enough, I did what I could to secure it for a few weeks. Did you need me for something?"

"Oh no, I just was surprised you weren't here mooching breakfast." Sandy felt her cheeks heat at the ridiculous answer and wondered what else she could say, when she was saved by her sister's arrival.

"I'm here!" called out Janet as she walked in the room.

Sandy made a beeline for her sister and gave her a big hug. Janet winced and pulled back, "I tripped on one of the kid's toys and bruised my back. Cindy, Brandon, give your aunt Sandy a hug. She hasn't seen you since Christmas."

"Hi, Aunt Sandy," five-year-old Cindy said as she hugged her aunt. Cindy pointed to her mouth that was open wide. "Look, I lost another tooth."

"I see that, but some of the others have started growing back in," Sandy said trying her best to hide her fury from the kids. *Tripped over a toy, right, and fell into a fist.*

"Hi, Aunt Sandy," eight-year-old Brandon said ducking his head as he shuffled over to give her a hug.

"Hi Brandon, have you gotten the new release of the game yet?"

The boy looked up, excitement written on his face. "No, will it be here soon?"

"I think the shipping confirmation said by Wednesday."

"Oh good, thanks for getting it for us, Aunt Sandy," Brandon said.

Cindy yelled, "Yay, I can hardly wait."

"My pleasure. My niece and nephew have to be the first to play it, you know."

"Hey, where's my hug? I'm the favorite uncle after all, and I deserve a hug too," Terry said.

Carol rolled into the room and said, "You're first after me, Terry. Grandma out-ranks uncle."

Terry moaned and rolled his eyes. "Fine, I can wait. But I'm not cooking until I get my hugs, so you all better get after it if you want to eat."

Hugs and laughter ensued and even 'uncle' Greg got hugs. And then everyone pushed Terry and Greg out to the barbeque grill—with beers in hand—to start the cooking.

TERRY AND GREG got the meat on the barbeque. Greg figured they were both seething about Janet's injuries. Sure enough, once the lid to the grill was closed. Terry said in a tight low voice, "Fell over a toy, my ass. That fucker was back in town this week and probably beat the crap out of her because he was trapped into letting her come over today."

Greg nodded, he wished he could refute Terry's logic, but he figured he was dead on in his assessment of the situation. "Yeah, probably."

"You'll keep an eye on her while I'm gone, won't you?"

"Of course. He should be gone for the next three weeks, so I'll check in once in a while and then pay a bit more attention when the asshole gets back in town. You can count on me to take care of all your girls while you're gone." Greg was serious. Terry's sisters and mother were just as important to him as they were to Terry. He would watch over them with his life, whether his relationship with Sandy changed or not.

Terry nodded. "Thanks, man. I know you will. Knowing it gives me the freedom to go on the road for a few months."

Greg nodded. "Wish we could convince Janet to leave that bastard, or at least admit he beats her, rather than pretending she's become the clumsiest person on the planet. Pisses me off that she protects him."

"You and me both, my friend. If she ever does admit it, the man is going to be behind bars so fast his head will spin."

Greg fist bumped Terry. "You got that right."

CHAPTER 6

As they sat down, with their plates mounded high, Sandy wanted to engage Greg. She'd felt kind of snotty since the last time he'd been at the house and it had weighed on her conscience. He was a good man and just because she felt sparks when she looked at him, was no reason to treat him badly. He was her brother's best friend. "So, Greg, tell me about this fundraiser you're setting up. It's to raise money for emergency flights to Chelan isn't it?"

Greg groaned, "How I got put in charge of this I will never figure out. But yes, we need some way to earn the money for the flights. The grant we've had for years has dried up, so we need to find a new source of cash. Insurance doesn't pay much, and you know people here don't have anything extra for emergencies. Gus plans to match whatever we bring in from fundraising. But tell me, why do people think I'm capable of running a festival?"

Terry laughed and said, "It was your idea. Therefore, you must know how to do it."

Greg told them about how Gus had meandered into his

bar all laid back and low-key, and basically forced him to be in charge. Sandy could quite easily imagine the scenario and found it highly amusing. Gus was the resident millionaire and he said he would match whatever they made. He wanted the townspeople to work for the funds and Sandy could certainly see his point, plus matching the amount would be terrific, if they brought in enough it might last another ten years.

Carol patted Greg's hand. "I have full confidence in you."

Greg folded his arms, and then unfolded them to run one hand around the back of his neck, and then up through his hair. Sandy was surprised. What was all this movement? Greg normally was a stoic guy and didn't fidget. Was he nervous about handling the fundraiser? It certainly appeared that way. Did he honestly think he wasn't capable and would let everyone down? He clearly did not see himself the way the rest of the town saw him, as a leader.

Greg shrugged. "I still don't think I should be the one to be running the whole thing, but Gus rarely takes no for an answer. When he does, there better be a damn good reason for it. I couldn't think of anything except my own insecurities. Just because it was my idea does not mean I know *how* to do it."

Terry said, "I'm sorry I'm going to be gone for most of the planning, but I will do my best to be back in time to help out."

Greg nodded and said in a low voice. "I appreciate that, and I will do my best not to eff it up. Anyway, Sandy, my idea was to do a festival at peak tourist season, in August, before schools start up again. I thought if we had booths where people could sell stuff, some of the proceeds could go to the town."

Sandy nodded, she hadn't thought about Terry being

gone when his best buddy was planning something of this magnitude. No wonder Greg was feeling out of sorts about it. "That's a good idea, we've never had a town festival before. Only the firefighters' picnic, and that is usually town people only, after school starts back up." She thought about other areas she'd heard of that did hold festivals. Chelan had their Winter Festival and Pirate Fest. Wenatchee had the Apple Blossom festival. Leavenworth had a couple of different ones. Over near Seattle there were lots more, the most well-known was probably the Tulip Festival.

If other small towns could do it there was no reason they couldn't, too. "But a lot of other towns have them all the time. Were you thinking to charge for booth space or some kind of percentage of sales? Booth space would be a flat fee, collected in advance. But a percentage could yield higher amounts, provided people are honest."

"What about a combination of both?" Terry said. "Like fifty dollars for the space and ten percent of the sales."

"That might be a good idea," Greg said. "I was thinking we would have food stations, craft booths, and games of chance."

"Maybe the town people could have the booth for free and then they can do the percentage, since they will most likely close their shops, to have everything centralized at the festival," Carol said.

Greg nodded slowly as he thought through that idea. After a few moments he said, "Good idea, that way the out of town vendors would be paying a premium, which might also keep out some of the riff-raff."

Sandy waived her fork. "I think rather than bringing in carnival rides you should have it by the amusement park and let those be the rides. You could work something out with Chris."

Terry said, "Don't most festivals have a parade and a king

and queen? And ribbons for the best pie, or the fastest runner or whatever?"

Greg, who loved sports of all kinds, said. "What about adding a marathon? That would bring in different people than we would normally have, we could do a swim and run, or something like that, not exactly a triathlon but something along those lines."

Sandy thought it over, once things settled down and she got the B&B schedule down, she might have some extra time. "Not a bad idea. You've got a couple of months to pull this together. Can I help?"

Greg looked at her like she was Wonder Woman in the flesh and heaved a huge sigh. "Sandy, you just made my day. I need so much help it makes me dizzy to think about it all."

They all continued to tease Greg about the ideas for the fundraiser, Sandy was actually excited to work on it. She could give back to the town and help her brother's best friend at the same time, and she wouldn't mind the eye candy, as long as it stopped there.

An attractive woman walked out of the door, that Sandy recognized as the photographer who was in town to start the work of a photography book of the Lake Chelan valley. The publishing company was wanting a photo study of the four seasons for the area.

Carol called out, "Deborah, please come join us. We've got a ton of food."

Terry looked around to see who his mother was talking to and a scowl covered his face. Sandy was so surprised to see her brother's expression she didn't know what to think.

Deborah walked over to Carol who was patting the seat, they had moved to the side for her wheelchair, in invitation. She'd invited all the B&B guests, but the family was clearly still at the amusement park and the engaged couple was having a tasting meal at Amber's restaurant, and a tour of the wedding facility.

Carol beamed as Deborah sat by her. "I'm so glad you could join us. Let me introduce you to everyone. You've already met my daughter Sandy. Greg, the local bartender, is here on my left and the good-looking blond man is my son Terry. Over there is my daughter Janet and my two grandkids."

Deborah smiled at each one of them and said hello, waving at Janet who was seated with her children at a smaller kid-sized table.

Terry was still frowning but managed to grunt out a greeting. Sandy wondered what was wrong with her normally affable brother, he was always friendly and charming to everyone especially women. Clearly Greg was thinking the same thing as he gave Terry a what-the-heck look.

Deborah filled her plate and took a bite, as a few more of Carol's friends came into the yard. Carol rolled off to greet them and invite them to have a seat. They had multiple small tables set up outside on the deck, each table could hold four to six people and had pretty umbrellas over them for shade. Carol joined the table with her friends, leaving the four younger people together.

Terry said gruffly, "So you're the photographer who's going to be taking pictures of our town."

Deborah answered easily, "I am. The publisher wants to do a photography book of the Lake Chelan area—"

Terry interrupted her, "One of the natives has recently published a book on Chelan and our town."

Deborah beamed. "Yes, Rachel Reardon-Kipling has a lovely book out. When she first pitched the book, she sent it to my publisher as well as a few others. By the time the powers-that-be decided they wanted to publish it, another house had beaten them out. So, they approached me to do one."

"In direct competition with Rachel? That seems low down and sneaky," Terry said angrily. Sandy could not believe her ears, she had never heard Terry take that tone with anyone, especially someone he didn't know, that was a tourist in their town. *What in the hell is wrong with my brother?*

"Not at all, they approached Rachel first about a seasons study like I'll be doing, but she's busy working on a Colorado book and turned down the offer."

Terry crossed his arms. "But your book will still compete with hers and draw sales away."

Deborah shook her head. "On the contrary, Rachel's book came out first, and will certainly point others to my book, but my work will also increase her sales. Since it will be out in approximately eighteen months, it will renew interest in the older book."

Terry glared. "I think you're making that up, so we don't run you out of town for poaching on Rachel."

Sandy was shocked at the attitude Terry was displaying. She said in a low but firm voice, "Terry, maybe you should see what Jeremy has to say about competition in the publishing world before passing judgment."

Terry rolled his eyes. "I doubt children's book publishing is anything like photography books."

Deborah countered, "That's where you would be wrong, Mr. Anderson. Publishing is not a competition, there are more than enough people in the world to buy books, it's usually a matter of getting the word out about a particular series. Synergy among authors is one of the best tools to encourage sales. We've already talked to Rachel about endorsing my book, and I'll be endorsing hers. Now, if you all will excuse me. I think I'll head in for the night."

Sandy looked at Deborah's full plate and frowned at her brother. "You haven't eaten yet."

Deborah's cheeks had turned red and blotchy. "I'm not hungry, but I'll take the plate to my room for a snack later, if you don't mind."

Sandy jumped up to help Deborah take her food and drink to her room and apologize for her jerk of a brother. "Please do."

GREG SAT THERE in total awe of what had just transpired. His normally laid-back-friends-with-everyone best buddy had turned into some kind of asshole. If Greg hadn't seen it with his own eyes, he would have never believed it.

He looked at Terry who was frowning after the two women who'd left the picnic.

"What in the hell was that?" he asked Terry.

Terry looked away from the door and shrugged. "I have no idea why that woman pissed me off. You know I wasn't in favor of her coming in the first place."

"Yes, I know, but I didn't expect you to go rabid on the woman," Greg said.

"I wasn't that bad."

Greg pointed at the door as Sandy stormed out of it looking ready to rip into Terry. "Wrong."

Terry muttered, "Oh shit."

Sandy marched over to her brother and sat down close to him, so Carol and her friends could not hear. Then she proceeded to give Terry a talking to that Greg was damn glad not to be on the other end of.

Terry had effectively torpedoed the barbeque, but Greg didn't know if he should leave or stay to try to help smooth things over. He was fascinated by the storm emitting from

Sandy and found her fury heightened her beauty. Her eyes were flashing and her whole being had become forceful and strong. It was so damn sexy he had to turn his back on the proceedings, so he could control his body.

He finally decided to go over and chat with Janet and the kids, so he wasn't in range of the lecture.

CHAPTER 7

On Monday morning Sandy's mom rolled into the kitchen after the guests had been fed. There was a fire in her eyes that Sandy knew meant trouble.

"I am going to start helping," Carol said.

Sandy wasn't at all surprised her mother was ambushing her on the day Terry had left to make his delivery run. She knew she had to be strong, so she mentally squared her shoulders. "Mom I haven't even been here a week, the doctor—"

"I don't care what the doctor said, this is my B&B and my life. I need to do something."

"Mom—"

Carol gave her *the look* and said in her sternest mother voice. "No, before you argue with me, just listen."

Sandy knew she had to listen, that look had always controlled her, but she wasn't going to back down. "Yes ma'am, what did you have in mind?"

"I want to take the calls and book the reservations. I need to have a feel for the guests that are coming, and I can't get that with you taking the calls."

That wasn't nearly as bad as Sandy had been expecting. Taking phone calls wouldn't hurt her mom, if they could figure out the logistics. "Oh, well, I suppose we could work out a way for you to answer the phones. We do have a portable phone with your land-line number."

Sandy thought about the reception desk. "Your current setup is designed for standing and I doubt you want that changed permanently, so maybe you could use my laptop to log into the reservation system."

Carol tried to look innocent as she asked, "Good, could I use your laptop to keep up with the books?"

Sandy nearly laughed out loud at her mom's expression. There was no reason Sandy could see that bookkeeping would cause her mother harm. As long as she didn't get too tired and overdo it. "Yes, we could arrange that. Although maybe you should think about getting a laptop for your business, that way you could be portable all the time."

Her mom looked like she was thinking that over, so Sandy kept quiet. "That's a good idea, let's do it. Can you order what I'll need?"

Sandy was relieved, since that seemed to be all her mom was asking for, she relaxed and teased her mom a bit. "Yes, ma'am. Anything else, ma'am?"

"No, that's enough. Thanks, Sandy. Except, try not to be smart-mouthed."

Sandy swallowed the laughter that wanted to burst forth. "Yes, mama. But you did wait to spring this on me until after Terry left, so you deserve some of it."

Carol's smile was a sly one. "I did. I admit it."

Sandy laughed, glad to see her mother feeling well enough to get sassy. On the other hand, her job was to keep her mom from doing too much, so she crossed her arms and firmed up her expression. "Until your new laptop gets here you can use mine. I'll need it to Skype into my team, but I can do that in the afternoon when you will be resting anyway."

Carol nodded in a defeated way. "As much as I would like to deny needing to rest. I can't. I do get tired in the afternoon."

Now Sandy felt bad for poking at her mom. "But you are getting stronger every day. It won't be long before you're back at it."

Carol said in a subdued tone. "If I can sit and answer phones, maybe do the bookwork, it will help me to be patient with the healing process."

"I know, mom. We can get you set up this morning."

"Set up doing what?" A male voice asked.

Sandy whirled around. How did Greg enter so quietly? He wasn't a little guy, but it seemed he was always catching her unawares.

Carol said, "Sandy is going to make me a workstation where I can answer the phones and use her laptop to book appointments. I can also do the bookkeeping."

Greg lifted one eyebrow.

Carol rushed to counter the questions he had asked with that lifted brow. "Don't look at us like that, Greg. If I don't do something, I'll go stir crazy. But if I can sit in the wheelchair or on the chaise and keep my fingers in the pie, I'll be much more content."

Greg laughed and winked at Sandy. "I take it she wore you down with all that?"

Sandy lifted her hands. "What else could I do but agree?"

"You noticed she waited to spring this on you until after Terry was on the way out of town."

"I did, indeed."

Greg sighed heavily and dramatically. "Well let's get the sneaky woman set up. I can grab the portable phone and the folding table we used to play Rummy a few days ago. You go get your laptop."

Sandy appreciated the support but didn't want to make him feel obligated to assist. "You don't need to help with this, Greg."

His eyes twinkled. "Sure, I do, that will earn me breakfast. I saw scones, didn't I?"

Sandy laughed. "You did. Very well, I appreciate your assistance. I'll grab my laptop."

~

GREG WASN'T sure this was the best idea, but Carol Anderson was a force to be reckoned with, and maybe it would keep her occupied enough, so she didn't push too hard or too fast. She didn't even let him push her along in her wheelchair. She was off into the parlor, telling him to grab some office supplies, too.

He chuckled as he gathered some pens and a spiral notebook and sticky notes. The portable phone was already in the parlor, since it was a bright sunny room that Carol enjoyed sitting in. When she actually *did* sit down, that is. While the older woman stationed herself on the chaise, he retrieved the table. Carol didn't wait for any help to move between the two chairs. Was she supposed to be doing that? Had she started physical therapy or was she simply determined not to be an invalid?

Sandy walked in as her mom finished the transfer. "Mom, you're supposed to wait for help."

"I'm fine. Greg was right here."

Sandy frowned. "With his hands full of crap."

Greg agreed with Sandy, but if there had been any trouble, he would have dropped the crap and been by her mom's side in an instant. They all knew that, so it wasn't worth saying out loud.

Carol directed both of them with the precision of a drill sergeant, she'd obviously thought through exactly what she wanted. Once they had her set up, she shooed them out of the room.

Sandy took him back to the kitchen, so he could have some breakfast. He muttered, "I wonder how long she's been planning that."

Shaking her head, she said, "Probably since she came out of the recovery room after surgery. Thanks for the help, Greg."

He took a scone and some eggs and link sausages from the warmers, while Sandy poured them both a cup of coffee. She set them on the table and took a scone for herself. He was glad she was planning to join him while he ate. He asked, "Do you need any other help this morning?"

"Not that I can think of right off. I'll give it some thought while we eat. Mom threw me for a bit of a loop when she came in demanding to be set up to keep her fingers in. But it might really be a good thing… if she doesn't overdo it."

Greg nodded as he swallowed a most delicious bite of scone. "It might keep her from trying to help in another area where she could slow down her recovery."

"Exactly. So, when do you want to get together to talk about the fundraiser?" Sandy asked.

Any day and any time would suit him, but better not scare the crap out of her with that answer. "Tuesdays are my slowest day at the bar, so I can take that day off. If Tuesday works for you, then you can set the time."

"I don't think Tuesdays are very busy here either. The weekend people are gone, and the new ones coming in are already here, or will be arriving later in the week. Any time in the afternoon or evening would probably work, once all the breakfast is dealt with."

Tomorrow was Tuesday, he would be happy to spend some time alone with her, talking about anything, including the fundraiser. "Want me to come here? So, we're within shouting distance for your mom?"

"Yes. Let's wait to start until next Tuesday. I still need a couple of days to get the routine down. But you coming here would probably be good at least the first few weeks. Maybe, later on, I can get someone to cover for me, if we need to go out and make arrangements."

He was disappointed to wait a week, but she'd only been here a few days and probably *did* need to get the routine down. "We have a plan. Are you going to come to the bar on Wednesday while your mom has her book club?"

"Yeah. I could use some down time. It would be fun to see some friends too. Should we put an ad in the paper? *Come see Sandy.*"

Greg would prefer to have her all to himself, but the idea of an advertisement did sound kind of funny. "No need for an ad, simply tell one or two people from your mom's book group and the whole town will know. You've been living in the big city too long."

She laughed and it made him happy to hear the sound. "A few at a time might be easier to handle anyway. So, what town gossip do you know?"

He was the town bartender. He knew it all, but the idea of letting anyone know that, sounded unmanly. "I don't do gossip."

Sandy frowned at him in mock disgust. "You and Amber. Your bar and her restaurant. Both of you are the ear of the town and your lips are practically sewn shut."

"Yeah, we are kind of alike in that respect. Did you hear Chris and Barbara are pregnant again?"

"Mom told me they're due pretty soon. What did you think of Terry's attitude toward the photographer?"

That had been weird and maybe it would be good to talk about it. "I know he was predisposed to not like her, based simply on the journalist that came for the amusement park opening, and the shit story they did on it. But I was astounded by his vehemence."

"Right? He's usually so laid back and likes everyone. That was a side of my brother I've never seen. Surprised the heck out of me."

It had Greg too. Was there something else going on, that had caused the two to go at each other's throats?

Sandy said, "Makes me wonder if there was some attraction there that he was fighting."

Greg lifted one shoulder. "That thought did cross my mind. We'll have to see what happens in the future, when she comes back and they're in the same town longer than twenty-four hours."

"Yeah, I'd like to see that, but I probably won't be here then."

The thought of her leaving at the end of the summer made his heart hurt, but he kept his response light. "I can send you updates. Do you want hourly or daily?"

Sandy grinned. "I think daily would be sufficient, unless there is some breaking news, then minute by minute might be good. I'm just glad I could smooth things over with Deborah, so mom didn't hear about the altercation."

"What did you tell Deborah?"

"I told her a little about the amusement park fiasco, and then explained Terry was stressed about going on the trip and leaving mom after her surgery. I don't know if she bought it, but she didn't pull her reservation for fall, so that's good. If I have to, I'll ban Terry from the property when she comes back. Or, I'll have you ban him since I will probably be back in Seattle by then."

Greg was surprised to hear the photographer wasn't planning to come back until autumn. It was only mid-spring so there was plenty of time for summer pictures and even some spring ones. "Won't she be back before then? Doesn't she need summer pictures?"

Sandy said, "Deborah hasn't booked any time here for summer. And I'm not sure if she's taking the real spring pictures yet. Maybe she's starting with fall."

Greg didn't necessarily want to publicize the fundraiser, but he did want to make sure everyone, that wanted to, had a chance to give. "Hopefully this fundraiser will be a one-time deal, or at least not every year. You might mention it to her, to see if she wants any shots of it."

Sandy smiled. "I'll do that."

He could sit and bask in her presence all day, but he'd finished his breakfast and didn't have any excuse to linger. He didn't want to look like a stalker or an idiot, so he carried the dishes into the kitchen and rinsed them in the sink. Sandy followed him in with her coffee cup.

He wanted to say something witty or enticing, but his brain had been fried by her smile. Then on pure impulse, he pulled her into his arms and kissed her cheek. He released her and murmured, "See you tomorrow."

Then he went out into the sunshine, feeling its warmth mingle with his joy as he walked down the street.

CHAPTER 8

It was time to beard the lion in his den, so Sandy dressed carefully in skinny jeans and a flirty top. She wore some sexy strappy sandals with three-inch spiked heels, she'd have to take them off if she danced too much, but they gave her legs and butt some nice definition in the skinny jeans. She put on some light makeup and pulled her hair into a French braid. Pretty earrings dangled, and she wore a bracelet that matched, both of which were Kristen's creations.

When she was confident in her appearance, she went downstairs to check on her mother. Sandy kissed her mom on the cheek and said hi to the book club ladies. They all assured her that they would be fine spending the evening at the house. By the amount of snacks and chocolate they had spread out, Sandy had to doubt anyone would go home hungry.

Carol said, "We usually have wine with our books and snacks, but we're refraining since my pain meds don't go well with alcohol."

"Very sensible of you," Sandy said with a grin.

Carol whined a little, "But not as much fun."

"It will only be a few weeks mom, then you can resume your normal behavior." All the ladies sighed, and she had to chuckle at their resignation.

It only took her a couple of minutes to get to the bar. She checked her face one more time before leaving the car and channeling Kalar.

Sandy sashayed into Greg's bar with a sassy strut. At least she hoped it looked like that. In reality it probably looked like the geeky girl she was, walking into a bar. Greg noticed her immediately, so she went directly toward him. "Got a beer for me, Greg?"

"Of course, there's a long neck right here with your name on it. Glad you could make it in. I'm sure everyone will be happy to see you."

She shrugged. "I doubt anyone will care much."

"I care… You're looking mighty fetching tonight."

Before she could tease Greg about his old-fashioned compliment, Steve Jameson walked over to her, and bumped into her shoulder, "Hey, Sandy, whatcha doin' here in the bar? I thought you were more of a fancy restaurant with a glass of wine kind of girl, not a rowdy bar with a beer."

"Nope, I'm just me and can be happy anywhere," she said giving Steve a hug in greeting. They had been great friends in high school, both geeks in math. In fact, Steve had been her partner in the very first version of the *Adventures with Tsilly* game. He hadn't wanted to leave home to attend the University of Washington where she had gotten her degree. He'd stayed close to home and gotten an education degree and was now teaching math and computer science in their high school, along with some drawing classes.

"I heard you were coming back, when did you get here?" he asked as if he didn't already know. The town was the size of a postage stamp and everyone knew everything about everybody. Always.

"Are you trying to tell me my arrival wasn't posted on Facebook or Twitter?" she laughed. "I got here Thursday."

Greg interjected, "Yeah, and she was going to clock me for beating her mom at Rummy."

"Greg, that was not my finest moment and you don't have to tell everyone everything."

"Hey, I enjoyed it, so simply spreading the joy. She came barreling in with the fireplace poker raised high. She made me think of Kalar."

"Well I did draw Kalar to look like her in the original version, so that's not a big surprise," Steve said.

Sandy rolled her eyes. "Yeah right. I am pretty sure Kalar looked more like Yvonne, who you had a crush on at the time."

Steve held up his hands. "Oh no, no, no. I am sure Kalar looked exactly like you. But even if she didn't back then, it seems like she's looking even more like you these days."

Pointing her beer at Steve she said, "Yeah, my team thinks they are very funny. When we go to conferences, they always think they are so clever when people call me Kalar."

"Do you wear one of those skimpy outfits at the conferences? I would come to one just to see that," Steve said, with Greg nodding along with the sentiment.

"No. I do not. And on that note, I'm going to mingle. I see a lot of people I haven't talked to in years."

One of the guys muttered "chicken" under his breath but she couldn't tell which one, so she kept walking. Sandy talked to old friends from high school and longtime residents. Her mother always kept her up to date on their lives, so she could talk to them like she hadn't been gone for years.

They told her about their kids and jobs, and as always, their suggestions on her next game release. Since a lot of tourism dollars came into the town because it was the birthplace of the game, there were always suggestions. She happily listened to their ideas, some she would use, others she would not.

She played a game of pool and did okay for being a bit rusty. Some of the girls got her out on the dance floor for line dancing, when the juke box played a country song. As it got later there were more slow songs playing and couples dominated the floor.

She danced with Jeremy Scott, who she had gone to homecoming with one year, and who had taken her bible stories and made them into self-published books for the kids in town. When the *Adventures with Tsilly* game had gotten popular he'd been commissioned to write and illustrate the stories that went along with each release of the game. After that he'd gone on to create other children's books, one whole series featured a beaver and his pals and was very successful. Jeremy was married to Amber Clarkson who ran the neighborhood restaurant.

She also danced with Chris Clarkson, who owned and operated the Tsilly theme park. They'd dated in high school, until he'd fallen hard for her best friend Barbara. It had taken some time to mend their relationship after that. He and Barbara had been married since right after high school. They had a really cute daughter, an adorable son, and another child on the way.

"So, what are you doing here at the bar instead of being home with Barbara?" she asked.

"She literally shoved me out the door and said she wanted some peace and quiet. Jill and Nathan are down for the night. Child number three will be coming along soon enough, so she wanted some time alone. I just hope she's resting and not cleaning the whole house in that nesting thing she does. Otherwise it'll be born tomorrow."

Sandy laughed at his expression. "So, I heard you didn't want to know the gender of this child."

Chris shrugged. "We have one of each now, so the third one can be a surprise. Gives everyone something to guess at. I think there is a pool going."

Sandy grinned. "That wouldn't surprise me one bit. What adventure are you featuring this month, Chris?"

"We're doing Venus, the kids love the outer space quests. So, it's a great start for the summer season. I assume you've got Mars in this latest release."

"We do. Barbara will have a hoot with this one. I let Peter talk me into putting Martians in it. It's silly but a lot of fun. I'll come by the park while I'm here and check it out, I love to see the way you re-create the adventures. I can't imagine what kind of costumes Barbara came up with for Venus."

Chris nodded. "That would be terrific, the costumes are great. I would love a preview of this newest release if you've got the time for a briefing."

Sandy laughed at Chris trying to be sly. "Greg was asking the same thing, maybe we should have a town meeting and I can give everyone that wants to know, a run down."

"Really? That would be awesome. If you're serious I can set that up for you."

"Give me a couple days until I see where mom is at, after her physical therapy appointment. Oh, maybe next Wednesday would work, since that's mom's book club night. If we have it early, Greg can still get over here to the bar in time for the evening rush. Like five thirty or six. Providing you aren't at the hospital."

"I shouldn't be, we're two full weeks out. I'll see what I can do to get everyone who needs a heads up, in the room at the same time, so you don't have to do it over and over again."

"That sounds good, Chris. I should stop by and see Barbara before she goes into labor."

Chris gave her a hug as the song ended. "Barbara would love that. But don't rush, when you've got time, even if it's after this one is born. You'll be here all summer, I hear, so plenty of time for a visit or two."

Steve asked Sandy to dance and she was happy to accompany him. "So how is this new release going on our game?" he said.

She winced at the "our game" comment, Steve mentioned that every time she saw him, even though he had worked on the game for less than six months, sixteen years ago. "It's going very well, we had a lot of pre-sales. And since it's been released it's selling strong."

"I heard a rumor you were going to be moving on to a new game."

Sandy was surprised by that comment. They had nothing else in the works. *Adventures with Tsilly* was still a hot product, and they wouldn't be moving onto something new until it wasn't. "No plans for that, must be someone's imagination running wild. Of course, you never know when sales will drop and what the company will decide."

Steve clearly didn't believe her. "Oh, come on, you can tell me. Maybe we could have a brain storming session."

Sandy thought back to their original "brain storming" sessions where he had made ridiculous suggestions and tried to eat everything in the house. The only real contribution he had done was the art work, she wasn't much of an artist. She had come up with the idea, coded the infrastructure, selected the adventure to use and determined a point system. Steve had done some decent drawings of Tsilly the lake monster and Kalar the warrior goddess. Although she had to keep nagging him to put more clothes on Kalar, they were not writing a porn game. He wasn't a brilliant artist however and as soon as her company had bought the rights to develop it, they had brought in professional game artists. She didn't think Steve would be that immature again, but she already had a team of professionals to brainstorm with.

"To tell you the truth, Steve, I'm really here to help my mom with the B&B, get her to physical therapy, and things like that. I don't plan to do much work on anything, but I'll keep your offer in mind."

"Fine, I can take a hint," Steve said testily, then he shook it off. "Thanks for the dance, Sandy, but I better get going, it's a school night. Young minds to teach and all that." Steve walked off the dance floor and out the door, leaving her standing there wondering what that was all about.

"Hey beautiful, do you have one more dance in you for the overworked bartender?" Greg asked.

"Oh, of course, sure," she said and tried to shake off the strange feeling she'd gotten from Steve.

"What's wrong, Sandy?"

"Nothing really, Steve just acted a little odd."

"Probably past his bedtime and he was getting cranky," Greg said with a twinkle in his eye.

That made her laugh, as he had clearly intended, and they started dancing to a slow George Straight song. "Chris is going to set up a town meeting, so I can brief everyone on the new release, maybe next Wednesday. I told him it should be early, so you can get over here after. Speaking of which, I've had a lot of fun here tonight, you run a great place. Everyone seems to be having a good time rather than getting hammered and obnoxious."

"Thanks. We still have hammered and obnoxious from time to time, but I have no hesitancy to cut someone off, or even call the cops if needed. Everyone knows that, so they tend to keep it friendly."

Sandy said, "Well it makes for a very enjoyable evening."

"Aw shucks, ma'am," Greg said trying to act embarrassed and failing miserably, which made her hoot with laughter, disturbing some love birds dancing nearby.

"Now, Sandy, this is a slow love song. Try to act with a little decorum."

"Love song, huh?" she asked leaning back with her hands around his neck and looking into his bright blue eyes.

Greg looked down at her and the laughter faded from his eyes. "Yes, Sandy. A love song."

She felt caught in his gaze with an intensity she hadn't felt for any other man. It seemed like the room faded away and he drew her in a little closer, breaking the stare to look at her lips, which had suddenly gone dry. She licked them, which caused a flame to light in his eyes. He pulled her a little closer and she tipped her face up to his. He started to lower his head, when there was a shout from the pool area, which caused them both to startle and break apart.

Greg looked toward the commotion and sighed. "Sorry, gotta go take care of that."

"Yes, go."

As Greg walked away Sandy quickly gathered her things and slipped out the door. *Oh my God! What was I thinking! I almost kissed Greg, right there in front of God and everyone. I must have had too much to drink and lost my mind.* Even though she knew she'd only had two beers. It had nothing to do with alcohol and everything to do with the man. *No more of that! I am not here to get cozy with Greg Jones, for goodness sake. I'm only here temporarily and then I'm going back to Seattle and my job.* But even as she said these things to herself another voice whispered, "Yes, but it's been a long time since you've been with a man, and that one is hot."

Maybe it could be a summer fling. No, no, no, that would never do, she didn't think a small bite of Greg would do anything but make her want more. Lots more, and that was not going to happen. She was not going there. "Well darn, you are no fun," said that other voice.

ONCE GREG GOT DONE TAKING care of the fools in the pool area, by sending them home, and telling them he wasn't going to tolerate that kind of nonsense in his bar, he looked for Sandy. Clearly, she had flown the coop, he wasn't sure whether to feel relieved or irritated that she had run off, probably a little of both, if he was honest. He didn't need to be acting like a dumbass in his own bar. That would be better to do in private.

He chuckled at himself for deciding it was okay to be a dumbass anywhere. But that woman made his blood boil and always had. Following through on that near kiss, however, would be better if it happened somewhere besides his own bar.

He got back to work, but the almost kiss didn't leave his mind. It kept percolating, running around and around in his thoughts.

There was always tomorrow.

CHAPTER 9

Sandy was clearly avoiding him. He'd stopped by the B&B every morning to see if they needed any help. Every morning this week she wasn't around. Carol sometimes called him into the parlor, sometimes there was a note and a couple of times she'd asked Judy to stay late.

Well today was Tuesday and they had made plans to work on the fundraiser, so he was going to sit at the B&B until Sandy showed up. He could wait. He had all day.

Greg was not only determined but desperate. He really did need the help. Sandy didn't seem to be the type to welch on her offer of assistance, but he wasn't taking any chances. He marched into the B&B prepared to spend all day if he had to. He figured a note or Carol would be waiting for him this morning with some lame excuse why Sandy wasn't there, well it wasn't going to work.

When he got to the kitchen, he was surprised to find Sandy waiting for him, which perversely pissed him off. He walked right up to her, backing her against the counter. "You've been avoiding me," he growled out.

She started to shake her head and he frowned. The shake

turned into a slight nod and shrug. "Maybe a little. But I did need to try to talk some sense into Janet, I didn't get far. And another day I needed to buy some things, so I took the ferry into Chelan to go to the Safeway, sometimes ordering online doesn't cut it. So not all of it was to avoid you."

"It's been six days and you haven't been here one morning since you came into my bar. Afraid I might kiss you? Afraid you might like it?"

She shocked the hell out of him by saying, "Frankly? Yes."

His ire eased. "Aw, Sandy, you know I'd never do anything against your will."

Sandy's laugh sounded self-depreciating. "Greg, that is one thing I was never worried about. I'm not afraid of you. I'm afraid of myself."

"Well let's take that off the table, right now." He took her face in his hands with the idea of kissing her hard and fast, but he just couldn't do that. He'd wanted to kiss her for years, and even though he was frustrated and angry he wasn't going to screw this up. Greg sighed and then laid his lips on hers, so softly, so reverently, it was almost a non-kiss. She pushed up, so their lips met in a firmer touch and he reveled in the taste of her. His head swam, he brushed his mouth over hers. Warmth and joy spread through his whole being as she kissed him back with no hesitation.

The kiss didn't last long, and it never became passionate but that small exquisite taste of her rocked his world in a way no other kisses before had ever done. He pulled back and she sighed.

Sandy put her forehead on his chest and he tried to gather his stampeding emotions. He didn't know what to say or do. Not completely sure he could say or do anything at all.

She pushed him and he complied with her request by taking a step back.

Sandy gave him a small smile. "That was nice, and

nothing to be afraid of after all. I'm glad we got that out of the way. Get some breakfast and let's sit in the dining room to make fundraiser plans."

Nice? Nothing to be afraid of? Breakfast? His blood was boiling, and he couldn't think clearly, and it was *nice*? Obviously, they were not on the same page. But he could fake it well enough, so he let her walk out of the room while he got some breakfast and coffee. Greg wasn't sure he'd be able to eat, but he was determined to do his best at acting nonchalant. *Suck it up Jones, don't act like an ass.*

SANDY ESCAPED the hot man in the kitchen. She wished she had time to go dunk her head in some cold water, but she only had a minute or two before he followed her. That kiss had really packed a punch. It had been a sweet closed mouth kiss that had totally rocked her world. She'd been terrified that he would be able to see her reaction to it, so she'd fallen back on her coping mechanism of running away and hid behind planning for the festival. She hoped it would take him a couple of minutes to gather up his breakfast, so she could calm down enough to use her brain. Providing it wasn't fried beyond usage.

Thank God she'd made notes in a spreadsheet, about some ideas she had so they could talk through those. Fortunately, her mom's new computer had come in yesterday and she'd hooked it all up for Carol's use in taking reservations and doing the financials.

Sandy opened up her laptop and tried to type in her password, but her hands were shaking so bad she flubbed it up twice. Once more and the tracking program would kick in, a new security measure they had implemented after the sabotage of the game. She could cancel the tracker with her phone, but she didn't want to trigger the tracker. *Dammit Sandy, calm down and get it right this time. Stop being a fool. Greg's just a man, your little brother's best friend.*

The stern self-talk did the job and she managed to open up the spreadsheet as Greg walked into the room with his plate and coffee. But as she looked up she knew he wasn't *just* anything. The man was much more than *just*.

She started babbling before he could even sit down. "So, I thought about another idea. That maybe you should have an auction, either a silent one, or a regular one, or maybe a combination. We could probably get people to donate some of their wares."

He looked at her and lifted his eyebrow as he chewed, so she barreled on. "For instance, maybe Chris could donate season tickets for a family of four to the amusement park. I think I could get my company to donate a set of Tsilly games."

Greg nodded. "Maybe Jeremy could donate some books. And Kristen some jewelry."

Sandy was relieved when he took up the idea. She'd managed to get him thinking about something else. "Exactly, if we hit up everyone here in town, we'd have a lot of things to auction."

"Lucille Thompson might give us one of her glass pieces and now her son Nolan, the police chief, is doing some glass work and making a name for himself."

Sandy grinned. "One of Lucille's pieces would bring in a lot of money and if Gus matched that, it would be amazing."

"It's a great idea, Sandy. We'd have to give everyone tax receipts, so we might have to make the fundraiser a non-profit, but that isn't too hard, and we've got time to get it done. I can look into that."

Sandy was happy that they were doing some positive planning and not being weird about the kiss. Best to simply ignore that and move on to important issues. "Good. I can draft up a flyer or plea letter and we can keep a list of who we ask, what they donate and how much it's worth, then we can decide on opening bids and track what they bring in. I'll do a mini database. A spreadsheet would work too."

"Whatever you want to do is fine with me. Some people would probably be best to speak to in person. So maybe the two of us can go around and ask them. Who else? Oh, I know. We could go wander around the Art Gallery and see what all we have available in town."

She happily typed in the suggestions they'd come up with into a tab on the spreadsheet named 'Auction'. "Yeah, they have pretty much everyone from town selling things in there. We might also want to contact Rachel about her publisher donating one of her books of the area."

Greg nodded, but his gaze was far away. "That was sure odd the way your brother treated that photographer. If I hadn't seen it myself, and someone was telling me the story I would have called them a liar to their face."

"Right? I've never in my life seen him act that way. It was like he'd been possessed or something."

"I couldn't agree more."

Sandy shook her whole body like a dog would, shrugging off her brother's oddness. "So back to the fundraiser. How many days are you thinking? One? Two? More?"

"No more than two. The weekend maybe. We could do the parade and a festival kind of thing on Saturday with booths and rides and stuff like that. Sunday we could do the mini-marathon and then in the evening upscale the event with the auction, and maybe a dinner/dance."

"That's a good idea. A family day and then an adult event. Maybe do a silent auction before dinner, where people could bid on the smaller items. Then save the big hitters like the glass sculptures for a live auction."

Greg frowned. "We'd have to find someone that could do the live auction calling. That isn't me for sure. Any ideas about that?"

"We can think about it. Maybe there is some kind of listing for people that do things like that, if we can't find anyone local."

"Non-locals would probably have to be paid."

"We could let it be known around the Chelan valley that we're looking for a volunteer and do tryouts," Sandy said with a smirk.

"I know you were kidding but that actually isn't a bad idea. Some people might like to do it just for fun."

"Stranger things have happened." Like for instance the man she'd always thought of as a younger brother kissing her brainless. Or if truth be told, she'd fought to see him that way and not always succeeded. But she didn't want to think about the truth, she wanted to stuff Greg back into the little brother box.

CHAPTER 10

Sandy had just finished talking to her team when her phone rang. Assuming it was her project lead, she answered without looking, "What did the brilliant boy come up with now?"

"Um, Sandy?"

She looked at the display, Steve. "Sorry Steve, I thought it was my project lead calling back."

"No just your former partner calling, no brilliant boy."

Steve sounded kind of snippy. Sandy rolled her eyes and said, "We have an intern this summer who is coming up with lots of ideas for the new game."

"I thought you said there wasn't a new game."

"I meant the next version of Tsilly, we're still in the brainstorming/feasibility phase."

"If you say so. I called to see if you wanted to go out to dinner tomorrow, since your mom has her book club and you had last Wednesday off. Plus, I heard through the grapevine that you are doing an update on this newest version for the town. I heard some people were invited to the meeting, but not your old partner."

Well heck, she'd planned to go to Greg's bar after the town's presentation, and now Steve had his nose out of joint. She inwardly sighed and decided she probably should go out with Steve, to sooth his ruffled feathers. And actually, it might be good not to see Greg.

She still couldn't get that kiss out of her mind. It popped up any time it wanted. Whenever she wasn't actively thinking about something else it sneaked in and she started fantasizing about it. It confused her and at the same time it had felt fantastic. Maybe going out with Steve would be a good thing.

"Chris set up the meeting and did the invites. I would be happy to have dinner with you after the talk."

Steve sounded surprised and some of the snippiness faded. "Really? That's great. Amber's?"

"Sure, that would be perfect. I'll be there after I talk to the folks gearing up for tourist season, and any other game fanatics that can't wait a week until their copies arrive."

He almost chuckled, but not quite. "I'll see you then."

Sandy wondered at his attitude, both times she'd talked to him he'd acted oddly. Had his personality changed that much? She couldn't remember him ever being cranky or bitter, but that seemed to have changed. She tried to guess what his deal was. But she didn't have much time for that, because her mom had an appointment at the physical therapist, so she needed to get her there.

It wasn't far away and she thought she would ask her mom if she wanted to go in the car or if Sandy could just push her in the wheel chair. There was only a couple of places where the wheel chair might be more of a challenge. One place an old tree root had pushed up the sidewalk making a bit of a bump. She thought she could handle it though and would enjoy the walk in the fresh air, if her mom was up for it.

She saw her mom was already up from her nap and in the wheel chair. "Mom, you're supposed to wait for me to help you get up."

Carol shook her head. "That's silly. I can manage to do it without putting any pressure on the bad leg."

"But if you slipped…."

"Sandy, don't be a worry wart."

Sandy gave up, her mom could only be bullied so much, better to leave it for something more important, besides she could rat her out to the therapist, Wendy, and let *her* be the bad guy. "Fine. So, do you want to go in the car or shall we take a stroll on this pretty spring day?"

"Oh, a walk would be nice. Do you think you'll have trouble with the tree root or that pot hole?"

"No, I think I can manage."

"Then let's give it a try."

The walk down the street was very pleasant, and Sandy didn't have any real issues with the not so smooth areas. The physical therapist had recently opened the bottom floor of her house to create an area for PT. Wendy was a nurse at the clinic and had started doing physical therapy as a side business out of her house. The clinic wasn't big enough for a full therapy area. Wendy even had a hot tub to ease out aches. The only thing she didn't have was a pool, but she'd worked out something with one of the hotels for when she needed to use water therapy.

As Sandy watched her mom going through the exercises, she started to feel uneasy about the trip back home. First her mom would be tired and sore, so a bumpy ride down the street might not be the best. Second going back was uphill, so it would be a more difficult journey on both of them. Sandy thought she should probably go get the car to get her back, but she wasn't sure if her mom would be too tired to get in and out of the car. Sandy could support her, but they were about the same size so anything more than support would be difficult.

If only Terry was in town, he would be happy to come help her. But since he wasn't, she decided that she would have to ask Greg, he'd been very adamant about being the substitute Terry as far as any help she, or her mom, or Janet needed. She didn't want to call him, but her mother's health was more important than her feelings. As she continued to watch the physical therapy workout, she knew it was going to be needed. This was the first real session after enough healing had taken place, her mom was looking weary and had another fifteen minutes to go.

She stepped out of the room and called Greg.

"Hey, Sandy."

"Greg, I hate to ask, but mom is at the PT appointment and I think I'm going to need some help getting her back into the house."

"Say no more, I'm on my way."

"Greg, can you bring a vehicle? We walked down here."

He chuckled. "A nice day going down, not so nice coming back?"

"Yep."

"Be right there."

Sandy was relieved he was coming to help, even if she did feel a flutter about seeing him. She needed to get over this weird reaction to him.

GREG WAS glad Sandy had called him. He'd been thinking about her all damn day and he wanted to see her again, even if it had only been a few hours since he'd left her house. She'd mentioned the PT appointment this morning as they'd talked about the fundraiser. He never thought Sandy would walk down to it, but it was a pretty spring day, so he could see the draw. Getting back was a completely different story and he would be happy to help. Miz Carol probably would need some help getting in and out of the car and wheelchair. She could do it well enough when strong and rested, but after a grueling therapy, not so much.

He decided to take his truck, he had a low-slung car, but he knew it would actually be easier to get in and out of a taller vehicle rather than a lower one. Most people would think just the opposite, but he'd helped enough of the folks at the senior center to get to appointments, to know the truth.

He walked into the office as they were putting Miz Carol into her wheel chair, she looked exhausted, in fact he'd never seen her look so tired. Her hair was damp with sweat and her skin was pale. He was doubly glad Sandy had called him.

Carol looked at Sandy. "You called Greg?"

"Yes. I thought—"

Carol sighed. "Thank God. Wendy wore me out. I was a little scared about getting back home."

Sandy let out a nervous laugh. "Me too, mom."

Carol looked at Wendy. "Then let's get out of here. I think my bed is calling."

Wendy patted her hand. "You did great. You can use some heat and ibuprofen if you need it. Don't sleep too long or you'll seize up. Do some of the cool down exercises I showed you, and let Sandy help you in and out of the chair today. Your muscles will be weak from your workout."

Greg said, "I've got tonight off, and can stick around and be helpful."

All three women looked at him like he'd just offered them diamonds. Sandy nodded. "That would be great, Greg. I'll feed you dinner."

"You don't need to—"

"Greg, you can help mom, I'll cook. It's the least I can do."

Carol yawned. "Can we…."

Greg snapped to action. "Yes ma'am, let's get you home and comfy."

He got Carol home and in her parlor within minutes. She had a heating pad and took some pain killers to help her relax. They would wake her in thirty minutes, have her move around some, and then if she wanted a few more minutes to sleep she could.

He and Sandy walked to the kitchen where she stopped and turned toward him. "I can't thank you enough, Greg. I sat there watching the energy drain out of her as Wendy put her through her paces and knew we wouldn't be able to get back. With Terry gone…."

He took Sandy into his arms as her eyes filled. "Shh, it's okay, that's what I'm here for, to help when you need it. It's an honor to be called." He ran his hands down her hair and back, soothing her, calming her, assisting her to let go of the worry.

He held her, hoping she was taking some of his strength for herself. He loved that she was allowing him to hold and comfort her. He would be happy to help out this way anytime, anywhere. It was close to heaven. The feel of her in his arms, trusting him completely. He wanted to kiss her again, but right now she needed comfort not some guy lusting after her. He could do that. He could do or be, whatever she needed.

He rocked her back and forth for several minutes before she pulled back. "Thanks, I needed that. This is all a little harder than I thought. Seeing mom so weak and tired is scaring me. She's always been so strong."

Greg squeezed her hands. "And she will be again. The injury and the resulting surgery would make anyone tired and weak. She's probably already doing more than most people would be."

Sandy gave him a wobbly smile. "Yeah, she probably is. Part of this is me, too. With the sabotage to the game and the frantic work to get it fixed. Then we had to launch it and go to New York for the press and to meet with some of the top gamers. It's been a hectic ride. Mom getting hurt in the middle of that, amped up my anxiety."

"Everything should be slowing down now that the game is out, and your mom is on the mend."

"It is, and I'll get stronger too. You're a good friend, Greg."

He cringed inwardly at the friend designation, he wanted so much more, but she did need a friend right now and he was happy to fit the bill. "I'm happy to have you lean on me anytime you need to. It never hurts to have a friend to prop you up."

After a big sigh she moved away, he felt her absence keenly. "So, what shall we have for dinner? Do you have a hankering for anything in particular?"

"Not really, anything that isn't fried would be great."

"I don't know how you eat all that deep-fried food all the time. It can't be good for your body."

He looked around mischievously. "If you promise not to tell I'll let you in on a secret."

"Cross my heart."

"I rarely eat what I serve in the bar. I eat a lot of salads and fresh foods. The apartment above the bar has food I can quickly cook. Not all of it is great, because I do sometimes have a microwave meal, but at least it's not deep fried."

She laughed, and the sound lightened his heart. Sandy said, "Your secret is safe with me. How about stir fry, with lots of veggies and some chicken?"

"Perfect. I can be the sous chef and chop some of those veggies."

"Hmm, I don't know if I can share the kitchen. I'm kind of territorial."

Greg raised his eyebrows. “I could go out on the porch.”

She giggled. “No need. I’ll suck it up and give you some of my space.”

He loved that giggle and he would be happy to take any and all space she would give him. In the kitchen, or anywhere else for that matter.

CHAPTER 11

The shrill tone of the fire radio could be heard above the noise of the bar. The jukebox was slapped off and the speakers now held the voice of the dispatcher. Greg immediately stilled to hear what she had to say.

A nearby tourist whined, "What the f—"

The waitress at the table next to the tourist whirled around and said, "Quiet" with such authority the tourist snapped his mouth shut.

Greg heard the dispatcher call out a house fire, *fuck,* and the address, *double fuck*. The Howe's place, deep in the woods. Thank God it was early in the evening, he didn't need a drunk crew on a house fire. The instant the dispatcher stopped speaking Greg started snapping out orders.

He barked out to the two men who had just walked in the door, "Been drinking?"

They both shook their heads. "No, sir."

"Good, Matt, take Pumper One, Craig, Ladder Three." He looked around and saw Adam spit out the mouthful of beer, the glass was nearly full. "Adam, that's your first?"

Adam nodded. "Pumper Two."

Greg saw Trey stand and noted his beer was full too. "Trey, get the tractor on the move, they had a good fire break, but—"

Half a dozen people said in unison, "That was six years ago."

Greg nodded. "Exactly."

He looked at Fred. "You stay here, eat some food and sober up. When you're good, if it's still going, come up. Report to me first."

Fred nodded and called out to the waitress. "Chicken and fries." Then he stuffed a hand full of pretzels in his mouth and started doing jumping jacks, right there in the middle of the bar.

Greg looked around. "Anyone else that's had more than one, do the same." Greg heard several people call out food orders and saw them get up to get their blood moving. "I'm going straight in, make sure the Howe's got out safe."

Jennifer, the mayoral admin and one of the female firefighters, said, "And their pets."

Shit, he'd forgotten about the menagerie they housed. "Jennifer, you're with me, then. You'll know what animals to look for." He looked at the dart area, saw Scott Davidson, who never drank. "Scott, grab your gear and come with me."

He called out to the rest of the volunteers in the bar, "The rest of you get to the station, catch a ride on the trucks."

Everyone started moving fast.

Greg double-timed it out to his truck knowing his staff would handle the bar. The siren on the fire department roof wailed as he pulled on his boots and bunker pants. He'd grab his coat and helmet at the scene. While Greg started his truck, Scott hustled over with his gear in hand, also already in pants and boots, and jumped in the back seat. Jennifer, dressed the same, slid into the front seat. Greg put his truck in drive and they tore out of the back of the parking lot, into the alley. Fortunately, everyone knew when the siren was blaring to stay out of the alley.

He radioed into dispatch to tell them he was in route to the scene. Shortly after that he heard the station chief radio the same and then the trucks started signing in.

Greg drove fast through town, confident that everyone knew to get off or stay off the roads when the siren was blaring. His truck had lights on top and a siren, that he'd engaged as soon as he'd put the truck in drive.

Scott, the town's pastor, said, "Praying the fire doesn't get into the trees."

"Yeah, we sure as hell don't need to start a forest fire this early in the season," Jennifer agreed.

"Yep, especially this close to town," Scott said.

Greg didn't comment, his focus was on getting them to the house as quickly as possible. There might be lives on the line, both human and furry. Every second seemed to take an hour as he roared up the road toward Ray and Betty's place, they were elderly and had gotten him through some rough periods in his youth, he couldn't let them down.

When he fishtailed into their yard, with dust flying, he could finally breathe. Ray had his garden hose on the front of the house and Betty was keeping their pets contained. The right side of the house was fully engulfed in flames. He barked out to Jennifer, "Make sure that's all the pets."

Jennifer waved as she hustled toward Betty. "Ten-four."

"Scott, go around back and get a second hose on the back."

"Got it."

Greg wanted to jump in and start helping, but the job of the assistant chief and first officer on scene, was to assess the work needed and give orders. He called into dispatch, "Tone it a second time. The front of the house is fully engulfed, everyone seems fine, but send the ambulance just in case."

"Copy, sir."

Jennifer ran up. "All the pets are safe, but both of the Howes ate some smoke getting them that way."

"Figured. Told dispatch to send the ambulance. Take over for Ray, so he can help Betty with the animals."

"Will do."

As equipment and volunteers streamed into the yard, he gave out assignments and dug into the strategy needed to keep this from spreading and hopefully save some of the Howe's home.

SANDY SPEARED A FORKFUL OF SALAD. "No, Steve, we really don't have a new game in the works. While *Adventures with Tsilly* is still as popular as it is, there is no reason to think about a new game." She was getting tired of this conversation, he'd asked her three times about a new game in the works and just wasn't listening.

"Of course, that makes sense." He nodded vaguely, and she wondered what he was really thinking. Clearly, he didn't believe her.

She tried again to change the subject. "Are you teaching the kids programming?"

He looked up. "A little... We have been talking about passwords recently. With all the hacking that seems to go on in the world, I am trying to teach them good habits on their accounts. I don't imagine you get to use the simple ones you did back in our high school days. Like your address or birthday."

She laughed. "Not even close, we have to have numbers and upper case and lower case and special characters. It's a nightmare. Plus, we have to change them out every ninety days and not use the last twenty passwords. Sometimes, I wonder if it's really necessary."

Steve nodded. "Right? How do people remember what it is without writing it down somewhere? It's one of the things we discuss in class. Any suggestions I can tell them from a real professional computer geek, like yourself?"

"Not really, only to keep it relevant enough to remember. Writing it down is never a good idea. We had one guy that used a sticky note attached to the underside of his keyboard. Not at all secure."

"Right out there for anyone to find." Steve chuckled as he shook his head.

A shrill tone sounded, and all sound and movement stopped in the restaurant. She saw Amber at the front counter turn off the soft music playing, and the dispatchers voice could be heard over the speakers.

Steve rolled his eyes but kept silent while the dispatcher spoke. Several men and one woman leapt up and rushed out the door, including Amber's husband Jeremy Scott, the children's book author.

She heard Barbara Clarkson say, "Go Chris."

"But—"

"No buts. Ray and Betty need you more than I do. Amber will make sure I get home. And Sandy's right over there."

Sandy turned and gave Chris a thumbs up. Barbara and Chris had been Sandy's best friends all through school, the rift from their senior year was all patched up. She would be happy to take Barbara home.

Chris looked back at Barbara one more time. "No baby urgings?"

"None whatsoever, get out of here, but be careful."

"Yes, ma'am." He called out, then he rushed out the door.

Sandy turned back to Steve to ask about joining Barbara.

He had a pissy look on his face. "I wish the whole town didn't have to stop every time the fire department is needed."

Sandy was shocked at his attitude. They had a volunteer fire department, so no one was sitting at the station ready for a call. That meant running the siren and nearly all the businesses and homes had fire radios, to alert the volunteers while they were out and about. In that instant she realized that Steve was a very selfish individual. She'd never thought anything about him not being on the department, not everyone was cut out for that. But to be angry about others responding to save lives and property, and disturbing Steve in the process, was ridiculous.

She didn't know what to even say. She sat there staring stupidly at the jerk across the table from her. She heard Greg radio that he was on the way. Now that was a real man in her opinion, leaving his business to go help people in need, not whining about his dinner being interrupted.

Sandy didn't want to spend more time with Steve, so she pushed her plate away. Barbara was finished eating but was now stranded at the restaurant. "I'm going to take Barbara home. It was fun catching up." She dropped some money on the table and went over to Barbara. Steve sputtered, but Sandy didn't look back.

"I'm okay, you don't need to end your dinner early," Barbara said when Sandy reached her side.

"No, trust me. I'm done. Let me help you get up. I can't imagine it's easy." Amber appeared on Barbara's other side and the two of them helped the very pregnant woman out of the chair. As they did so Sandy heard the trucks signing in as they left the station.

Barbara said, "I need to pay."

Amber chuckled, "Don't be silly. I'll collect from my brother later. I probably need to get some coffee and snacks ready. If they tone it out a second time, we'll need to take more than snacks."

Sandy was ready to spend the evening assisting the firefighters. "Once I drop Barbara off, I'll come back and help with that."

Amber nodded. "As long as Barbara or your mom don't need you."

"I'll check with mom and see if one of the book club ladies can stay with her." Sandy looked at Barbara, "Can your baby sitter stay, or should I see if one of the book ladies can come over and keep you company?"

"I'll be fine, I've got a high school kid watching the littles. She'll need to go home."

"I'm sure you will be fine, but someone hanging out at your house while Chris is fighting a fire would ease his mind, and mine."

Sandy could tell Barbara couldn't argue with that. "All right, I guess it's not a bad idea."

Sandy made arrangements while Amber helped Barbara into the car.

Sandy said, "All taken care of, I'll be back in a few minutes to help with the coffee." She turned to get into the car and heard the radio tone out a second time. "And other food, sounds like a long night ahead."

Amber nodded. "Go and I'll get coffee on and put together the snacks. My cook is probably already started getting the heartier food going."

CHAPTER 12

Greg sighed with relief when the ambulance arrived to check out the Howe's. Once the EMT's had examined them and given them oxygen, they had released Betty and Ray. Currently they were sitting in some lawn chairs with their pets surrounding them, watching the fire slowly being put out in their house.

It was clear to Greg that the kitchen and living room were destroyed, but he thought they had saved the bedrooms. Water and smoke would have caused a lot of damage but at least some of their personal items and furniture would be saved. They'd kept the fire from spreading into the trees too and he was definitely grateful for that.

Greg had been surprised to see Sandy pull up a bit ago with some food, water and coffee for the firefighters. After her talk about the newest version of the *Adventures with Tsilly* game he'd asked her if she wanted to get a bite to eat. But she'd told him she was going out to dinner with Steve.

He couldn't imagine they were done eating when the house fire came in, so she must have cut her dinner date short to be here with food and drinks. All the men and women on the line would appreciate it. They'd be here for many more hours, and the food would keep them going.

She came over to him with a sandwich, a bottle of water, and a cup of coffee. "The man in charge needs fuel, too. Eat. While I talk."

He couldn't argue, and took a big bite out of the sandwich after pounding down half of the water.

Sandy looked toward Betty and Ray. "I talked to mom and she said to have Betty and Ray come stay at the B&B tonight, and for however long they need to. We aren't full and won't be for at least a month."

He nodded as he chewed, and she continued. "I don't know what to do about the animals though, we don't have a fenced yard or anywhere to house them."

"I've got that covered," said a voice from behind Sandy. She turned to see police chief Nolan Thompson. "Kristen called me and said Barbara had called her to ask about keeping the animals. Kristen said that would be fine, our yard is plenty big enough to handle more pets."

Sandy asked, "But what about Farley? I heard he chased a cat all through town a few years ago."

Nolan laughed. "He did, but that's because the cat took off and Farley thought it was playing. He was barking and wagging his tail the whole way to the park where the cat finally climbed a tree. The Howe's cats live with other dogs, so they won't be skittish like that tourist's cat."

Greg took a big gulp of his coffee. He was relieved that the town was rallying around the now homeless couple and their menagerie of pets. "The two houses are close enough for the Howe's to visit their animals frequently."

Sandy nodded. "Good. I'll go talk to Ray and Betty."

Greg watched her walk off. He'd wanted to quiz her on her date with Steve but didn't feel he had the right to, at least not yet.

Nolan was still standing there, so he asked. "Barbara told Kristen? I guess you guys don't have a fire radio."

"Nope. Barbara was with Chris at Amber's when the call came in. Sandy drove Barbara home, so Chris could take the car."

Greg nodded. "Makes sense. You can have a fire radio at your home, being that you're the police chief."

"I know, but I don't think Kristen would really want to have one. She doesn't mind helping out with the animals but hearing the chatter of everyone over the radio might drive her a bit up the wall. Even though she now lives in town and has the gallery, she's still an introvert."

"Yeah I imagine she is, and if Barbara calls her to give her a heads up when needed, I guess that's easier for her to handle."

Nolan grinned. "Exactly, that's what sisters are for. And to be honest I'm not sure where we would even start, the house, both studios, the art gallery, the apartment above the art gallery? That's five."

Greg laughed.

Sandy came back to say that the Howe's were happy with the plans and were relieved they hadn't unloaded the car before taking a nap, after the drive up from Portland.

Nolan snapped his fingers. "That's right, I remember, they were looking to see if they could find a place to buy nearer their daughter, now that the grandkids are getting older, they don't want to miss so much."

Greg said, "They've been gone a couple of weeks, maybe three."

Nolan looked around. "Didn't they put their house on the market? I don't see the sign."

Greg grimaced. "It's under the stabilizers for the ladder truck."

Sandy laughed. "Oops. I'm sure Kyle has more."

Greg grinned at Sandy's amusement. "Since he's the one that was stabilizing the truck and smashed it, I would guess so."

Sandy guffawed. "You're kidding me."

"Nope, Kyle smashed the hell out of his own sign."

Sandy shook her head, her eyes sparkling with mirth. "And you guys are going to tease the crap out of him."

Greg smirked. "I can neither confirm nor deny such actions will take place."

Trey had walked up in the middle of the conversation, now that the fire break had been dug and they had dampened down the trees. "Well I can sure as hell confirm it. It took me hours to get the cling wrap off my car when you guys *welcomed* me to town. What do you want me to do next?"

They all laughed as Greg gave Trey a new assignment to help rotate the firefighters through the food line. Sandy and Nolan went to get the Howe's and animals on their way to their temporary locations.

Sandy chuckled to herself about Greg trying to look innocent about the pranks the firefighters all pulled on each other. She didn't believe for one minute he wasn't in on the silliness they came up with to tease the unwary.

She wondered what they would do to Kyle as she refilled the food and helped hand out drinks. The Howe's had gone off with Nolan to get settled into the B&B. Before Sandy had come to help at the fire, she'd made sure the room they would be staying in was ready and had clued in her mom and the friend that had stayed after the book club meeting. Carol's friend would probably spend the night, too. The B&B

wasn't full, so it wasn't a problem, and that way Sandy could help out at the fire.

When her mom was the mayor of their town, her family had always helped, so it was naturally ingrained and even expected. Her mom would have been horrified if Sandy had stayed to hover, instead of helping at the fire.

Amber drove up and gestured toward Sandy. Sandy went over to help carry the second round of food. "Do you really think they'll eat all this?"

Amber nodded. "Every bite."

Sandy waved at the table. "Some of the spouses have brought some things, too."

"Good, a couple of them called me to coordinate." Amber looked over the spread that held the offerings of granola bars, bottles of water, fruit, and even a whole ham that had been hacked away at.

"I brought chili, because when the fire is fully out, and the temperature drops, they are going to need something hot. Since I have catering warmers, I filled them up. Thank God I have lots of paper bowls and spoons. I wouldn't want to haul all this back to wash. An industrial dishwasher is awesome, but still."

Sandy laughed at Amber's expression. "Plus, some of them would inevitably end up in the trash."

"Sad but true. I had to buy a lot of new silverware after one wedding. Fortunately, I hadn't used the really good utensils. Why everyone threw them away I will never know. I guess maybe because the plates were disposable, and they didn't think to separate. Now if a bride wants real it's all or nothing. Not that many want it now days, the plastic plates and forks are so nice that there's no reason to want china and silver, especially since I charge a huge deposit for them. I learned that lesson."

Amber was suddenly whirled around, and Jeremy laid a

big fat kiss on her. "Thanks for bringing more food, sweetheart. I assume there's more in the car."

Amber flushed, but managed to stammer out a yes.

Jeremy grinned and winked at Sandy as he went off to carry more food over.

Amber shook her head. "Who was that masked man?"

Sandy laughed. "I believe that would have been your husband."

Amber gave her a happy smile. "And the guy can kiss, let me tell you."

Sandy decided to tease Amber just a bit. She nodded dreamily and said, "You do know I went to homecoming with him one year, right?"

Amber narrowed her eyes. So, Sandy laughed. "In middle school, before we knew how to kiss."

"Good, well no more second chances."

A male voice said, "Second chances at what?"

Sandy knew that voice and her cheeks turned pink as Amber said, "Sandy kissing Jeremy."

Greg's eyebrows lifted so high they disappeared into his helmet. "You want to kiss Jeremy?"

Sandy stammered, "N-no, of…of course not. That's silly, he's… he's married to Amber."

Amber laughed and turned away to direct Jeremy in the food placement.

Greg nodded and said quietly. "Good, because I'm the only one that gets to kiss you."

"What? Who decided that?" Sandy blushed so hard she thought she might put the lights on the fire equipment to shame.

"I did, of course I wouldn't do it unless you wanted me to, but so far you've been a willing candidate."

"We've kissed exactly once."

"Yes, and you did not protest. Maybe later after all this

mess is cleaned up, we can give it another try."

While her body cheered a resounding "Yes!" her mind told her to run. And be quick about it.

Greg said, "Don't worry. I have to get back to work now. The fire is out, and the crews are checking for hot spots before we start the cleanup. We'll be here for hours yet. Good thing Amber brought more food, the guys are going to be starving."

Sandy finally stammered out, "What about you?"

Greg looked at her mouth and whispered, "I'm starving all right, but not for food." Then he turned and went back to the command post.

Sandy's hands were shaking when she joined Amber at the food table. Did she want Greg to kiss her? She couldn't lie, even to herself. Yes, she did. But she wasn't sure she was ready for a real kiss. That tiny one they'd shared—was it only yesterday—had rocked her world. A real full on kiss might kill her.

She had hours to think about that, if she didn't sneak off to avoid the whole thing. Greg would need to be part of the team that would give the preliminary look at what might have caused the fire. The full investigation would start tomorrow in the daylight, but sometimes the night gave a different perspective.

Greg was back in command of the crew. The man was so damn sexy, the idea of him kissing her after he'd worked all night on the fire was so hot, she worried she might go up in flames right where she stood. Maybe she should leave before he finished. Not that she could avoid him forever, they were working on the fundraiser together. But… She needed to stop this craziness and help feed the men. She took one look back at Greg, he turned as if he could feel her staring, he held her motionless in his powerful gaze for a few heartbeats, before turning back to the fire, and she could breathe again.

CHAPTER 13

Greg had to work to keep his mind on the job. They had hours to go before he could even think about indulging his desire for Sandy, and by then she would probably be gone.

But duty came first. They had to make sure there were no hotspots and then they could pull the hoses out of the house and do whatever cleanup was possible. All the hoses had to be drained and returned to the trucks to take back to the station to be hung up, so they would finish draining and dry. Then the trucks would be restocked with dry hoses, in case they were needed again, before tonight's hoses were dry. Pretty long odds on that happening in their one-horse town, but better safe than sorry.

He, the station chief, and the fire investigators would need to do a quick look at what might have caused the fire. Then seal up the place for the formal investigation tomorrow. He decided to start with letting the squads get some food. The officer in charge had to look out for the men, low blood sugar could cause a lot of problems, even more than alcohol consumption with some people. They'd rotated out earlier when the sandwiches had arrived, but there had been a lot of energy used since then, the chili would hit the spot.

Now that the fire was fully out, they could have short breaks to refuel before they dug back into the cleanup. Getting the fire out was only half the job, the most important by far, but not always the most time consuming.

He spoke into the mic, "Beta squad take over for Alpha team. Alpha squad, refuel." As the firefighters started changing places on the line and the Alpha team headed for the food, he looked over at the table one last time. Sandy was looking right at him and he locked eyes with her for a moment. That woman packed a punch even from ten yards away. He tore his gaze from her and went back to work. Directing the teams on what was needed, coordinating the jobs with the chief, and the squad captains, communicating with the dispatcher and police.

As they worked, he occasionally looked back to the food area and was happy to see Sandy back there, bustling about.

SANDY WAS NOT STALLING WAITING for Greg to get finished. She was merely assisting with the cleanup. She carried food to Amber's car and wrapped up leftovers for others to take home. She bagged up the trash and washed down the tables. Nope, she wasn't stalling at all, she was helping.

Greg had gone into the house with a couple other senior guys twenty minutes before, and she was keeping an eye on the door. She knew they were careful and had the training necessary to determine their own safety, but she would still be happy when he was out of the burned building.

She looked around and realized she was alone. She sighed. Just because nearly every other support person had happily gone home to their beds, knowing the firefighters would be a while longer back at the station, was no reason for anyone to suppose she was waiting for Greg.

Shit. She was clearly stalling, and when she finally realized there wasn't one more thing to pretend to be doing, she gave up and walked to her car. She got in the door and shut her eyes, she hoped no one had seen through her pitiful excuses for staying. They probably hadn't, people were more interested in their own lives and feelings, to bother with the likes of her, and why she was the last civilian off the property.

She heard a knock on her window and startled, Greg was leaning on the door. She powered down the window.

"Are you sleeping in the car, beautiful? Waiting for me?"

"No, just getting ready to leave and needed to close my eyes for a second."

"Yeah, the smoke can make them sting some, and you've been here a long time. We all appreciate your hard work on our behalf."

Smoke, what a great excuse, much better than hanging around waiting for him. Before she could say anything, she looked closer at him. He wasn't really smiling, and his eyes held a weariness she didn't think was from the fire. "What's wrong?"

He sighed. "Nothing."

"Want me to sign an NDA?"

A chuckle burst forth. "No need for a non-disclosure. We just found some odd things inside the house."

"Odd as in…."

He shook his head. "We can't tell for sure, but the origin of the fire is not where it should be. It should have been near an appliance or even the fireplace, but it wasn't. It was next to some drapes that do not have anything electrical by them. And it appears there might have been some accelerant used."

She gasped. "You're not accusing the Howe's of setting their own house on fire."

Greg shook his head wearily. "No, at least not yet. Fuck, Sandy. I can't even start to believe they would do something like this."

Sandy said firmly, "No they didn't, and you'll discover the truth. In the morning, maybe it will all look different then." No way would she believe the Howe's had set that fire, it wasn't logical or part of their personality.

"I hope you're right. How about a little goodnight kiss to seal the deal?"

She laughed at his silliness which brought out a tiny almost smile from him. "Sure."

Leaning in her window he softly kissed her. When he started to pull away, she grabbed his coat and pulled him back down for a hotter kiss. His lips on hers, their breath mingling, she opened her mouth and his tongue swept in. He tasted like smoke, and Amber's chili, and all man. A little growl came from the back of her throat and the kiss got hotter.

He pulled back panting and looked at her for a long moment. "I have to get back to the station, but if I didn't…."

She thrilled at the fire in his eyes. But now was not the time or place. "Another time maybe. I need to get back, too."

"I'll take you up on that. Drive carefully."

"I will, and don't worry, we both know Ray and Betty had nothing to do with starting that fire."

He nodded. "Yeah, but I'm going to have to prove that."

"You will. I have full confidence in you." She started her car and drove off, leaving him standing there with a surprised look on his face.

CHAPTER 14

Greg was delighted with the response he'd gotten from Sandy last night at the fire. The kiss had knocked his socks off. So passionate and yet sweet at the same time. If the car door hadn't been between them it might have escalated, right out there in the open where anyone could see. When his brain had reminded him that's where they were, he'd had the strength to pull back. One of these days he was going to make sure they were somewhere without the possibility of onlookers.

He'd also been floored at the total confidence she had in him regarding the fire investigation. There was no question in his mind that the Howe's had not set their own house on fire, but it sure looked like arson from what they'd found last night. He couldn't think of any plausible reason for this. Did they have an arsonist loose in their town? Or what? It simply didn't compute.

So why had Sandy been so confident he would figure it out? Greg had every intention of getting to the bottom of it. But Sandy didn't really know him that well. Unless she'd gleaned more from Terry than he thought was possible.

He parked his truck in front of the Howe's home and saw them standing in the yard. Ray had his arms wrapped around his wife who was clearly crying as she looked at her house. They shouldn't be here, it might not look good if they were brought up on charges.

"Hey, Ray. Hey, Betty. The property isn't cleared for you to go in yet," he said as he approached them.

Ray cleared his throat and said, "Yeah we know, but we needed to see it in the daylight. We couldn't tell anything last night. It looks pretty bad."

Betty squeaked out, "It's horrible." Then she started sobbing as Ray tried to soothe her.

"How bad is it inside, Greg?"

Greg probably shouldn't talk about it, but he couldn't leave them in the dark. "The living room and kitchen are bad. The bedrooms are fair, mostly smoke and water damage in them."

Betty sobbed as she said, "I wanted… to take our furniture… to… to our new place… and now we can't."

"It's going to be all right, sweetheart. At least all the photo albums are in that blanket chest in the spare room. Maybe they're still okay."

Betty nodded and wiped her eyes, clearly trying to get the crying under control. "Oh, I hope so. Matty put them online, but I like to look at them the old-fashioned way. The kid's graduation pictures were in the living room though, I suppose they're destroyed." She sighed, and Greg felt the weight of it on his shoulders. There was no way these two had set their house on fire.

"We can get prints made of them, darling. Matt scanned those too, when he did the photo albums. We are safe, and so are our pets, and that's what really matters."

"I know it's just stuff, but it was *my* stuff. Things we picked out from the time we were newlyweds right up until today. I loved those things. My poor Roomba you just bought me for Christmas is ashes. It made me so happy."

"I know honey, I know." Ray held his wife tight as the tears started again. "Any idea what started it, Greg? We always unplug everything when we are going to be gone for a while. Did we forget something? Or was it bad wiring? I think that was up to code. We've been having things looked at in preparation for selling. I can't think of any reason for it to go up in flames like that."

Greg couldn't say any more without compromising the situation. He felt like a jerk for keeping it from them, but he had to follow the rules. "We'll be looking into that, Ray. Can you give me an idea of your return, so we can narrow down the timeline a bit?"

"Sure thing. We got to Chedwick on the ferry about five thirty. We noticed something big seemed to be going on at the school. We wondered what. Hey, your truck was there."

Greg knew that was right. "Sandy was giving us a run down on the new game release."

"Oh, sure that makes sense. Did I hear she's here for the summer to help out at the B&B, so Terry can take his delivery run after all?"

"Yes, you heard right. So, after you got home?" Greg prompted.

"Right, so we thought about stopping by the school, but we were too darn tired, so we drove home. We decided to take a quick nap before unloading the car. It was packed with luggage, and food for both us and the animals. Plus, the food bowls, and crates for the cats, and dog beds, and well just more stuff than we had the energy to bring in. So, we decided to take a nap first."

Betty said, "We set the alarm for an hour. Any longer than that and we would sleep all night."

Ray chuckled. "When the smoke detector started going

off, I thought it was the phone, and kept punching the button, but it wouldn't stop. I finally realized it was too loud to be the phone and was the smoke detector. Plus, the dogs were barking."

"They've got their own sleeping room across the hall. Ray doesn't like animals in the bed," Betty said.

"No. I don't. Anyway, by that time Betty was awake, and we could smell smoke. I checked the bedroom door for heat and didn't feel anything, so I looked out and could see flames down the hall. I yelled at Betty to get out the window and that I would get the animals out the same way in the other room, so for her to come around to that side and take them."

Betty said, "I called 911 before I crawled out the window. Needed to get you boys on the way."

Ray shook his head. "That never even occurred to me. Good thinking, sweetheart. I ran across the hall and lunged into the room. The animals were all going crazy. They normally sleep in crates, but those were still in the car, so they were a little frantic. As soon as I opened the window and called them the dogs jumped right out and most of the cats too, they are all pretty smart animals. Our old dog Brutus needed a little help, he's not as spry as he used to be."

Betty nodded. "And the kitten."

"Betty called up to me to find the kitten, that she was missing. I hoped to God she hadn't gotten through the door when I ran in, but I hadn't seen her. So, I started searching. Finally found her in the closet under some old blankets. The smoke was getting really thick, so I tucked her in my shirt and went out the window."

Betty shivered. "I was getting pretty scared when he finally showed up with the little rascal."

"I dropped the kitten off with Betty, who said you were on the way. Then I turned on the front hose and was trying to shoot it into the front window that had shattered. Thank God you showed up a few minutes later."

Greg thought this all sounded reasonable. "So what time did you set your alarm for?"

Ray shrugged, "I don't remember exactly what time it was. I just set it for an hour."

"Good, that gives me an idea of how things went. We're going to be doing some investigation to see if we can figure it all out. I'll give you a call when you can come back and go into the house."

Betty nodded. "Thanks, Greg. Ray, let's go back to Carol's. I need to rest; all that sobbing made my head hurt."

"Sure thing, darling. Sandy can make you some nice soothing tea, and you can put a cold cloth on your forehead."

Greg watched them walk away as Jeremy Scott, the other fire investigator on their department, walked up. "What were they doing here?"

"Crying over the destruction of their home."

"But they are moving to Portland."

"They are, but they hadn't moved any of their belongings, they were looking at places to buy in Oregon first. I had them give me a timeline and a recap of events."

"Good. Well let's get after it. When is the investigator from Seattle coming?"

"Tomorrow is the plan, but he said to go ahead and take a look, see if we can get anything for the labs to start on." Greg worried about his friends and what he and Jeremy were going to find in the house, but he had a job to do.

SANDY WAS FINISHING up the breakfast cleanup when Ray and Betty came into the kitchen. Betty's face was tearstained, and her eyes were puffy and red. Clearly, she'd been crying. Sandy's heart went out to the older woman.

Ray escorted her in and sat her gently at the kitchen table. "Sandy, would you mind making Betty a nice cup of tea, she's had a rough morning. I'm going to get a cold cloth for your eyes, Betty. I'll be right back."

"Of course. Did you go over to your house?" Sandy filled the teapot and turned it on. She took down a mug rather than a teacup, this didn't look like a teacup-sized problem.

Betty's shoulders drooped. "We did. Oh, Sandy, it's such a mess. We couldn't go in yet, and Greg said he would call us to come back when it is safe to go in."

Sandy's heart lurched when she heard Greg's name and she told herself to knock it off. Betty needed her. Now was not the time to moon over Greg Jones. "I know it's hard, Betty, but it's best to let them do their jobs. How did you get out? It looked like both doors were in flames to me."

Betty started to tell the story, while Sandy made her tea. When Ray came back with the cold cloth he helped with the narrative, so Betty could sip her hot drink. Sandy was surprised at the older couple's ability to keep their wits and get everyone to safety. She'd heard stories of elderly couples not being so fortunate. Her heart broke as they told the tale, but she was really proud of them at the same time. Sandy wanted to be exactly like them when she got older. Their relationship was so sweet. She had to wonder if she would ever have someone in her life like that.

When they finished their recounting of the events Sandy said, "Oh my, that is quite the experience you had. I'm so glad you and all your pets are safe. It's hard to lose your possessions, but much better than lives."

Betty sat up straighter. "You're right Sandy, and I'm going to be thankful about that, instead of crying over the belongings we lost."

Sandy patted Betty's hand. "You'll still have some crying, it's natural to feel loss."

Betty nodded. "I think I'll go lie down for a while. I want to refresh this cold cloth to put over my eyes, they feel gritty. Ray, you might want to go check on the animals."

"I'll do that, Love. You rest for a while."

Betty stood to make her way upstairs. "Make sure that kitten is all right, she's only a baby. Give her some extra loving."

Ray kissed his wife's cheek. "I will. Now you rest and stop fretting."

Sandy had an idea. "Ray, give me a minute before you go."

He nodded, and Sandy went off to have a word with her mom.

When she came back, she told him her plan and he was grinning as he left to go to Kristen's house. Just as he was leaving, she had another idea and called Kristen.

CHAPTER 15

Greg was back at the bar, he'd had a shitty morning. They had found concrete evidence that the house fire was arson. They'd also found evidence of the story Betty and Ray had told them. But that didn't outweigh the arson. He still didn't believe, for one moment, that the Howe's had set their house on fire and then crawled out the bedroom windows, but he had no other ideas about how it had started. Unless they had an arsonist in town. But that seemed nearly as far-fetched as the Howe's starting the fire.

He was in a piss poor mood and doing his damnedest not to take it out on his staff, or his customers. It was probably obvious to anyone who knew him well, and he hoped everyone would behave tonight, so he didn't rip anyone's head off their shoulders. Since it was a Thursday, he probably wouldn't have a full house. Lucky for them.

Sandy surprised the heck out of him when she strolled in the door. But some of the tension he'd been feeling did settle as she walked right up to him. "Do you have a minute and somewhere we can talk in private?"

Private? Hell yes. "My office would work." He nodded to

one of the waitresses to take over the bar and led Sandy back to his work space.

She said, "I have some good news, and you look like you need some."

Good news would be amazing, but he finally had her alone without any eyes on them, so he had to go for it. "I could use some, but a kiss would be even better."

She laughed. "I've got one of those I can spare."

When he locked the door, she walked right into his arms. He could feel the frustration leaving his body as he wrapped his arms around her and she melted into him. The woman had some kind of magical power, he lowered his head and she reached up toward him, opening like a flower after a long cold winter. He couldn't believe he was getting all sappy, so he ramped up the heat of the kiss to burn the foolishness away.

Sandy tasted like heaven, her hands were around his neck pulling him to her, her body was pressed to his from knees to chest. He could stay like this for a week, but he knew he had only a few minutes before he needed to get back out front. He lightened the kiss slowly, giving them both time to get their wits together.

He pulled back and put his forehead to hers. When he'd caught his breath enough to speak, he whispered, "Thank you. I needed that."

She patted his chest and looked up, still dazed. "Anytime."

"So, what is your good news?"

Sandy shook her head. "I have no idea, you just kissed all the brain cells away."

He chuckled at her bewildered expression. She was adorable all flushed and confused.

After a deep breath she said, "Oh yeah, I remember. Kristen is going to let the Howe's use her house up on the mountain while they wait for the next step. Mom's letting them keep the kitten at the B&B tonight and until they can get up to Kristen's. That cheered Betty up."

The weight came back in full force. "That's good, they'll feel more comfortable at Kristen's with all their pets. The next step might take some time. We need to wait for an investigator from Seattle."

"That doesn't sound good."

He turned and paced away running his hands through his hair. "It's not. The investigator will be here tomorrow. The Howe's won't be able to get back in their house until after he's had the time to investigate and we can make sure it's safe for them to get some of their things out. I don't like the looks of this fire. It's not adding up. I don't like what I'm seeing one bit… I can't say anything else."

Sandy walked back over to him and ran her hands up and down his arms. "It's okay, you'll figure it all out. Just take it one step at a time. Ray and Betty can stay at Kristen's. They have enough clothes and animal supplies to stay up there a couple of weeks. They were ordering groceries from Chelan when I left the house. Once the food arrives, they'll take it all up to Kristen's. You just do your job and it will be fine."

He sure wished that was true, but he didn't think it was going to be. He shook his head. "I don't know."

Sandy put her hand over his mouth. "I do. Now, no more fretting. One day at a time. Give me one more quick kiss before your staff starts banging on that door."

He laughed and gave her a fast but firm kiss, before they went back to the crowd.

SANDY FLOATED INTO THE BAR, that man knew what he was doing in the kissing department. He'd literally kissed the thoughts right out of her head. She'd come to the bar on the hunch that Greg was worried about the outcome of the fire investigation. The nagging feeling that he needed some good news had persisted and since the Howe's were at the house, she knew her mom would be fine for an hour. The three of them were playing cards when she checked in to see if her mom needed anything. Carol had shooed her off saying that Ray or Betty could help her if she wanted something and she could always call.

When she'd arrived at the tavern, she'd taken one look at Greg's face and knew she'd done the right thing by coming. She'd been shocked right down to her toes when he'd said he needed a kiss. Shocked, but totally willing. He'd then kissed her like a starving man and she'd kissed him right back with pleasure.

When he'd been reticent to talk, she knew he was worried. Not that Greg was a gossip, because he wasn't, but saying he *couldn't* say any more boded trouble. She'd tried to encourage him, but when that didn't work, she'd asked for another kiss, and he hadn't hesitated.

Sandy knew her blood was still racing, and she imagined her cheeks were flushed, but hoped the dim lighting would hide it well enough. She got a hard cider from the bartender and went over to join some friends from high school. Greg had disappeared into the kitchen.

She'd stay and drink her cider and then go home. The nagging feeling had left, and she knew she'd done everything she could.

Greg came out from the back with a plate of food and a large glass of water. He brought it over to the table where she was sitting. "Mind if I join you guys?"

Fred laughed and moved over. "It's your bar. Feel free."

Sheila looked at his plate piled high with chicken strips and fries. "Did you miss dinner?"

Greg shrugged. "I wasn't hungry."

Sandy knew there was more to that statement than everyone else realized. He'd probably been too upset to eat. That made her even happier she'd followed her instincts and come into his bar. She stole a French fry off his plate, he grinned at her and kept right on eating.

A fun song came on and the rest of their table got up to dance. One of the guys asked her to join him, but she declined. She was happy to sit by Greg as he finished his food.

She stole another French fry and dipped it into the pool of ketchup.

He swallowed. "Thanks for coming in tonight. You helped me calm down. Nothing changed, but your support makes a difference."

A warm glow filled her at his words. "Happy to be of service."

He finished eating and gulped down the water. "I better get back behind the bar. Can't slack off all night because a pretty girl is here."

She laughed. "I need to get home anyway. The Howe's being with mom is great, but I don't want them to have too much responsibility."

Greg nodded and kissed her on the cheek. "Have a good night."

He carried his plate and glass to the back, and she was sorry to see him leave. But he made a fine figure as she watched him walk away, and more than one lady turned to watch him go. He could probably have any woman in the place, other than the married ones. Even some of them, might be interested. So why he was spending all his time with her and giving her kisses, she didn't know.

CHAPTER 16

The fire investigator from Seattle would be here today, and Greg wasn't all that excited about it. The fricken fire looked like arson and there wasn't a damn thing he could do to shield the Howe's from that.

He was certain they hadn't set it, but with their plans to move to Portland and the house on the market, a quick insurance claim would be faster than waiting for the place to sell. Their home was a little too remote to be an easy purchase. The right buyer would be harder to find than one of the in-town houses, not that there were a lot of places available right now, but still.

He'd decided last night after Sandy had left the bar that he should consult with Nolan to maybe get the ball rolling on the investigation. Nolan might have some good ideas. Greg had called and asked for a morning appointment with the Chief of Police. The dispatcher had laughed at him and said he could come by any time without an appointment, but Greg wanted everything official and above board.

She'd given him a ten o'clock appointment and the ferry would be landing at eleven thirty, so that gave him an hour and a half with Nolan. Greg probably didn't need that long, but he didn't want to feel rushed either.

When he walked into the police station, Greg saw Nolan in his office. Nolan glanced up and waved Greg in to join him.

Nolan gestured toward the coffee pot. "If you want coffee, grab some on your way in."

Greg first thought to decline, but then decided maybe something to drink or at least hold might be a good thing. So, he stopped to make a cup, they had both paper cups and also ceramic mugs with cutesy sayings on them about police officers. Greg took a mug that said, "The police never think it's as funny as you do", and wasn't that the truth in a nutshell?

He took his cup into Nolan's office. "Mind if I close the door?"

Nolan shook his head. "So, I take it this isn't a social visit. What's on your mind, Greg?"

"The fire the other night. It looks like arson."

Nolan leaned forward. "Is that right? I would never have guessed that. The Howe's don't seem the type to do something like that."

"I am fully confident they didn't set the fire, but that's because, A. I know them, and B. I saw them the next day totally devastated about the fire. That's not going to convince anyone else, however. So, any suggestions?"

Nolan sat back in his chair and folded his arms. "First, let me get this clear, do you think we have an arsonist in town?"

"It sure looks that way. We've never had anyone who has any significant pyromaniac tendencies. So, unless someone is acting out in a new way, it must be someone from out of town."

The chief of police nodded, and Greg could see him thinking it through, so he waited until Nolan spoke. "Not a lot of tourists yet, but it only takes one. We could look for like crimes if you can get any kind of signature. How it was started, did they use an accelerant? What kind, those types of things. Did you find anything to send to the labs in Seattle? When will the fire investigator be here?"

Greg relaxed as Nolan peppered him with questions, it indicated he was open to the idea. "We took some samples where it looked like it started. Which wasn't near any appliances or even a light socket, only some drapes. It did look like accelerant was used and based on the smell my guess is kerosene. Jeremy thought the same. The investigator from Seattle will be here on the ferry today. I thought it looked fishy the first night, after we got it out, so I called immediately."

Nolan jotted down notes. "Good. I'll go out and dust for fingerprints, on the outside of the house, I won't go inside until the fire inspector has his turn. You guys all wear gloves on scene, so maybe we'll find something. Doubtful, but you never know, we could get lucky. I'll start a search for arson fires started with kerosene. We'll start with Washington and then branch out from there."

Nolan tapped his pen on the page. "I'll go by Carol's B&B and see if the Howe's have washed their clothes from the fire. If they started it with kerosene it would have splashed and gotten on clothes or shoes."

"They said they went out the windows, so they wouldn't have gotten any on themselves accidentally."

"That's helpful. We could probably check here, and in Chelan for recent purchases of kerosene. Although they'd driven in from Portland and could have stopped anywhere along the way to buy it. Or had it on hand. Although at their age, I doubt they go camping much."

Greg chuckled, Nolan was taking him seriously and planned to look into ways to prove, or rather disprove, the

Howe's culpability. It wasn't the end of the issue, but it was a step in the right direction, which allowed Greg to finally breathe. "Anything you need or want me to do?"

"No, you just handle the inspector. Make sure he knows we're looking into it as a crime against the Howe's."

"Will do."

"If you can stall him a half hour to give me time to dust for fingerprints that would be superb."

Greg smiled. "I'll see if he wants to grab lunch and emphasize the house is in a remote location with no readily available food."

"Perfect. You know if it is an arsonist or pyromaniac they tend to stick around to watch. Did you see anyone who didn't belong?"

He hadn't even thought of that. Greg searched his memories of the night. "I can't think of anyone, but I'll give it some thought. I was pretty focused on the fire and crew, plus that far out, I didn't expect onlookers. Someone else might have noticed."

"Or he could have been hiding in the woods," Nolan ventured.

"So many avenues to look down. I'm sure glad this is your job and not mine."

Nolan barked out a laugh. "This is the most activity I've had since I moved here."

Greg smirked. "You mean to say the thief and the homeless vet weren't much of a challenge."

"The kid was for a few days. Owen, not so much."

Greg wondered about how the kid, Theodore Beaumont-Jordon, had faired moving back into society after living off the grid most of his life. His father had kidnapped him at a young age and moved him to the mountains near Chedwick. When his father had died, Ted hadn't known to go anywhere else. Until a forest fire forced him into town, where he'd stolen some food and supplies to survive. "Have you heard from Theodore recently?"

"As a matter of fact, he's going to be spending the summer here working at the amusement park. He's been playing the game and talked his mom into coming here. Not that she had a lot of choice, he's of age now and can do as he pleases, but they're not ready to be separated so she's coming too. He graduated from high school only one year late. He must be smart as a whip to start going to school at sixteen and be able to graduate so quickly. He's continued to send Kristen his sculptures to sell in the gallery, and they are magnificent."

Greg was impressed by the success of the boy. "That's amazing news. I'm glad it all worked out for him."

"Yeah, it's a great success story. Well, if I'm going to beat you out to the Howe's place, I better get a move on."

Greg stood and shook hands with Nolan. "Thanks for your time."

"Give the investigator my number so we can coordinate."

"Will do." Greg put his empty coffee mug on the tray designated for them and walked out the door, feeling more confident than he had in days. He thought about texting Sandy and decided that was weird. He didn't think they were quite there yet in their relationship. But the urge to text her was stronger than he expected.

SANDY WONDERED how Greg felt today. He'd not come to breakfast, so she assumed he'd been busy with the fire aftermath. The Howe's said he'd called them to tell them the investigator would be here today, and he would need to talk to them. They hadn't seemed concerned about that idea, so Sandy doubted Greg had said anything to them about the suspected arson.

She spent the morning making some phone calls for auction donation items for the fundraiser. Marking in her spreadsheet exactly what would be donated, the value of the item, when they planned to ship it, and email addresses for easier correspondence. She was making some headway on their list. She doubted Greg had had much time to work on his half.

They would start with local people next week or the following one. Now was the time to contact remote artists that needed extra time to ship items. It was time consuming, but she had the time on days her mom didn't have PT appointments, so she didn't mind.

After making her mom lunch and checking on what Carol had done that day, she spent afternoons on a conference call with her development team in Seattle. Making decisions and looking at story-boards. The story-board part of the planning took months. They had to design all the different scenarios a game player might take and how that affected the game world.

Sandy liked being busy, and she certainly was. It did not however keep her from thinking about the hot kisses she and Greg had shared. Sometimes she felt mortified that she was kissing a man three years younger, who was her brother's best friend, but then the memory of the passion those kisses had evoked burned away the embarrassment. It was definitely nothing she expected to feel. But every time she thought about those kisses her blood heated and she craved more.

The doorbell interrupted her musings and she was startled to find Nolan, the police chief at the door. "Nolan, what brings you here?"

"Hi Sandy. I need to talk to the Howe's for a few minutes. I need to get their observations from the fire."

"An alibi?" she squeaked.

"No, but I do need to hear what they have to say about that night while it's fresh in their mind."

"Oh, yes, of course. Have a seat and I'll go get them. They only got back from playing with their animals at your house a few minutes ago."

He chuckled. "The animals are having a fun time all together, even though Farley is getting up there in age. Thanks Sandy, and don't worry Greg and I are not leaving one stone unturned."

Sandy was relieved to hear Nolan say that, he clearly was of the opinion that the Howe's needed those stones turned over in search of the arsonists. She decided to stay close during the interview in case they needed something. Drinks, tissues, whatever.

Sandy found her intervention was not needed. Apparently, Nolan had gotten to know Betty and Ray through Kristen, and although they talked seriously for a while it was comfortable. She'd gone in to offer them drinks at one point and there had been no tension in the room. So, she stopped hovering and sat with her laptop looking at some of the story-boards her team had sent.

Greg and the fire investigator came later in the afternoon after Ray and Betty had rested for a while, so they were more than ready to talk to the man from Seattle.

Greg joined her in the kitchen while Betty and Ray answered questions.

Sandy said, "Nolan was here earlier and interviewed the Howe's."

"Yeah, I talked to him this morning and he volunteered to work on the police side of things. He's going to look for like crimes."

"Oh, that's good, I guess. I still can't believe we have an arsonist in our town."

Greg nodded. "I'm right there with you. It does seem like

something that would happen somewhere else, not here. The main thing is, unless we can find the person, this investigation could be drawn out for months."

"Really? On television the perps are always found in a few days."

He rolled his eyes at her. "Yeah, but you do realize that's fiction. Real life takes longer. They won't release the house to the Howe's until all the lab results are back, in case more evidence is needed."

"Well I'm glad they can go up to Kristen's mountain house then. I noticed they get tired after they go visit their pets. I imagine the separation is taxing on both humans and animals."

"Probably. I'll ask them when they want to go up and see if we can't give them a hand getting settled. I don't think Kristen brought much down from up there, so furniture should be fine. But the gas might need to be turned back on or refilled or whatever," Greg said.

"Yeah. It might be worth taking Kristen up there to get them settled."

"Good idea."

Sandy laughed. "That's why they pay me the big bucks."

Greg had gone still when she laughed and the atmosphere in the room had changed. If she didn't have people in the very next room, she might have been tempted to see how far the electricity between her and Greg went. But there *were* people in the other room, so she cleared her throat and asked Greg if he wanted something to drink, or if he thought she should offer something to the investigator.

He seemed to shake himself out of whatever he'd been feeling and agreed to a glass of iced tea. But before she could stand to get it, he said, "But no more laughing. It's too sexy."

She started to laugh again but stopped. "Sexy? My laugh? That's silly."

He said in a gruff voice, "Silly maybe, but true just the same."

She turned toward the living room to avoid looking at him and popped her head around the door. "Would you all like something to drink? Iced tea? Lemonade? Water? Soda?"

The atmosphere was thick in the room, all three of them looked relieved at the interruption, and agreed to a beverage.

She looked at Greg and whispered, "The tension in that room is off the charts."

Greg looked worried but resigned. "He's probably telling them it's suspected arson. It's not easy on the investigator and Betty and Ray are probably devastated by the news. I'll help you with the drinks."

When Greg and Sandy took the glasses in, Betty had silent tears running down her face and Ray was holding her close. The investigator quietly watched them, but Sandy could see a slight bit of stress around his mouth. She hoped it was because he wanted to believe their innocence rather than their guilt, but she supposed his job was to remain impassive. She didn't think she'd want his job.

The investigator looked up as they entered the room. "Please join us, we're finished with the interview for today."

Greg sat in the chair next to the investigator. Sandy sat on the couch by Betty after they put the drinks on the coffee table.

Betty looked at Sandy. "Someone set our house on fire with us inside it. Do you think… do you think they were trying to kill us?"

Sandy gasped. "No not at all, maybe they thought you were still gone, or the house was vacant or something." She looked at Greg for help.

Greg said, "I agree with Sandy. I can hardly imagine an arsonist in our town, let alone a murderer."

Ray asked Greg, “Do you think we’ll be safe up on the mountain at Kristen’s house?”

Greg nodded. “Yes, I do. It’s too remote to get to easily. Your house is remote, but it’s still a relatively easy location to find. Kristen’s? Not so much.”

Ray relaxed and chuckled a bit. “True, unless you’re a Billy goat.”

Betty said, “Well let’s get up there then. I need some rest. Running back and forth to see our pets all day is taking a toll on these old bones of mine.”

Greg said, “We’ll get that taken care of tomorrow. Now that you’ve answered everyone’s questions you don’t need to stay in town. If any other things need to be asked, we’ll come up to you.”

Sandy was impressed by the compassion and gentleness that Greg was showing to the elderly couple. He could be hard as nails in his bar when someone was acting out, but he clearly had a gentle side to him. Sandy found that dichotomy very sexy.

CHAPTER 17

Greg got the Howe's settled with Kristen's help. Kristen had given them the grand tour and had shown them everything they would need to know. While Kristen did that, Greg checked the gas tanks to make sure they had plenty of fuel for heat, cooking, and hot water. It was still early in the spring, and they were high enough on the mountain that they might need to turn the heat on.

Greg said, "You've got plenty of propane."

Kristen nodded. "I keep the tanks filled enough for a month or two, but not any longer, that way if we have another fire up here it's easier to evacuate."

Greg remembered six years ago when Kristen had waited for someone to come help her haul out all the tanks while the forest fire had been breathing down her neck. She'd had not only the household tanks, but large ones she used for her jewelry design business. They'd been so busy getting everything squared away in town, they'd completely forgotten Kristen up on the mountain—in the path of the fire—with all that gas ready to blow them all to kingdom come. "Yeah, a couple of months is easier to manage, for sure."

Kristen shrugged. "It all worked out."

Greg grinned at that, while the guys in town had forgotten her, Nolan had been a new cop in Chedwick and tasked with evacuating the residents on the mountain. Fortunately, he and one of the hotshot firefighters, that had been brought in, had helped her get them loaded in her truck.

Greg guessed Kristen had fallen in love with Nolan a little bit that day. And Mary Ann who had been up helping Kristen might have felt the same way, about her own current husband, who had been the hotshot firefighter. One just never knew how tragedy—or near tragedy—might affect a life, or four.

By the time he'd gotten back to town after securing Ray and Betty in their temporary home with all their animals, the investigator had interviewed all the firefighters and the police that had worked the house fire.

He met Greg on the way to the ferry. "I've been called back to Seattle for an apartment fire. Thank God no lives lost, but some injuries and the fire chief didn't like the looks of some things. I'll circle back here when the lab results come in and we can write up the docs to file then."

Greg nodded. "Sounds good, have a safe journey back over the mountains. I'll give you a call when the results get here."

With everything calmed down, Greg and Sandy went back to working on the fundraiser. They had gotten a lot of pledges for donations by calling and emailing people that were remote. He'd had to hustle to catch up on his half of the list. Sandy had offered to help but he wanted to put his share of work into it.

She already had an impressive list of items on her laptop. They would start chatting with the local people soon.

Sandy had made some very handy forms that people could fill out on the spot. Or they could leave the forms, with information about the fundraiser and auction, for people to look over in their leisure.

Greg joined Sandy at the B&B and had an amazing coffee cake, it was filled with butter, and cinnamon, and nuts. When he was stuffed to the gills with eggs, bacon, coffee, and the sweet delight, he had to force himself to put his fork down. "Sandy, that is the most amazing thing I've ever eaten. If we don't get out of here right now, I'm going to keep eating it until I explode."

Sandy laughed at him. "I'll put the rest in a storage container and you can take it home for tomorrow's breakfast or a late-night snack."

"Deal. Now let's get out of here. I need to walk some of that deliciousness off."

They spent the morning on main street, stopping into every business, even the ones they couldn't think of anything that could be donated. They'd been pleasantly surprised by the reactions of all, and came away with some very unique prizes to auction off.

Little by little the breakfast wore off, so they stopped at Amber's for some lunch. Greg decided after the decadent breakfast he'd had, that the salad bar would be a good choice.

When he said as much to Sandy she laughed. "You go right ahead and eat your rabbit food. I'm having one of the Reuben's. No one makes a Reuben like Gary does. I suppose I could skip the shoestring fries and have a salad instead."

Greg could tell she didn't really want to swap the fries for salad and was probably only doing it because he was. "No, get the fries, you can have a few bites of my rabbit food, and I'll have a handful of fries."

Her smile lit up the room. "Awesome."

Amber came up while he tried to get his brain cells to function after being blinded by the mega-kilowatts that had just been expended from a smile.

"What are you two doing out and about?"

Sandy answered, thank God, because his brain was still shorted out. "We're collecting donations for the auction we're having at the fundraiser."

"You haven't asked me or Jeremy yet," Amber folded her arms and glared at them.

"We started on Main street and were working our way towards you, but got too hungry. Being charming, and begging for donations, is hard work."

Greg sputtered out a laugh. "Charming? Begging? Who've you been out with?"

"Well *I* was charming and begging, while you glared at them like they were slackers if they didn't pony up something." Sandy looked at Amber. "We've got quite the eclectic group of items. I didn't think the plumbers would have anything to donate but they managed to give us a gift certificate for a free roto-rooting session. They also said they knew a couple of families that would fight over the prize."

Amber giggled. "That's amusing. I'll donate a family of four for lunch in the café and a couple's night out in the fine dining section. Oh, and I should do something for the wedding venue." She tapped her lip in thought. "I can't think of anything right off. Let me get back to you on that. I'll talk to Sheila and see what we can come up with."

Sheila was the wedding coordinator for the town, so that might end up being a great prize. Sandy pulled out a packet of information and added three of the signup forms. "You can fill them out now, or we can collect them later, or both."

"Great. I'll talk Jeremy, or his publisher into donating a bunch of books. I'll make copies of the form for them, or you could send me an electronic copy that Jeremy can send on. Are you getting some Tsilly games from your company, Sandy?"

"I've put in the request. I should hear back in a day or two. It's still a big corporation."

"And they move slow as molasses in the arctic." Amber looked at Greg. "Are you going to add some toys to the auction? With all the babies coming, there might be fights over those."

Sandy gasped. "Who else is preggers besides Chris and Barbara?"

"Mary Ann is huge, I take it you haven't been to the gallery yet."

Sandy shook her head but kept quiet. Greg noticed Amber had an odd look on her face, so he was silent too.

Amber looked around and then said quietly, "And, well, I haven't said much, but Jeremy and I are expecting a little one toward the end of the year."

Sandy shrieked and jumped up to hug Amber. "What? You don't look like it. At all. Congratulations, that's so cool."

Jeremy had just walked in the door, so he made a beeline toward them. "I see hugging, did you tell them?"

"I did. I couldn't contain it."

Jeremy smiled at his wife and Greg knew the sweetness in the room had amped up to monumental proportions, so he stood to shake Jeremy's hand and slap him on the back, to calm down the estrogen overload, just a bit. "Congrats, man. That's great news."

"Thanks, Greg."

Sandy wormed her way in to give Jeremy a hug and Greg tried not to be jealous. He knew the two of them had a history, but it was over and being jealous of a happily married man was ridiculous.

Jeremy took his wife's hand. "Amber, honey, let's give these two some space."

Greg saw their waitress hovering behind Amber, not wanting to interrupt, but still needing to do her job. He grinned and said, "Congratulations to both of you. Amber don't forget to talk to Jeremy about the auction."

Amber nodded and walked off with her husband. He looked at Sandy and winked. She was clearly trying to keep from laughing.

~

SANDY KICKED Greg under the table as the waitress came up to give them water and take their orders. Amber was normally so efficient and ran a tight ship, so Sandy found it hysterical to see her all befuddled and sappy about being pregnant.

When the waitress left Greg leaned in, his blue eyes drilling into her. "I saw you trying not to laugh at Amber, so don't deny it."

She giggled. "How could I, she was being such a zoom. I've never seen her like that. She had no idea the waitress was behind her. Normally Amber knows exactly where each waitress is, who she's waiting on, and what they need at every moment. I never really believed there was such a thing as pregnant brain. I always thought people used it as an excuse, but it was on full display just now."

"Then why did you kick me?"

She giggled again. "I didn't want you to say anything in front of the waitress."

"You don't think they've all noticed?"

"Of course they have, but still, no need to emphasize it."

He smirked and got to his feet. "I'll go get us some salad. Ranch or vinaigrette?"

"Either, both are good, about the only thing I don't like is blue cheese. I mean who wants to eat mold?"

"I couldn't agree more. Be right back."

While the hot man walked off to the twenty-foot salad

bar running across the back of the room, Sandy thought about Amber being pregnant. She'd felt an odd sensation when Amber had told them the news. Was she jealous? Did she wish she was pregnant too? Not without a husband. She had a friend at work who had wanted children bad enough to use artificial insemination, because she wasn't married. Sandy couldn't imagine doing that. But she would like to have kids someday. There was plenty of time she had only turned thirty a couple of years ago. Of course, if she wanted a husband she would need to start dating seriously. Who had time for that?

CHAPTER 18

Sandy finished up the breakfast service and gave Karen a list of what needed to be done. She had decided last night with all the talk about babies, that she needed to get over to see Barbara before she had hers. She felt bad that she'd put it off as long as she had, Barbara had been her best friend most of her childhood. Chris had said after the baby was born would be good too, but by the time Barbara was ready for company, the fundraiser prep would be heating up, so now would be better.

She'd called Barbara to make sure she was feeling up to it and told Greg that she would be busy until about noon. He'd agreed that there were some things he'd been ignoring and said he could get those done in the morning and meet her to keep working on business owners afterward. Sandy figured she could mention the auction to Barbara while she was there and kill two birds with one stone.

She took some scones with her to give to Barbara, before Sandy could knock, Barbara whipped the door open and said, "For God's sake don't ring the bell. I just got the monsters to sleep for their nap."

Sandy jolted at the near hysteria in Barbara's tone. "I was going to knock."

Barbara held the door open and Sandy stepped inside. "Oh, well good, some people are clueless about doorbells and children. I've told Chris to dismantle the damn thing over and over, but he refuses."

Sandy had nothing to say about that, it did seem like kind of a severe thing to do for a couple of hours during nap time. She looked around and saw that the house was spotless. She was a little surprised, they had two small children, how could it be so clean? Sandy wondered if Barbara had "done her nesting thing" as Chris had called it, where she cleaned the house from top to bottom and then had the baby immediately after. She didn't think it was her place to ask so she held out the scones. "I brought scones."

To Sandy's horror, tears filled her friend's eyes. "Oh, you are the best friend ever. Come in. Let's go into the kitchen and I can make some tea." As Sandy followed Barbara into the kitchen, Barbara complained, "What I really want is a cup of coffee. But no, coffee is not allowed." Barbara huffed as she pulled out some tea cups and tea bags and put them on the table, motioning Sandy to have a seat. "The baby will be out in a day or two. I don't think one cup of coffee is going to kill him or her."

The tears had turned to anger, which was still uncomfortable, but since it wasn't directed at her, Sandy didn't mind.

Barbara filled the tea kettle still muttering to herself and slammed it down on one of the burners. The sound clanged through the kitchen and Barbara stilled. Not moving, just staring terrified at the ceiling, Sandy didn't think she was even breathing.

Finally, after a minute of total silence Barbara took a deep breath. "That was close, I would have killed myself if I'd woken the littles with my temper tantrum. How stupid can one person be? What a terrible mother."

Sandy sat in shock at the self-loathing she saw on her friend's face. Sandy was getting whiplash with all the wild emotions Barbara had shown in the last five minutes. Did every pregnant woman do this or was it only Barbara? This was totally insane.

Sandy cleared her throat. "I brought the baby something, it's not much."

Barbara's eyes filled with tears again. "You are such a good friend. I don't deserve you." She tore open the gift and smiled at the tiny Seahawks jersey. "Oh, how sweet, thank you. He or she will love it."

Sandy wanted to try to stop the rollercoaster of emotions and she'd just thought about how to do it. Business, Barbara was always on target when she talked about her business. Sandy grabbed that idea like a lifeline, praying it wouldn't let her down this time. "So, have you heard about the auction?"

Barbara's head snapped up and her eyes cleared from all the sappy emotions. "I have."

Sandy breathed a sigh of relief. "Would you like to donate something to it?"

Barbara nodded. "Yes, I've been thinking about it. I hear you have forms and information. Let's go sit at the dining room table and look at them."

Sandy was thrilled to move into an area where she was in control. As they talked about the different auctions and the items Barbara was willing to donate everything went smoothly. They also talked about the booth Barbara and her partners planned to have. Sandy relaxed more and more as the discussion became normal and not fraught with so many emotions.

As Barbara handed her back the paperwork, she got a sly look on her face. "So, you and Greg Jones?"

Sandy was so caught off guard by the question she felt her face heat and stammered out, "J-Just helping him with the f-fundraiser. He's in over his head. H-His words, not mine."

"He's a fine-looking man. No reason you can't have a little fun while you slave away. He's not dating anyone."

"I'm only here for the summer, then I'm going back to Seattle and my job."

Barbara shrugged. "No reason you can't have some summer fun. A little vacation fling might be good for our hard-working game engineer."

Sandy had to admit even if it was just to herself it did sound like a tempting idea. But she wasn't about to say that out loud. "No, I don't think so. I've never been much into flings."

Barbara's eyes filled with tears again. "I'm so sorry about stealing Chris away from you."

Oh, for crap's sake that had happened over fifteen years ago, and they'd been through it already. "Barbara, no, don't be silly that's old news."

"But it was still a horrible thing for us to do," she wailed, the sound getting louder and louder with each word.

Sandy worried about the napping children. "Shh, it's all right, you don't want to wake up the little ones."

Barbara clamped a hand over her mouth and stilled, staring toward the stairs. A minute or two passed and there was no noise. She took her hand off her mouth and whispered fiercely, "Oh my God. What is wrong with me today? That's twice I almost woke them up."

"I was kind of wondering the same thing, you've been a little emotional."

Barbara stilled again like when she was waiting to see if the kids had woken up. Sandy listened intently but didn't hear anything.

Barbara jumped up. "I forgot. I was so happy you were

coming. I didn't think. Oh my. We need to get moving. I need to call Chris and the baby sitter. My bag is by the door."

Sandy was back to being confused. "What is it?"

"I'm in labor. I didn't notice because you were here. My emotions always go haywire right before I have the baby. With this being number three, we've got no time to lose."

"What can I do?"

"Do you have Chris's phone number?"

Sandy nodded.

"Tell him to meet us at the clinic. I'll call the neighbor, she's going to stay with the littles."

Sandy was shaking as she tried to scroll to find Chris's number. Thank God he wasn't further down in the list. As she pushed 'send' she saw Barbara point to the scones and mouth "bring them".

She was chuckling when Chris answered his phone. She quickly relayed to Chris the pertinent facts and he said he'd meet them. The neighbor charged in the door as Sandy hung up and she was relieved to see it wasn't old Mrs. Erickson, who was the neighbor on one side, but a young woman carrying a baby of her own, who looked to be about six months old.

Sandy grabbed the scones and put them back into the container she'd brought them in and then carried Barbara's bag out to the car. Barbara gave her neighbor last minute tips and then waddled quickly out to the car.

When she was buckled in, she said, "I'm going to call the clinic and let them know we're on our way. You drive, and don't spare the horses."

Sandy laughed at the old term but didn't dawdle on the short drive to the clinic. The staff met them on the sidewalk and Chris slid to a stop right behind Sandy's car. Barbara grabbed the scones and let Chris help her out of the car.

Sandy got the bag out of the backseat and handed it to

Chris once his wife was in the wheel chair and moving toward the clinic.

"Thanks for being there, Sandy."

Sandy was still in shock but managed to say, "My pleasure."

Chris kissed her on the cheek and took off to go help with the birth.

Sandy collapsed back onto her car and simply stood there. She couldn't have moved if she wanted to. She was completely drained from her visit with her friend.

GREG KEPT himself busy all morning. He'd been slightly disappointed when Sandy had postponed their getting together today. But then he'd metaphorically slapped himself. He had things he needed to get done, he'd been slacking on a few things. With spending all his time with Sandy and on the fundraiser, but that didn't mean he could ignore everything else.

He needed to put in an order for the bar, he was getting too low on a few things. He always kept a large supply of everything, because the orders took a long time getting to them in their remote town and he didn't want to run out of anything. Some of the things had gotten dangerously low and if it had been any other time of the year besides early summer he might have run into trouble. He quickly took care of ordering after looking through his supplies, there were only a couple of things he hadn't been aware of that were running low.

Next, he knew there were some reports he needed to work on at the fire department. Some he needed only to read and rubber stamp, and others he needed to work on. He walked to the station, it wasn't far and a good stretch of the legs, not that he hadn't walked over half of the town with Sandy yesterday, but that had been slow and a lot of standing around. This would be a quick walk to give his heart a boost.

No one was at the station, so he let himself in and jogged up the stairs to the office space above the trucks. They had a kitchen and a couple of bunks, plus a pool table and another for ping pong. Sometimes after a call some of the guys would hang around to shoot the shit and play a few rounds. There was an office he and the station chief shared, they were about the only two that did a lot of paperwork. It was his job as the assistant chief to help with the reports. A third desk occupied a corner, it could be used by whomever needed to write something up.

He dug into the paperwork. It didn't take long, for the most part he needed to look over what the other guys had written up. He wasn't always first on scene and when that happened whoever was, would start the report. He or the chief would add to them if needed, but most of the time it was simply reading through and verifying the information, then filing them away.

The Howe's house fire was still on his desk since they were far from being finished with that one. He hadn't heard from Nolan about the investigation. Maybe when he was finished with the reports he should wander over and have a chat with him. He hadn't seen anything come back from the lab yet, that wasn't a big surprise they sometimes didn't get to the samples for a few weeks.

Greg finished up the reports and answered his emails, but nothing was important. A training company had sent him some information on programs to use with the volunteers here in town. There was one about a planning meeting for the fire department picnic to be held at the end of the summer. And a couple of people had emailed his fire department account about the fundraiser, even though he'd set up another account for that. He assumed it was easier to use the one they'd used in the past. He forwarded those to the other account after looking them over. With nothing left to do at the station, he turned off the lights and locked up before walking to the police department.

He hoped Nolan would be in, but if he wasn't Greg would leave him a note to say he had stopped by and would talk to him another day. Nolan was in his office, concentrating on his computer. Greg knocked on the window of the office. Nolan looked up and gave him a smile motioning him to come in.

"Greg, welcome. You saved me from dealing with some tedious crap. What can I do for you?"

"I was wondering about the fire and if you'd found anything."

Nolan shook his head. "Unfortunately, not much. I found a fire or two that were started with kerosene, but they were in abandoned buildings, nothing like our house fire. But I'm still looking. It takes time. I'm doing concentric circles further and further out. I'm at Helena, Montana and Redding, California. So, lots more searches to make. Hear anything from the lab yet?"

"No, but I didn't expect to yet, they are almost always booked solid, it usually takes a while."

"Yeah, plus this isn't terribly high priority since no one was hurt."

"Exactly." Nolan's phone buzzed with an incoming text. He read it and looked up. "Barbara's at the clinic in labor."

That surprised Greg. "Oh, Sandy planned to visit her this morning."

Nolan stood. "Well come along then, let's go see if everything is all right. Kristen still freaks out even though this is Barbara's third. Plus, that gives me a great excuse to avoid the computer."

Greg figured it wouldn't hurt to ride along. Nolan told the dispatcher he'd be out of service at the clinic.

After they climbed into Nolan's official vehicle, Nolan slid Greg a look. "So, you and Sandy."

Shit. Greg didn't know what to say exactly. "Yeah, she's helping me with the fundraiser."

Nolan didn't answer as they drove toward the clinic.

Greg felt like the cop was waiting for more. He was a very observant man. Had he noticed Greg's interest. "She's been very helpful."

"She's a very beautiful woman."

Greg sighed. "Yeah, she is. Always has been."

"Terry's gone for the summer."

"He is."

With a twitch of his mouth Nolan asked, "So, are you going for it?"

Greg cleared his throat, if he'd had a collar on, he would have been yanking on it. "I wouldn't mind. She's pretty special."

"I've noticed her catch your eye when I've seen the two of you together. Good luck, for what it's worth."

"Thanks."

They drove up to the clinic and Greg saw Sandy leaning on her car looking a little shell shocked. "She's looking a little rattled."

"She is." Kristen's car screeched to a stop on the other side of the street. Nolan shook his head. "But not as much as that one."

Greg chuckled. "You have fun with that."

Nolan sighed and got out of the car.

Sandy turned her head as he got out of the police car and her shaky smile showed relief at his appearance. He stepped in front of her and took her ice-cold hands in his. "You doing okay?"

"Sure, now that she's in with the doctor, and you can drive me home. I'm feeling a little drained."

He ran his hands up her arms and back down. "Tell me what happened."

As she talked, Greg was damn glad he'd spent the whole morning working on paperwork. Compared to Sandy's morning he'd gotten off easy. He didn't want to laugh, but Sandy's description of her friend's manic mood swings, sounded very similar to some of the things Chris had mentioned.

"I can see you trying not to laugh, Greg Jones. It might be funny on a second-hand hearing, but living it, not so much."

"I'm sorry, it's just that Chris has mentioned similar behavior in the past. I always thought he was exaggerating."

Sandy shook her head. "Nope, probably not. In fact, he probably downplayed it. The woman is nearly psychotic when she goes into labor."

Greg couldn't help it, he could feel his mouth twitch.

Sandy glared at him and then he saw her mouth twitch too, and her eyes filled with amusement. She chuckled. "Go ahead and laugh. It is kind of funny to think about."

He chuffed out a laugh. "It is. She's normally so businesslike and calm."

She giggled. "Yeah, not so much today, except for the few minutes we spent talking about the auction and her booth. She was nearly normal then, all business."

Greg snickered. "No silly labor is going to interfere with business."

Sandy's eyes were filled with mirth. "Right? Business comes first with her, always."

"Come on, let's get you home. You can tell your mom about it. She'll love the story."

Sandy laughed. "She will."

CHAPTER 19

Greg and Sandy went back to canvasing the town. By the time they had finished talking to all the business owners, they had a pile of papers to enter into Sandy's spreadsheet, and sore feet. They decided to meet in the morning to enter everything into the computer. That way Greg could read it to her and she could type it in. Some of the handwriting was atrocious, and they had decided that two trying to interpret the hieroglyphics, would be better than one.

Plus, waiting until tomorrow gave Sandy time to hang out with her mom and not feel like she had to get it all in tonight. Like a free pass tonight and then a concentrated effort tomorrow. Sandy was in favor of that.

When they pulled up in front of the B&B Greg turned off his truck. "Do you mind if I come in to say hi to your mom? I haven't seen her in a few days."

"Not at all. Come on in."

Sandy's mom was so glad to see Greg that when she asked if he was staying for dinner Sandy couldn't argue. She'd put a pot roast in the crockpot before she'd gone off with Greg, knowing that when she got home, she wouldn't feel like cooking. So, all she had to do was pull it out and make some gravy. There were carrots and potatoes in with the roast, so it really was no trouble at all to have an extra mouth to feed. She decided to put some pre-made rolls from a tube in to bake, to go with the roast.

Sandy set out the butter and an assortment of jams to go on the dinner rolls. Then she put the roast on the counter to rest. The vegetables went in a bowl with a lid and were covered with a towel to keep them warm. She made gravy while the rolls baked.

Greg came in the last five minutes, so she put him to work carving the roast. "This looks and smells delicious, Sandy. You've got quite a feast going here for the fifteen minutes I talked to your mom."

"That's because it's all been in the crockpot since this morning. The wonder of technology."

He laughed. She pulled the dinner rolls out of the oven and slid them into the basket she'd prepared with a cloth napkin to cover them. She and Greg worked well together, which she had to admit surprised her a little. They had such different personalities, but it didn't seem to matter.

Between the two of them they got all the food on the table and Carol joined them. They filled their plates and settled in to eat.

Carol said, "So tell me about all the auction items you've collected."

Sandy enthused, "We've had such great response by everyone. Not one person in town has told us no. Every business on Main Street and the next one over has something to donate. I've got a stack of papers to enter into the spreadsheet."

Greg nodded. "And nearly all the people we called or emailed agreed to something, too. We've got vacations all over the state to offer. And quite a few art objects. Nolan's mother asked all her friends to donate."

"Yeah, I would guess there is at least thirty things already on my spreadsheet. It's been very gratifying to see the support. We're going to get all the papers entered into the spreadsheet in the morning. After breakfast and the few guests we have, head off to their activities, and Greg mooches breakfast."

Greg looked aghast, but Carol ignored his fake outrage. "My book club is in the evening."

"Did you rest this afternoon? After Karen finished the cleaning?"

"I tried, but I kept waking up. I don't know why. I would doze off, and then wake up, almost startled. It happened a couple of times. Very odd. Maybe I've had too much rest."

Sandy thought that sounded off, but what did she know? She'd never had surgery. Maybe her mom was getting too much rest now that she was feeling better.

"But now I'm kind of tired, so the no nap thing seems to have back-fired. I'm sorry to cut the evening short, but I'm going to go to bed."

Greg stood and kissed her mom's cheek. "Now don't you worry about that, Miz Carol. I'll give Sandy a hand with the cleanup. You get a good night's sleep."

"Stay and keep Sandy company, if you don't need to rush off, Greg. If you don't, she'll just get on that computer and work all night."

Greg laughed and winked at Sandy. "It would be my pleasure to keep her from working too hard. Good night."

When her mom had gone back to her room, they carried the food into the kitchen. Sandy didn't want Greg to feel obligated, so she said, "You don't really need to keep me company. We've been together all day."

Greg backed Sandy up against the counter, which she

absolutely loved him doing. He could back her up to anything he wanted, as long as his large warm body covered her in front. "If you're tired of me I'll go, but I would be more than happy to stay and keep you company. Even though we've been together all day, it's been around other people. I would enjoy spending a few minutes alone with you."

Sandy looked up at him and her mouth went dry at the look in his eyes. She licked her lips and his breath caught. "Or hours, I could spend hours with you alone."

She whispered, "Okay."

His head lowered, and she stretched up, so they met in the middle, in a slow searching kiss, that sent lightning racing through her body. When she sighed his tongue swept into her mouth and the kiss went from slow to volcanic in a heartbeat.

Sandy edged closer to the big warm male kissing the stuffing out of her. She wrapped her arms around his neck, so her breasts pressed into his chest. Greg took the hint and pulled her hips into his. She marveled at the feel of him. She couldn't get close enough and there was a lot of clothes between them. She muttered, "Too many clothes."

He squeezed her tight and then broke off the kiss. "We're in the kitchen, your mom is less than a dozen yards from here."

Sandy looked around the room in a daze. Kitchen? Why were they in the kitchen? As her thoughts coalesced, she remembered that they were supposed to be cleaning up after dinner. "If you hadn't kissed all my brain cells away, I might have remembered where we were."

Greg chuckled. "Not that I would fight the less clothes idea, but maybe not here. I know your mom is tired, but probably not quite that tired."

Sandy was embarrassed by her forwardness and pushed past Greg to start cleaning up the dinner mess. He let her bustle about for a few seconds, while she longed to run out the door and far away from him. After about two minutes he stopped her and pulled her around to look in her eyes. "Sandy, sweetheart, I've dreamt about kissing you like that for years and years."

That surprised the heck out of her. She'd always thought of him as a very attractive male, but she had no idea he'd felt the same about her. "You have?"

"I have. Since I was old enough to have the slightest inkling about a boy-girl relationship. I've been crazy in love, or lust, with you. I would love nothing more than to have you in my bed or be in yours, for that matter. But we've got time and I'm a very patient man."

"I don't feel very patient, Greg. I felt kind of slutty, in fact."

"Not slutty, but so damn sexy you made my eyes cross. You'll hear no complaints from me about not being patient either. I only stopped because I think we would both be mortified if your mom caught us naked in the kitchen."

She nodded and sighed. "Yeah, that would be embarrassing."

"How about you give me a rain check on the less clothes idea. In the meantime, we can clean up the dishes, and then watch TV or talk or play your game."

"Are you talking about a play date?" she laughed at the idea, but kind of liked the thought of hanging out without another project on their minds.

"Why not?" He shrugged and then turned his laser focus on her. "And a rain check?"

She parroted back, "Why not?"

His eyes heated, and she scurried away before they *did* end up naked in the kitchen.

~

Greg let her go. This time she was avoiding more heat, not being embarrassed. He didn't want her to feel shame for her attraction to him, so he was going to do his best to make sure that didn't happen. He hadn't planned to blurt out his feelings for her, but it had helped her be rid of the humiliation, so he wasn't sorry, and nothing he'd said wasn't one hundred percent accurate.

After they cleaned up the dinner mess and put the food away Sandy asked, "So what adventure in the new game do you want to play?"

She was going to think he was a geek after he answered, hopefully she wouldn't run away screaming. "My favorite is always the US history adventures. You mentioned at the meeting the other day that this most recent release has the Boston Tea Party in it."

"It does."

Greg thought he detected a note of hesitancy in her voice. "I love history, but the wars might be hard to portray, politically speaking."

"Yeah, history is hard. Ideas and opinions have changed so much in the last thirty years."

"They have, but you can't rewrite history, so unless you skipped that whole period you had to include it. How did you go about telling the story and at the same time not offend people?"

"We had a lot of discussions around that. But compared to the release before, this one was a piece of cake."

"Yeah, I can see that. The Native American wars, or what we called Cowboys and Indians in my youth, had to be the worst."

Sandy shuddered. "It totally was, it was hard not to vilify any one group. Atrocities were meted out on both sides. For the game we basically tiptoed through history on that topic."

He thought about how difficult it would be to give history

a place in the game, without causing a lot of hard feelings. He'd never considered her games in that light. "Since it's a worldwide game, I imagine you'll have more challenges that are similar."

"Yes. But it's still ninety percent US purchased. Not a lot of other countries have embraced it. With this version including the UK, and the next Europe, for world geography, that might change."

"You'll have some issues with the Revolutionary war and the Civil war too, I imagine."

Sandy groaned. "Don't remind me. We did the Boston tea party, so now it's the American revolution we're working on."

"One of my favorite times in history, all those laws being made. The leaders coming together to hammer out what they wanted this fledgling country to be like. So much of that purity and hope, has been warped over the decades." He'd had such enthusiasm learning about the law, the founding fathers, and delving into what they had hoped to set up.

Sandy looked at him for a long time. "I didn't know you were such a history buff. Is that why you went to law school for a while?"

Greg sighed. "I did. I had all this passion about going into law and making a difference. I learned pretty quickly that I wouldn't be changing anything."

"Is that why you left school?"

"Yeah, I did a couple of internships with a big law firm that showed me exactly what a lawyer did. It wasn't pretty. I couldn't turn a blind eye to the clients and just take one stand. If they were guilty, I didn't want to defend them. And being on the other side I didn't want to prosecute someone who I thought was innocent. I finally decided that I couldn't be a neutral shark, and fight for what I didn't believe in. So, when the bar dropped in my lap it was an easy decision."

"That way you can do what's right, without anyone paying you to do the opposite."

Greg was surprised at Sandy's insight. "Yeah, that's it in a nutshell."

"I admire that, Greg."

He wasn't comfortable talking about his psyche, so he picked up the controller and busied himself with getting the game set up for two players. She didn't say anything else and he relaxed while they played the game. She showed him some hints and tricks to gain his way into hidden areas.

They played until it got to be late and both of them started to lose their edge. He put down his controller. "I need to go home. We've got a lot of work to do in the morning."

"Yeah, I'm getting sleepy."

He stood and pulled her up with him. "Do I get a good night kiss?"

She smiled. "Sure. At the door."

He pulled her quickly after him until they were by the door. She turned the tables on him by pushing him back against the door and covering his body with hers. He planned to go slow and gentle, but when her body hit his and she stood on her tiptoes to lift her mouth to his, he lost control and plundered. She met him stroke for stroke and had her hands gripping his hair, nearly pulling it from his head by the roots. Only she was pulling him down to her, until the kiss became voracious. Lips and teeth and tongues fought and clashed, as they strove for every taste, every touch.

Greg's body clamored for more and Sandy moaned into his mouth, her body plastered against his, squirming for a closer contact and amping up the friction. It was so damn erotic to have her practically climbing him like a tree.

He finally pulled back and they stood gasping for air, their bodies heaving as they drew in oxygen. Surprised to find he had managed to stay standing, when it felt like every bone in his body had gone up in flames and there was nothing left but ash and smoldering ruins.

Sandy put her head on his shoulder. "That was… I don't know what, but all I can say is, wow."

He muttered, "More than I've got. I feel like my whole body went up in flames and there's nothing left."

She chuckled. "We do seem to have a combustible reaction to each other."

"Yeah, I better go before we burn the house down."

"That would be tacky if the fire chief caused a house fire with his kisses. Go. I'll see you tomorrow."

"I hope I can get some sleep. I might be awake all-night reliving that kiss."

She laughed and pushed him out the door. Before she closed it, she said softly, "Dream of me."

He shook his head as he walked to his truck. How could he do anything else. The woman had him tied in knots. He loved it.

CHAPTER 20

Sandy danced to the radio as she made a strawberry and cream cheese, puff pastry braid. Fortunately, her mom had some frozen puff pastry dough. She could certainly make her own homemade, but it took a long time to do it up right. Mostly because the dough had to be chilled over and over again after each set of layers. Just the chill time added together was two hours.

So, buying it already made allowed for a quick breakfast. She felt like something a little fancier today than the normal muffins or cinnamon rolls. The braid was fun and fancy and didn't take too long to make. They didn't have a lot of guests, so she only made two braids. In the height of the summer tourist season it would take a lot more than two.

If she was honest, part of the reason she was fussing a little more is that she was nervous to see Greg this morning. Why did everything have to feel weird in the daylight that hadn't at night. But that's exactly the way she felt, awkward, about last night and her practically propositioning the man. It seemed kind of slutty in the sober light of day, and not at all her normal behavior.

At least she'd slept well, after all their walking and talking to people she'd gone straight to bed after Greg left. Then slept like a baby until it was time to get breakfast started. Once she had everything ready and in a buffet line, she would go get her laptop and the papers they collected yesterday. She didn't know exactly what time Greg was coming, but they had a lot of work to do, and if she got started before he arrived, that would be good too.

She didn't get a chance to grab her laptop because some of the guests nearly beat her to the serving area, then they asked all kinds of questions about things to do in Chelan. They'd spent the day before at the amusement park and wanted to do something different, maybe on the lake. She told them about the different options and they decided to ride the ferry up to Stehekin. It was a fun ferry ride and explored the upper part of the lake. The layover in Stehekin would be long enough for them to have some lunch.

Once everything was squared away after breakfast, she waited until Karen arrived to ask her to clean up after her and Greg last night. They hadn't made a mess, but it could use a bit of tidying. She'd put the game pieces in a cabinet under the television. It was available for guests to use, but wasn't kept out on display because it didn't go with the décor.

Karen called out, "Hi Sandy."

"Good morning, Karen. I made a strawberry puff pastry braid if you want to try it."

"That sounds amazing, but I'm trying to watch my calories. When you're old and have had kids, it's easy to put on the pounds."

Sandy laughed. "We're the same age, and I refuse to believe we're old."

"Well we're not in our twenties anymore."

Carol said, "You're still a youngin' in my book, Karen. Just because you've got a couple of kids doesn't make you old or fat. Have a sliver of the braid, it's wonderful."

Karen grinned, "I suppose a sliver wouldn't hurt."

Sandy said, "Now mom, it's not nice to make light of someone's health choices."

Carol nodded. "That's true, Sandy, but I've gotten to know Karen and sometimes she does want someone to talk her into it, so she can have a taste and not feel guilty."

"Busted," Karen said and then took a bite of the pastry. "Oh my God, Sandy, this is amazing. I think it's a good thing I don't live with you, because I would be hard pressed to pass up your cooking."

Sandy laughed. "Not cooking so much as baking. My cooking is mediocre, but I love to bake."

Karen took another bite and moaned in exaggerated approval of the treat.

"Okay, I heard that moan out at the street, what did Sandy make for breakfast this morning?" Greg asked as he walked into the kitchen.

Karen swallowed and said, "The most amazing strawberry and cream cheese braid thing I've ever had in my whole life." Karen whacked off a large piece for Greg, put it on a plate and gave it to him with a fork. "Try it, you'll like it."

He laughed and cut into it. "All right I'll try it, but I think I'm going to need some coffee to go with it and maybe some eggs. Protein to counter the sweet." Then he put the bite in his mouth.

His eyes lit up and he moaned almost as loudly as Karen had. Only his moan did something to Sandy's body that Karen's had not. Every nerve stood up and goosebumps covered her.

"That is delicious, Sandy. You were totally right, Karen."

Karen nodded and then turned toward the buffet to get

him coffee and protein. She filled a plate and took it over to where he'd sat to eat the pastry.

Sandy still couldn't move so she just smiled at his praise. She was rooted to the spot watching him eat. Eating had never, ever, in her whole life, enthralled her. But right now, watching Greg eat her pastry and other foods was mesmerizing. She needed to get a grip.

She finally shook herself free from the haze she was in and said lightly. "I'm going to go get my laptop and the papers from yesterday." Greg nodded absently, as he continued to shovel food into his mouth like he'd never eaten before.

Sandy ran up the stairs and into her room. She gathered up the papers off the dresser where she'd laid them last night. Then turned toward the desk to get her laptop. Only it wasn't there. Confused, she looked around the desk, in the laptop bag, and even glanced at the bed. The charging cord was also gone. She frowned. Where was her computer?

Maybe her mom had borrowed it for some reason. She went downstairs where Greg had apparently eaten enough, since he was sipping coffee and chatting with her mom and Karen.

"Excuse me for interrupting, but did you borrow my laptop, mom?"

Carol shook her head. "No, you bought me my own, so I haven't needed to."

Sandy said, "It's not in my room."

"It was yesterday morning," Karen said. "When I was cleaning, it was on the desk. I picked it up to dust underneath it and then put it right back where it had been."

"Well it's not there now."

"You didn't use it after I left, did you?" Greg asked.

"No, I went straight to bed, all that walking and talking to people wore me out."

"Yeah and you beating the pants off of me in the game," Greg complained.

"I did write it. I hope I could beat you since you've not played it," Sandy said. "But where is my laptop?"

Carol asked, "You don't suppose someone stole it do you?"

"What? Walked right in here and boldly went up to my room and took my laptop with everyone here?"

"No, but what if they came in when no one was home, well except me of course, I didn't leave yesterday. But I did keep waking up from my nap. Maybe someone was in the house then and making noises that woke me up. Is anything else missing?" Carol asked.

"Not that I noticed. Maybe we should all look around and see if anything looks disturbed. Karen, you were probably the last person to see what things looked like. Maybe you should go upstairs and look around. Mom, you check down here. Greg, please help mom. I'll go up and check my room, since we know they were in there."

Sandy checked her room, she looked in her jewelry, but nothing was missing. There was cash in her sock drawer and it was still there. She'd had her purse with her yesterday with Greg. When she'd cleared her room, she coordinated with Karen and took some of the upstairs rooms, but nothing looked disturbed. One of the guest rooms had a nicer laptop than hers sitting on a desk.

When they were done, they all met back in the kitchen. The reports were the same, nothing else was missing, even the cash they kept at the check-in desk for people that wanted change was all still there.

Greg said, "You should call the police and make a report."

Sandy pulled out her phone and called the station.

A few minutes later, as Nolan knocked on the front door,

Sandy's phone rang with a ringtone that gave her chills. Someone was trying to access her computer.

She answered the silent phone. "This is Sandy Anderson, alias S-A-N-D-Y-A. No, it's not me, start the trace."

Nolan came in and Sandy quickly explained to him and the rest of the group. "My laptop's been stolen. That call was from the security we put in place when we had some sabotage at my company. After a certain number of failed login attempts, the security program calls the cell phone of the employee. If it's the employee being forgetful, or having butterfingers, they can tell the computer it's okay. The program doesn't say anything, so if someone stole both the computer and the phone the person would think it was a prank call and hang up."

Nolan said, "Ingenious, so then what happens?"

"If I tell them to start the trace, then they allow the person to get into a fake profile. We all put enough files and apps on that profile to give the person hacking it time to look at stuff. A trace takes a few minutes to get proper coordinates, so we want them to stay on for a while. I had enough time on my flights to and from New York, to set up a pretty real looking account. I never really believed it would be seen, so I had some fun with it." Sandy shrugged, thinking whoever got into her fake profile was either going to be amused or freaked out.

"Once the laptop is found, the program uses the coordinates and one of the map programs to find what building and address it's at. Then the program will alert the company and me, so I can call the police. But you're already here, Nolan. My phone will have the coordinates so once we get to the building it's in, my phone will lead us right to it."

"Well, that's very handy."

Sandy's phone rang again with the chilling ringtone. "This is Sandy. Yes. Alias S-A-N-D-Y-A, Games division,

AWT group. Thank you, the police are with me now. I'll call back when the laptop is retrieved."

She hung up and there was a text with the name of the building and address. Sandy looked at it and frowned. The text read "Chedwick public school." That didn't make sense to her, but that's what the program had found. So, she said, "It's at the school."

Nolan looked at Greg and then at Sandy. "You two, come with me. Carol, Karen, you need to stay here. We'll be in touch."

~

GREG WAS SURPRISED to be invited along on official police business, but he was also relieved. He didn't want Sandy walking into something alone. At least with the three of them, he could help if needed.

Nolan said when they got to the car. "The backup officer had to go up to Kristen's this morning to talk to Ray and Betty. He wouldn't be able to get down here in time. So, Greg, you'll be backup. I doubt we're going to run into any trouble, but you never know."

Greg hoped like hell that Nolan was right and there wouldn't be any trouble. He thought it odd that someone at the school had the laptop, and the time to try to break into it. It seemed to him like everyone would be in classes. It wasn't lunch time. Maybe a study hall? He couldn't figure it out. "I can do that."

They drove fast to the school. It wasn't far. "I'm going to park in back. We'll go in the high school wing and follow your phone to where ever it leads from there."

They got out and Greg saw Nolan unsnap his gun. Sandy was intent on the phone and probably didn't notice, but he had seen it, and that made the whole thing more intense.

Sandy whispered, "It looks like it's in the high school wing."

Greg said, "Makes the most sense, little kids wouldn't take a laptop. But a teen might. Still seems odd to me though."

Nolan said, "If the kids are in the hall, simply act natural. If they aren't, that's even better. Sandy if I tell you to get help you go straight to the office and tell them to lock down the rooms. The code word is Tsilly. Greg if that happens, I want you to stay close and keep everyone nearby out of harm's way. Got it?"

Sandy squeaked out a yes and he also answered in the affirmative. They walked into the school and it appeared everyone was in class. The halls were deserted, which helped him relax a little. Sandy pointed the way with her phone. Greg thought they were in the math section of the high school wing, but he hadn't been in the school in years, so he wasn't certain.

Sandy kept her eyes on the phone until they got to a door where she stopped. "I think it's inside."

Greg looked at the name on the door and sighed. "Steve Jameson."

Sandy looked at him. "What?"

He pointed at the name on the door.

She frowned and then her face turned furious. "Steve stole my laptop?"

"Looks like it."

"Why that little—"

Nolan cut her off. "Quiet. I'll go in first. If it's clear, I'll say so and you two can follow. Quietly."

Nolan turned the handle and slowly opened the door. He turned back and rolled his eyes and nodded for them to join him.

The three of them walked in the room to see Steve staring at the laptop, jotting down notes as fast as he could. He didn't even hear them enter his room. They managed to get all the way to the desk without him noticing.

Finally, Nolan cleared his throat and said, "Whatcha doing, Steve?"

Steve jerked and slammed the laptop closed.

Sandy said, "Hey, be careful with that, it's mine."

Steve looked from Nolan, to Greg, to back at Sandy. "I know, you loaned it to me, remember?"

Sandy nearly growled. "No. I did not. You stole it from my house yesterday and broke into it today, here in your school office. Exactly what were you trying to do?"

Nolan said, "Wait. I need to read him his rights."

Sandy folded her arms and glared at Steve, while Nolan read the revised Miranda to the man. When Steve agreed that he understood his rights, Sandy started back in.

"What the fuck, Steve. What were you looking for?"

Steve glared right back at her. "The new game you're working on. You wouldn't tell me anything about it and I wanted to know."

Sandy nearly shouted, "Dammit, Steve, there is no new game."

"Yes, there is, I saw all kinds of information on a new game with the code FUD."

"Did you notice there is an execution file?"

Steve shook his head. "No. I was reading the docs and the code."

Sandy rolled her eyes. "Open the laptop back up and pull up a command prompt."

Steve did as she suggested.

"Now type in, run FUD."

When he did all kinds of fireworks and streamers flew across the screen and whistles poured out of the speakers. Then a little sign started growing and unfurled. When Greg could read the sign, he saw it said, "Fuck You, Dumbass!"

Steve groaned and slumped in his chair. "It's a fake profile, isn't it?"

"Yep, it sure as hell is, and while you sat there playing with it, my security program led me right to you."

"Well, hell."

Nolan had put on gloves and pulled an evidence bag out of a pocket. He put the laptop and charging cord into it and said to Steve. "You get an all-expense paid trip to the city jail, Steve. On the accounts of burglary and attempted sabotage."

Steve sputtered. "I wasn't going to sabotage anyone, I only wanted in on the new game. I need some extra money to pay off some debts."

Greg finally spoke up. "Getting a second job would have been a smarter option."

Steve flipped him off. "Fuck you, Jones."

Greg just grinned. "Back at you, Jameson. Come on, Sandy, sweetheart. I'll walk you back home."

Sandy asked Nolan, "When will I get my laptop back? Or at least the files from it."

"The computer we'll need to keep until sentencing. The files you can have anytime."

"There's only one I don't have backed up. The spreadsheet for the fundraiser auction."

Nolan nodded. "Give me an hour or two to process everything and then come by the station and you can retrieve it."

"I simply need to upload it to the cloud. My company will probably want me to use a new computer anyway, just in case Steve is smart enough to plant a virus."

Steve sighed. "I didn't plant a virus. I obviously didn't get anywhere. I only had it unlocked ten minutes."

Sandy looked back at her phone. "Nine point five."

Greg wanted to laugh out loud, but he managed to keep a straight face.

"Let's go Steve. If you don't try anything, I'll let you walk out without handcuffs, but I won't hesitate to slap them on you, if needed."

"I'll go with you. But I do have classes this afternoon."

Sandy smiled in a very scary way. "I'll be happy to go by the office and let them know you've taken ill and won't be teaching the rest of the day, and probably the rest of the week. You'll have to tell them the real story."

They watched as Nolan led Steve out the back and got him into the patrol car, then they went to tell the office about Steve's sudden "illness".

Sandy said exactly what she'd told Steve she would say, but her body language and tone of voice said something entirely different. When one of the office staff mentioned seeing the patrol car on the premises, she did not deny it having to do with Steve.

Greg realized right then and there he never wanted to get on Sandy's bad side, for any reason. The woman was scary.

He was surprised when Sandy sat on the benches in front of the school and called her company. To let them know the thief had been caught, and the laptop was fine. But she would need a new one shipped out. She told them she would send the stolen one back for them to wipe.

Then she called her mom and told her everything, saying she wouldn't be home for a couple of hours while everything got processed. He wondered what she was planning to do for those couple of hours. Maybe go talk to more people about the auction, since they couldn't record their list from yesterday. That's the only thing that made sense, to him anyway.

CHAPTER 21

Sandy hoped Greg would be on board with her idea, once she got off the phone relaying all the information about the theft. She wanted to go back to his place and get cozy. They couldn't work on the auction spreadsheet for at least a couple of hours, even if she had a machine to put it on. So why not spend the time naked? With Greg.

It seemed like the perfect opportunity and her body was hyped up from the adrenaline that had poured into it with that first chilling ring tone.

She'd made her final phone call; now did she really have the guts to tell him what she wanted? His house wasn't far away, she'd been to it once or twice with Terry, for a barbeque or something. She decided to just start walking towards his house and maybe she wouldn't have to say anything at all.

Kind of a chicken attitude. But if he didn't take the hint, she'd let him know in a more obvious fashion.

"I'm so relieved we found the laptop. All I could think about was having to reconstruct the auction list. I know it's not a big deal, but I made a lot of phone calls and had a ton of information in it. I should have backed it up, but it never occurred to me that someone would steal my laptop."

"It's not a scenario that most people would think about. What was Steve talking about wanting to get his hands on a new game? Are you working on a new game?"

Sandy turned the corner and Greg walked along with her. "No, not at all, *Adventures with Tsilly* is still raking in the money and until it stops, we've got no plans to change anything."

"Do you think his obsession with there being a new game has anything to do with the sabotage?"

What? She stopped dead in her tracks and stared at him as her mind processed the idea. Finally, she shook her head. "No, I don't think so. The sabotage might have hurt our reputation, but we would have fought to gain back the trust of the buyers. It would have been a PR disaster for sure, but I don't think it would have tanked the game." She started walking again.

"I can't understand why he would be so adamant about there being a new game otherwise."

Sandy frowned as she thought about it. "Yeah, I know what you mean. But I can't imagine him knowing anything about the sabotage. I think it was just wishful thinking on his part."

"I hope you're right. Edward, Steve's older brother, does live in Seattle, and he's in the high-tech world. He doesn't have a lot of scruples. Does he work at your company?"

"I have no idea. We kept everything pretty hush-hush but if he does work there, he might have heard about it. Besides wasn't his primary lack of scruples—as you call them—directed at the female population?" Sandy turned another corner, moving further away from the central part of town.

"Yes, he seemed to think all women would want to jump in the sack with him, and if they didn't, he got aggressive.

That is until Ellen took him down with a knee, and Hank Jefferson threatened to clean his clock. He's laid low when he's been in town since then. What he does in Seattle, no one knows."

Sandy said, "No reason why I can't mention to the security team to check to see if Edward is in the company. Might have them alert the investigators looking for the sabotage source."

"I think that would be a good idea. So why are we on my street, this is a residential area. I thought we were going to talk to more businesses."

"No, I don't want to do that. I thought you could invite me in to show me your etchings."

Greg barked out a laugh even as his body tensed. "Do people still say that? Isn't that from our grandparent's era?"

Sandy shrugged. "I have no idea, but you know what I meant, right?"

He didn't answer. Instead he took her by the hand and started walking fast up to his front door. By the time he got there he had the key in his hand. It took him only seconds to get the door open and pull her inside with him. Before she could even glance around he had her backed up to the door with his mouth on hers.

She did not complain at his high-handed treatment. In fact, she was perfectly happy to let him take the lead. He kissed her with a passion that shocked her to the core. His kisses had been ardent in the past, but this was above and beyond anything that had happened previously.

Her brain turned to mush, and her legs were emulating cooked spaghetti noodles. But since he had her pressed up against the door with his body covering hers, she wasn't going to slide to the floor anytime soon. Sparks and lightning were erupting all over her body, and she dragged her hands through his hair holding on tight.

When they finally had to breathe, he put his face in her hair and drew in deep breaths. After a few minutes he said in a low tight voice, "Yes, I know exactly what you meant. Are you totally sure about it?"

"Oh, yeah. I'm sure." She looked down at her shirt. "I can't understand why our clothes didn't incinerate from all that heat."

Sandy thrilled hearing his gruff laughter. Even as aroused as they both were, he still found her funny. She didn't think she'd ever had a man laugh while in the throes of passion.

He said, "Instead of letting them burn up let's take them off. Come with me."

"I don't think I have the strength. My legs turned to spaghetti."

"I can take care of that." He picked her up and carried her, Rhett Butler style, to his bedroom. She barely had time to take in her surroundings as he walked quickly down the hall to his room. When he dropped her on the bed, he said, "Sorry, the bed isn't made. I wasn't expecting a sleep over."

Sandy noticed the sheets and blankets were pulled up. The blankets were a dark chocolate brown and the sheets beige. It wasn't a military-style made bed, but it was adequate in her mind. "I don't intend to do any sleeping. This isn't a sleepover, it's a sex marathon."

His eyebrows raised. "Marathon?"

"Well as long as you have enough condoms. Although, I suppose we need to go by the jail in two or three hours."

"Two or three hours? You're planning a sex marathon for two or three hours?"

Sandy decided to tease him. "Well if you can't handle that, I suppose we could play a Canasta or something."

Greg growled and joined her on the bed. "No worries. I'll manage to keep you entertained, right here in my bed, until it's time to go to the station to get your file. And yes, I have plenty of protection. I bought a new box just last night."

Last night. As in, on the way home from her house, after she'd practically propositioned him in the kitchen. "Oh, well then, I guess you didn't want to take any chances."

"No. I didn't, and there is a second box in my truck, and a third in the car, just in case."

Wow, the guy was serious about being ready. She didn't know whether to be flattered or scared. She decided to be flattered. "How many in your wallet?"

"Four."

Sandy laughed. "And you were giving *me* a hard time about a sex marathon?"

He grinned, then covered her mouth with his.

GREG WAS SO DAMN glad to have Sandy in his bed he felt giddy and light-headed at the same time. But there was no way he was going to act like an idiot. He wanted to savor his first time with her, and he wanted to make it so amazing for her, that she would want to spend all their spare time in bed. Naked.

Which meant he needed to start that getting-naked process immediately. He was torn between ripping her clothes off and unwrapping her like the most precious gift. His body wanted the former, but his heart and soul wanted the later. He told his body to wait for another time. This first time needed to be special. He'd waited for this woman half his life and he wasn't going to rush it to appease his lust. He wanted to worship her.

He gentled the kiss and pulled back to cup her face in his hands, and let his fingers get tangled in her hair. He kissed her forehead and both eyelids, her cheeks and nose and chin.

Then he went back to her sweet mouth, it was like sipping nectar from a flower. He internally rolled his eyes at himself. Nectar, really?

Sandy grabbed his head and pulled him down to her for a harder more passionate kiss, he was more than happy to oblige, but he wasn't going to let her rush him. He broke off the kiss and moved to her neck where he kissed his way up one side to her ear. He kissed and suckled her ear, and she squirmed under him. He nipped the earlobe and she moaned in delight, so he did it again.

He repeated the process, up to the other ear, and she clutched his arms. She was holding on tight enough that he might actually have bruises tomorrow. They would be well worth it. He kissed back down her neck to her shoulder and started pulling the clothes aside, so he could kiss all the soft spots.

She squirmed. "Greg, we need to start getting rid of clothes. Like now."

He kissed her shoulder one last time and then pulled up, so he could drag the blouse off of her. While he was dropping it on the floor she reared up, unfastened her bra and tossed it on top of the shirt.

He was elated she was eager, but the sight of her stole his breath, she was so beautiful. He felt a little frozen. Where to start with all that delicious skin for him to explore? Before he could begin, her busy hands were on his shirt, pulling it off him. Running her hands up his chest.

He reveled in her touch on his skin. Her soft hands tracing the contours of his chest. She was inciting a fire in him with every tiny movement. He had to stop her hands, so he could return the favor.

"Sandy, baby, we need to slow down. Just a little."

She ran her hands over his pecs and pinched his nipples.

Fire raced through his body. “I don’t want to slow down. I think we need to speed things up.”

“But I want to savor our first time, to learn your body and what you like.”

“You can savor next time. This time I want to kick it up and get to the main event.”

His laugh was strangled, as his body fought between amusement and passion. But instead of arguing he leaned down and licked her nipple. She stilled, so he did it again, and then drew the turgid bud into his mouth to suckle. Sandy gripped his hair and held him to her. He bit down lightly and dragged her nipple between his teeth as he raised up. When she moaned, he gave the other breast the same treatment. After the nipple popped free, he filled his hands with her breasts and rubbed his thumbs across the tips.

She grabbed his ears and pulled his mouth down to hers in a scorching kiss. Wrapping her legs around his hips and rubbing against him, made his eyes cross in pleasure.

All those years of dreaming about having her in his bed were not even close to the real thing. Foolish fantasies. This was pleasure so intense he wasn’t sure he would survive it. This woman, the one he’d been fascinated by for twenty years, was making his blood boil.

They were still half dressed. The jeans needed to go, asap. She had him locked down tight with her arms and legs wrapped around him. He managed to growl out, “Sandy, baby, jeans off.”

She let go of him so fast and pushed him to the side, he nearly fell off the bed. He managed not to fall to the floor in a messy heap, but just damn barely. Sandy stripped out of her clothes so fast he was shocked. When she looked over to him in his still dressed state she frowned, and he decided he better get after it, but he was having trouble not staring at her luscious body completely bared to him.

Shit, his hands were shaking as lust and desire and passion and just plain want, poured through him in such a powerful mixture that he wasn't sure he could free his erection. But he didn't want to disappoint the lady, so he clamped down on his own emotions and got busy stripping.

When his lower half was unclothed, he heard Sandy purr, and that tiny sound sent shockwaves through his body. He wondered if she had any idea what she was doing to him. He managed to look from her delectable body to her face. There was such a pure look of wickedness painted there, that he decided that she knew exactly what she was doing and was having a fine time tying him in knots.

Time for paybacks.

He didn't know if his appreciation of her body would affect her the same, but he could test out that theory. Steeling his mind and body, he looked over at Sandy. Starting at the top of her head. Her hair was messed up from him running his fingers through it. Her lips were swollen from his kisses. Her nipples hard from his mouth and hands. There might be a tiny bit of razor burn on her soft breasts. His eyes continued down taking in her sweet waist and sexy hips, down to the strip of hair guarding her womanhood. Lust roared through him and he groaned, which made her breath catch, so he took that as an affirmative on his experiment.

Greg stalked over to her and took her in his arms. Her soft skin touched his, and her curves filled in all the valleys on his body. It was like they were specifically designed for each other. He put his face in her hair and breathed in the fragrance of her. It was addicting.

He could hold her for hours, even days, but Sandy had other ideas and her demanding hands were running over his body, her mouth licking his neck. When she squeezed his ass, he realized it was time to step up his game, so Greg caressed her shoulders and back, trailing his hands down until he reached her sweet derriere and gave it a squeeze, pulling her hips in closer to his.

Sandy started taking tiny steps, backing him toward the bed. He allowed her to think he wasn't noticing and let her have her way. At the very last minute he twirled them both around and swirled her onto the bed, with him right there with her.

She giggled. "That was sneaky."

"It was."

She smiled devilishly. "I loved it."

"So did I, and I liked you trying to pretend you weren't pushing me backward to the bed."

Sandy giggled. "I was. Standing in the middle of the room was nice but it's time to move things along. We didn't get naked to only stand around. Did we?"

He laughed at the wicked look she gave him. "No, we did not."

"Then suit up mister, and let's get this show on the road."

Greg couldn't help the smile that spread across his face, she was a demanding little miss, and he loved it. "As you wish."

He pulled a condom from his night stand and rolled it on. But before he entered her, he wanted to make sure she was good and ready, so he kissed her, while caressing her body. Moving his hand lower and lower until he reached that sweet warm area between her legs. She was wet all right, but he planned to make her wetter. He reached inside the folds for the bundle of nerves hidden there, and set up a stroking rhythm to drive her right to ecstasy. His thumb was on her clit and two fingers pushed into her wet sheath. It did not take long before she stiffened and called out his name while her thighs clenched his hand, stilling the motion and drenching his fingers.

He waited, watching the emotions flit across her beautiful face, and felt the tremors in her body. When she opened her eyes and looked at him, and her legs relaxed, releasing his hand, he could hardly stand to not be joined with her. He wanted to love her and bring her to climax over and over.

She let her thighs fall open. "That was wonderful. Thank you. But we're not finished yet, so come on in and join the party."

He didn't have to be asked twice, he slid between her thighs and kept right on going until he was fully seated within her. It was the best feeling of his life. Until Sandy wrapped her legs around his waist, tilted her hips, and he slid in deeper. Her inner muscles squeezed him, and he couldn't think. His body, however, was happy to take over for his brain, and started moving on its own accord.

Sandy moaned. "Now we're talking. Like that, Greg. Perfect."

Her hips reached up for his on each stroke, and the flames of passion grew hotter. He felt her body start to tense and knew she was getting close to a second orgasm, so he sped up the thrusts to carry her up into the conflagration. She screamed his name and he pounded into her three more times, before he let himself join her.

The flames roared, and sparks of light floated upward, taking bits and pieces of them, swirling around into the atmosphere.

When he could breathe again, he thought about his foolish feelings. But he couldn't deny the way he'd felt at that moment, even if he would die before admitting to those feelings.

Sandy whooshed out a breath when he rolled off of her, pulling her along with him, so they lay face to face.

She looked sleepily up at him. "I loved your weight on me, but it does make breathing a bit of a challenge."

He chuckled and kissed her nose. "Can't have you suffocating. Although the mouth to mouth might be fun."

She muttered. "Silly man."

He dropped the condom in the trash and pulled a sheet up over them, so they could rest for a while without getting cold. Sandy snuggled in next to him and he held her close as the joy of their union washed over him. This was way better than anything he could have hoped for. The woman of his dreams was in his arms, and in his bed.

CHAPTER 22

Sandy dozed, cuddled up next to Greg. He was so warm and smelled good, and best of all he seemed to like her being right next to him. He'd pulled her in close and had his arm wrapped around her so there was no space between them. She'd never had a man do that before, most of the time once the sex was over, they were ready to move on.

Greg didn't seem to be in any hurry to do anything. He wasn't asleep. She wondered what he was thinking about. She kissed his chest and looked up. His eyes fastened on hers. "What are you thinking about?"

He tensed and then relaxed, she was curious what that was about. He finally said in a quiet voice, "You, in my bed."

Was that a good thought, or a bad? Maybe he wanted her to leave, although he was still holding her tight. She stiffened questioning if she should pull away and get up.

He continued speaking, "And how magnificent it feels to have you here. It's a dream come true." The smile that slid across his face was a mix of a child at Christmas and a man with sex on his mind.

She relaxed and laid her head back on his chest. He inched her another millimeter closer. “I thought maybe you wanted me to leave.”

“Sandy, there is no way in hell I want you to leave. You could stay right here in my arms for the rest of your life and I wouldn’t mind one bit. Other than maybe needing to eat, occasionally.”

“Or being called out on a fire, or maybe needing to go to work. Silly man.” She knew he was teasing, but it still felt nice to hear he wanted her with him.

He chuckled. “I didn’t say it was a practical idea, just that I would enjoy it.” He ran his hand down her back and squeezed her butt. “And we would need more condoms.”

She pinched his nipple and he sucked in a breath. “If you keep that up young lady, we might run out of condoms, today. Before we get your auction file back from your computer.”

Sandy didn’t want to think about Steve stealing her computer, but since Greg had brought it up, she said, “Why do you think he was obsessed enough with a new game idea to steal my computer? Everything is locked down and encrypted, he’d have to be a far better hacker than he is, to get to anything.”

“I’m betting he had no idea. He probably used passwords you’d had in high school.”

She barked out a laugh. “That would be ridiculous. I have to use complicated passwords now, numbers, letters, special characters. You know Steve asked me about passwords and what he might tell his students. Do you suppose he was fishing even then?”

“I would bet on it. Didn’t he ask you about a new game the first night you came to the bar? I remember you saying something about him acting weird.”

Sandy looked up at him. "I think you're right. It seems like that's about all he's talked about. I kept telling him there is no new game."

Greg leaned down and kissed her nose. "Clearly, he didn't believe you."

"No, he did not. What do you suppose he was going to do, if we were creating a new game?"

"I have no idea. Maybe he was going to sell it to a competitor or have his brother do it."

Sandy was mystified. "How did he think he would get away with it? We had him within a day. Less than an hour from when he started trying to get into the files."

"Steve had no idea you had a tracing program on your laptop. He was probably going to get what he could off your machine and then dump it in the lake."

"That wouldn't be good for the fish in the lake."

Greg shrugged. "I doubt he cares about the environment. Or anyone or anything else for that matter. He was probably trying to make some quick cash. Instead he'll be spending time in jail."

"But he has a good job. I know teachers don't make a ton of money, but he was still working and he's a single guy. Why did he need so much?"

"No idea. Toys, maybe? A gambling problem? Loan sharks? A mistress?"

Sandy laughed and slapped his chest. "Now, you're just getting silly."

"I could be silly. But I think I'd rather be sexy. Are you ready for round two?"

In answer to his question, she licked his nipple and pulled it into her mouth. His breath caught, and she could feel his lower body stirring to life.

"I'll take that as a yes." He whipped her onto her back and

covered her mouth with his in a steamy hot kiss. He looked up and into her eyes and she could see the flames burning in them. "You promised me I could explore your sweet body slowly and thoroughly this time."

Sandy's lady parts cheered at that idea. "I don't think I was quite that descriptive. I think what I said was that we could slow it down a bit the second time."

"And that I could savor. So, you be a good girl and let me investigate every inch."

Her body tingled at the look in his eyes and the words coming out of his mouth, so she relaxed and let him have his way.

She learned something new about Greg Jones. The man was painstakingly meticulous, when he had a mind to be. Her body was thrumming, and she'd lost count of the orgasms he'd given her by the time he was finished savoring every inch. She'd never been so totally aroused.

Only one thing was lacking, she wanted him to fill her. But she didn't have the energy to say a word. Hopefully he would figure it out on his own.

SANDY'S FACE glowed with satisfaction. He'd done that. Greg had spent long minutes on her body, kissing, licking, suckling, and fondling every bit. His own body had screamed for release, but he'd beat his arousal down several times to be able to give Sandy the complete attention she deserved, and that he wanted her to have. It had been magnificent watching her come undone, drawing every bit of pleasure from this woman.

His body was demanding release, so he reached over for a condom. For just a second, he hesitated, what if she was finished and not interested in more. He held up the condom. "Do you want me to continue?"

A beautiful, sexy smile moved over her face and she nodded. *Hot damn*, she was still on board. Exhausted maybe, but ready for more. He rolled the condom on and climbed between her legs. He lifted her hips and slid in.

She sighed and then purred. It was the sexiest sound he'd ever heard. Then she wrapped her arms around him and held on while he loved her.

He whispered into her neck. "You are so beautiful. Your body is a delight. I want to stay right here with you, inside you, loving you for hours."

She muttered back, "Not enough energy left for hours."

He chuckled and sped up his pace. "Next time?"

"Sure."

That was the last word either of them said as he pulled them both along into the heat and the fire. The flames roared, and their bodies ignited, until they exploded in a supernova of passion and satiation.

Greg tossed the used condom in the trash and pulled the sheet back up over them. Sandy was already passed out. He didn't blame her, he'd worn her out.

He watched as she slept. She was so beautiful and trusting to let him have his way with her. Could he be with Sandy like this and not crave more? She would be going back to Seattle in a few weeks. Would it break his heart when she left? Probably. Maybe he shouldn't do this, maybe he should pull back. But would he rather guard his heart than spend this time with her? Hell no.

Greg was in this for as long as he could be. If it didn't last past the summer, then it didn't last. But he was damn sure he was going to put it all out there. He would have no regrets that he didn't go for it. He was all in, balls out, going to spend every minute loving this woman in every way he could.

With that decision made, he pulled her into his arms to rest a while, before they needed to get up and go to the police station.

They still had a fundraiser to put on.

And an arsonist to find.

And a saboteur to discover.

Yep, they had their work cut out for them.

CHAPTER 23

Sandy was enjoying her time in Chedwick as the summer sped by. She helped her mom with the B&B in the morning, cooking breakfast, chatting with guests, and managing the work done by employees. Most afternoons she Skyped into her team in Seattle, they looked at storyboards and finalized ideas for the next release of the game. It was typically a three-year process from design to release, but because of the sabotage last summer the time for this version had been cut short by almost six months. They could have also lengthened it by half a year, to get back on track with a Christmas release, but no one liked that idea, so they were trying to work quicker than normal.

Many evenings she worked on the town's fundraiser. Sometimes she worked with Greg, but mostly it was by herself. His job was a night job and she didn't mind the effort she put in, especially when he came by late at night, and snuck in her bed.

A few weeks ago, her mom had noticed Sandy let Greg in one night, and had handed him a key the next morning, so he didn't have to wake Sandy to let him in. Greg's ears had turned pink and Sandy knew her face was fire engine red.

Carol had rolled her eyes at them and said, "What? You think you two invented sex? For goodness sake, you're both adults. If you weren't having relations, then I *would* be concerned."

So now Sandy stayed snug in her bed until the big warm man joined her. She was glad her mom had given him a key. Sometimes she thought about what she was doing, spending nearly every night with Greg. Was she capable of this much intimacy without getting her heart involved? She didn't know the answer to that, but she did know that when she thought about breaking it off with him, she didn't like that idea one little bit. So, she stuffed her doubts down and focused on having the best time with him she could.

No thinking about the future.

No dwelling on leaving at the end of the summer.

No plans for going back to her cold, solitary apartment in the city.

She was simply taking it one day at a time. One glorious night of sex and cuddling after another, until she went back to the city. When she left, she would survive it and so would he. Until then she wasn't going to think about it. A little bit of Scarlett O'Hara type thinking was fine with her.

The two of them spent nearly every Tuesday together, primarily working on the fundraiser, occasionally they went out in nature, hiking or out on the lake. Wednesday night during her mom's book night, Sandy went to the bar and hung out with friends and danced with Greg.

The weeks flew by.

The fundraiser was coming together. People had purchased booths. There were food booths, and game booths, and craft booths, and even some political booths. They had to do some quick thinking when the political people had asked for booth space. Since they wouldn't be selling anything for the town to get money from, they'd decided to charge the politicians five hundred dollars for a booth. The town would have plenty of activities for all ages on Saturday. They had an election for king and queen of the parade that would be held on main street.

The auction items were coming in daily. Amber was allowing them to keep the larger donations in a storage area at her place. They would be using Amber's banquet hall for the auction, which would have desserts for people to munch on during the live auction. The silent auction would start two hours earlier before a plated dinner.

As the fundraiser weekend grew closer, all the places people could rent a room were packed full. Sandy wasn't sure if that had anything to do with the fundraiser or the fact that the Tsilly amusement park had a very attractive package deal going for the weekend, the proceeds of which would be given to the fundraiser.

Sandy's mom was back on her feet, Sandy still helped with breakfast, and some of the running up and down the stairs that was needed but Carol was very nearly ready to take the full reigns of the B&B back. Which meant Sandy could go home soon. She'd decided she would after the fundraiser was over. Leaving didn't sound nearly as attractive as it had when she'd first arrived. She was very much enjoying helping the town and spending lots of time with Greg. It would be hard to leave, but her job was in the city, maybe she and Greg could plan some rendezvous. Although with him working weekends and her job being a Monday through Friday thing it would be challenging.

Terry would be arriving in a day or two and Sandy was a little concerned about that. So, she decided to talk to Greg about her concerns.

She and Greg had just made love and were wrapped in

each other's arms. Their breathing returning to normal and their bodies cooling. Sandy murmured, "Terry will be back soon."

"He told me he'd be here tomorrow or the next day."

"Did you say anything to him about us?"

"Us? Like what?" Greg ran his fingers lightly down her back and she shivered.

"That we're sleeping together."

"No, I didn't think it was any of his business."

She sighed and relaxed, she hadn't realized she was worried about it. "I agree. So, I'd like to keep it that way."

"What do you mean?" he asked and then kissed her shoulder.

"I don't want him to know."

The kissing stopped, and he stiffened. "As in you want to hide it from him?"

She shrugged. "Yeah. I guess, or at least not tell him directly."

He rolled to his side and sat up leaving her alone on the other half of the bed. "Are you serious? You don't want me to tell my best friend that I've been dating his sister? You do realize the entire town has seen us out together?"

Sandy crawled over to where he was sitting. "Well, I suppose. But not all of them know we're sleeping together."

Greg huffed out a half laugh. "My truck is parked in front of this house every single night, until morning. What do you think they believe is going on? That we're playing Monopoly?"

Greg was pissed, and she didn't want him to be. She simply didn't want Terry sticking his nose into their business, especially since she'd be leaving in a few days.

"Greg, don't be mad, I just don't want his two cents worth on how we've spent the summer. I'll be leaving soon, and I don't think it's any of his business."

Greg rubbed his chest like it hurt and stood. "Well in that case I better stop spending the night. So, he can't see my truck out front."

No, she didn't want him to leave. "But he's not here yet. You can stay tonight."

He pulled on his jeans and t-shirt. Sandy suddenly felt cold and naked. "I don't think that's such a good idea. It feels devious to me."

"But..." she stuttered.

"No, it's okay, really. I knew this was going to end, so it's fine." He took the keys out of his pocket and removed the house key. "Thanks Sandy, this has been the best time of my life."

He kissed her on the forehead and carried his shoes out of the room.

Sandy flopped back onto the bed and felt tears slide down her cheeks. Her throat had a horrible lump in it and she felt like kicking her feet like a child.

GREG REGRETTED his decision to leave before he even got his truck started. So what, if she didn't want Terry to know. He'd deliberately kept the news from his best friend, why was this so different? Because it felt shady. Not gossiping to Terry when he was hundreds of miles away was a lot different than hiding it once he was in the same town.

Was she embarrassed by the two of them? Was she already moving on? He hated the idea of her leaving and he could admit he'd deliberately pushed that inevitability away, so he didn't have to think about it. But when she'd mentioned it so blithely, it had sent an arrow straight through his heart.

He was dreading her leaving with an extreme loathing,

and she was ready to go at any time. Well hell, and now he'd walked away and given the key back and might never get to hold her again. What a dumbass. He should have put his damn pride in a cage and locked it and reveled in being with her for the last week or two she would be here. She was committed to the fundraiser that was coming up at the end of the week.

He could have one more week with her, sure he'd have to sneak around some to keep Terry from finding out but.... No, he couldn't do it. It felt dishonest and cast their relationship into a place he didn't want it. Like it was something shameful. It wasn't. Their connection was glorious. He didn't want to hide it. In fact, he wanted to shout from the rooftops that this woman was his. At least for now. And that was the whole crux of the matter. It was a temporary love affair. And it was love for him. Clearly it wasn't for her. Well, fuck.

And not only that, but tomorrow was Tuesday and they had countless things they needed to do for the fundraiser. They'd planned to start as soon as the guests were fed, since he'd planned to spend the night, he'd even brought a fresh change of clothes which were still in a backpack in her room. Dumbass.

He'd go home tonight and give it all some more thought. The radio in the truck toned out and the dispatcher started speaking, well that would keep his mind busy, it almost made him glad a call had come in. Right up until he heard her give the address and state it was a structure fire. Dammit.

It was a remote barn, fortunately not near the forest, but there would still be plenty of brush around it, and at the end of the summer it would be dry and easily ignited. He called into dispatch to say he was on the way to the station to grab a pumper truck, just as the city siren went off, calling the volunteer firefighters into the station.

He got to the station before anyone else, since he'd been

up, dressed, and in his truck. So, he opened the bay doors and pulled the first pumper out onto the pad. Two other vehicles roared into the parking lot and the firefighters ran over to join him. He didn't hesitate, now that he had some help, he radioed into dispatch to say they were rolling. Others were on their way to bring the remaining trucks, he needed to get there asap to access their needs, and to get water started on the fire.

As he drove, he thought about a second structure fire in only a few months. They really must have an arsonist in town. When nothing had come to light from the tests that had been run, he'd talked himself out of a fire bug. But now he was beginning to doubt that idea. They'd have to see if the incineration pattern was the same, to give them a better idea.

Nolan had found some like crimes, but nothing very near to them. There'd been an incident in Lake Tahoe a few months prior to the house fire. Another one that looked similar had been in Grand Lake, Colorado. And a couple of other ones near national parks in Utah and by the Grand Canyon. All of those had been abandoned buildings like the one he was headed toward. They'd discounted those other fires, since their fire had been an occupied house, but nothing else in the database matched that.

What if the arsonist hadn't known the Howe's were still living there? What if it had looked like it was abandoned? Ray and Betty had been gone for weeks. It was an interesting thought, but he didn't have time for any more speculation. They had arrived on the scene and the building was fully engulfed. The fire was starting to spread into the brush surrounding the house.

"Both of you grab a hose and start on the fire in the brush, we'll have a helluva bigger mess if all those weeds catch fire. I'll get the next pumper in, started on the barn."

Both the firefighters confirmed his commands and he had

the pumper parked as close as he could get. Within seconds the water started flowing. Greg wasn't sure where the closest fireplug would be, so they would get started with the water the pumpers carried in their belly.

More personnel and trucks started arriving and he directed the firefighting efforts. The station chief took the plug book and was looking for the nearest working water to tap. When he found it, Greg radioed to the last truck coming in to hit it and lay hose into the fire. It wasn't close, but they could manage it.

His chief said, "Gotta wonder about this one. Seems much more like some of the ones that the cop shop found."

"I was thinking the same thing on the way in."

The older man said, "If the MO matches it might give us more to go on."

"Yeah. It should clear the Howe's of any wrong doing, too."

"Never thought it was them to begin with."

Greg nodded. "Neither did I, but you never know about the state or the insurance people. I'd like to see them cleared so they can get their money and move on."

"Agreed."

The last truck rolled into the yard as hose slipped off the back making a long line in the dirt. The firefighters on the back of the truck pulled off enough to get close to the fire and uncoupled it from that left on the truck. Then they twisted on a Y coupling and pulled another length off the truck to give them two heads. They put on two nozzles and ran up to the fire, two men on each line of the Y for safety. When they were set and ready, Greg radioed to the plug man to turn on the water.

With all the water being pumped on the fire, it didn't take too long to get it knocked down to size. The barn hadn't had much of anything left in it, so it was just the old structure, which had burned fast. The best part was that the fire hadn't spread into the weeds and brush surrounding the barn. They'd gotten that stopped swiftly. The land was flat here, and it was a hundred yards or so until it met the trees, but the fire would have gotten there eventually, if it hadn't been put out immediately. Weeds caught fire easily and spread from the top—not from the bottom—as most people would assume. Which meant getting them out needed to be done quickly and efficiently. He was damn proud of his crew for doing so.

Once the fire was out and the crew started cleanup, Greg, Jeremy and the chief went into the barn to see how the fire had started. They found a nice little pile of old boards and other random flammable objects. And it was obvious accelerant had been used to draw the flames out across the building. They gathered some samples.

Greg took a sniff and it smelled like kerosene to him. Not that he was an expert, but the other men thought so too. They would send the sample to be evaluated in a lab and they would call in the inspector from Seattle. But Greg felt in his gut that this was the same person who had started the house fire and maybe even some of the other ones Nolan had uncovered.

Nolan himself met them when the three of them left the building. "So, what did you find?"

The chief said, "Sure looks like those ones you dug up on the internet. And the Howe's home."

Greg and Jeremy both nodded.

Nolan frowned. "So, the arsonist is here in our town right now. I'm thinking to set up a watch post on the road and one at the ferry to check some ID's and gather information. Might be able to smoke out the guy or gal starting these."

Greg looked at the other two firefighters, who nodded. "Sounds like a damn fine plan to us, Nolan. Maybe we can keep this pyromaniac from causing real trouble. If this keeps escalating, he might actually kill someone in a house fire."

"I'll get it started immediately. I think this will allow the Howe's to get on with their life, too."

The chief nodded, "The investigator will have to take a look, but yeah, I think so."

"Good to hear. Let's see if we can't catch this asshole."

CHAPTER 24

Sandy was nervous to see Greg. They were supposed to work on setting up the auction over at Amber's and work through a hundred other little details. He'd been pissed last night, but she sensed that under the anger was a large dose of hurt. She'd hurt him by not wanting to tell her brother and indicating she was ashamed of the two of them

She wasn't ashamed, exactly, she didn't know what she was, to be honest. She wished she had time to talk to someone about her feelings, Barbara or even her mother would work. But she didn't have time. There were guests to feed, the place was packed.

Her mom was already in the kitchen when Sandy walked in. They started working in companionable silence until they had everything in the oven or in serving trays. Then her mom turned to her. "I heard Greg leave early last night. Before the siren went off."

Sandy hung her head. "Yeah, I think I hurt his feelings. I told him not to tell Terry about us."

Carol snorted. "That's ridiculous. You do know the whole

town knows about the two of you. You don't think someone else isn't going to mention it? Besides why don't you want your brother—and Greg's best friend—to know you've been enjoying each other over the summer."

Sandy sighed. "I don't know, mom. I just don't want Terry butting his nose in or making sarcastic remarks."

"Or teasing his big sister?"

"Maybe."

"So, you've pushed away the best man you've ever had in your whole life because your brother might tease you a little?"

"I'll be leaving in less than two weeks anyway."

Carol shrugged. "Seattle's not that far away. And you seem to be doing fine working from here now."

Sandy looked at her mom. She'd not thought about continuing the relationship past the summer. Maybe it was something to think seriously about. But not now, the food was ready, and she heard guests stirring upstairs. They needed the baked goods carried out for breakfast.

"Let's get the stuff out mom, I hear people."

Her mom wasn't going to be derailed, however. "You just think about it, Sandy. This doesn't have to be the end."

Sandy picked up the sweet rolls. "I will, mom."

And she did, all through breakfast, and the cleanup and even on the drive over to Amber's restaurant.

Did she come to a conclusion with all that thinking? No, she did not. But she did decide to tell Greg she wasn't ashamed of their relationship, and if he had his heart set on telling Terry he was welcome to do so. Because the fact of the matter was, she didn't want to end this now. Maybe when she left, she would feel different and be ready to end it, but today? No, not ready.

She didn't see his truck parked in the lot but decided he might have left it at the bar and walked down. She went in through the restaurant to say hi to Amber on her way to the back.

Amber saw her and waved her over. "Is something wrong with your phone?"

"Not that I know of, why?" Sandy pulled the phone out and looked at it. She didn't see anything wrong.

"Oh, it's just that Greg called and said he would be running late and asked me to tell you. He said he has to go by the fire from last night and do some more investigation into what caused it. I was a little surprised you didn't come by to help. It was that old barn at the edge of Chris's land, but still, it took them a while to get it out."

Sandy didn't know what to say, she would have been there if she'd known, but her mom didn't need a fire radio in the B&B and Sandy had been too upset by Greg walking out to investigate why the siren had gone off, and what the call was. Since it didn't go off a second time, she'd assumed it was something minor.

She shrugged in answer. "I'm going to get busy. If Greg is delayed for long, I'll need to work faster than if it was the two of us."

"Let me know if you want lunch later."

Sandy waved as she walked toward the banquet hall. She wasn't sure she could eat if she didn't get this worked out with Greg soon. Her stomach was tied in knots. Why hadn't Greg called her instead of leaving a message? That seemed a little extreme. Was he being childish? He didn't seem to be the type.

She would wait and ask him later. She really did need to work faster if he was going to be busy today. They didn't have a lot of spare time to get everything ready. Relief filled her to see that Amber's crew had set up the room to be ready for the auction and dinner. The long tables were against the back wall and had been draped with white table cloths. Each item would be placed on the table along with an auction signup form and a couple of pens.

The live auction items would be on the stage. But they would set those up later. Today's focus was the silent auction setup.

She'd been working about a half hour when Kristen walked in. Kristen was a pretty woman with long dark curly hair, her petite form was dressed in jeans and a tank top, with no makeup whatsoever. Some people had mistaken her and Barbara as twins, but Kristen was a few years older. "Greg called me and asked if I would come over to help you set up. Apparently, the investigation from the fire last night is taking longer than he thought it would. Nolan's decided to put some officers and volunteers on the road out of town and the ferry dock."

"So, the barn was arson too?"

Kristen nodded. "It's looking like that, so they're being careful with the investigation. It looks like some others that have happened in different areas."

"Really? So, does that let the Howe's off the hook?"

"For the most part yes. Nolan is talking to the investigators in other states."

"That makes this a bigger deal then, doesn't it?"

"Yes, and with Greg being the first officer on scene and also an investigator it's taking some time. He was worried about you trying to get everything done that the two of you had planned, so he sent me to help."

Sandy was glad for the assistance. Kristen was an artist and had an eye for design plus she had her own art gallery, so she knew how to create a flow for traffic.

While the two women worked Sandy kept thinking about Greg. Was he pawning her off onto others, or was he really busy? She didn't like the uncertainty of it. If she hadn't promised to help him with this, she might have just left to go back to Seattle without seeing him again. Kind of a chicken attitude, but oh well.

However, she had promised—so she was stuck—until at least Monday.

When it got to be lunchtime Kristen went out and ordered food for the two of them. Sandy wasn't sure if she would be able to eat it. It seemed like she got tenser and more worried as each minute passed and Greg didn't appear. She was almost certain he was avoiding her. It couldn't possibly take this long to investigate an abandoned barn.

When the door opened with the food she didn't turn, she was trying to arrange a quilt so that the best part of it could be seen by the people who would be bidding. It needed to stay in its thirty-six-inch area of the table, but it was for a king-sized bed. It simply didn't fit well.

A man spoke low into her ear. "You need to stop and have some lunch, you can fuss more later." She whirled and there was Greg, smiling gently at her.

She threw herself into his arms, which locked tight around her. "I'm so sorry about last night. I don't really care if you want to tell Terry or the whole damn world."

"I'm sorry too. I shouldn't have gotten on my high horse and stormed out. I regretted it before the fire alarm went off."

"You did?"

His hand caressed her back. "Of course. I understand that you don't want to answer to your brother. But I don't want you to be ashamed of us either. What we have is good, and honest."

"I know, and I'm not ashamed. I mostly don't want his teasing us or being grumpy about it."

He hugged her tight again. "If he does either, I'll punch him. But I don't have to tell him the instant he gets off the boat either, we can let him find out naturally."

"It's up to you. I just want you back. I was lonely and cold last night. You left your backpack and I'm holding it hostage."

He laughed and kissed her nose. "I'm sorry, I would have had to leave anyway for the fire. I only got a couple of hours sleep before I had to be back at the sight to investigate."

"Why did it take so long?"

"We found some interesting things. Possible footprints that led off toward some brush. Then it looked a little, to we untrained types, that someone had crouched behind the bushes for a while and maybe watched. We had to document all of it, without disturbing it, for when the investigator comes from Seattle. We can't trust that it will all be there in a couple of days when he gets here, it could rain. So, we wanted to take careful pictures, but not contaminate it, so he could see it, if it doesn't rain."

"So, do you think it was the same person as the Howe's house fire?"

Greg nodded. "It looked that way to me. Come on, let's eat. I'm starving."

Sandy realized that she was hungry too, now that her stomach had settled down. She looked around and didn't see Kristen. "Where did Kristen go?"

"Out into the restaurant to eat with Nolan. I wanted a few minutes with you alone, without an audience."

Sandy put her head on his shoulder as they walked over to where their lunches were waiting. They'd made it past *this* hurdle. She hadn't decided about the future, but she was happy with the present.

GREG WAS RELIEVED Sandy had been glad to see him. He'd been concerned about her reaction all morning, as he and Jeremy had spent the time at the fire site. He didn't think she would turn him away, but there had been women in the past that had done so, for far less than him walking out on them. Some of those women would have probably shot him dead, rather than taking him back after pulling that stunt.

Sandy had also relented on her stance about telling Terry. Which only made him want to keep it to himself. Terry would probably know within minutes of being home. He loved to be in on all the gossip. Although he might hole up for a while too. Sometimes he did that when he first got home from one of these trips.

Especially if he was in a hurry to get home, which was probably the case, since Greg knew Terry wanted to be home for the fundraiser. Greg wouldn't be at all surprised if Terry was still a little concerned about his mom. Terry knew Carol was feeling better and that she was up and around now, but the last time he had seen his mom she'd still been in bed, or on good days, in a wheel chair for a few hours.

This homecoming with Sandy in town and his mom feeling so much better, would be a good one. Of that Greg was confident.

As they ate their lunch Sandy filled him in on all she and Kristen had accomplished. "Kristen is a mover. She got a ton of stuff done. Of course, she had to redesign part of it, because she said we had too many big-ticket items lumped together, and it would cause a traffic jam. I decided she was right, so didn't complain, but it did slow us down."

He looked around the room and thought it looked great, there was one tiny area that was not yet finished, but he figured that would take them less than a half hour to do. So, he asked her about some of the other things they needed to do today.

Sandy swallowed the bite she had been chewing and looked down at her plate for a moment. She said quietly, "I couldn't sleep last night, so I got up and worked on the newspaper ad, and the flyer we're going to put up along main street, and at the ferry and hotels."

Well, hell, him walking out on her was the reason she couldn't sleep. He reached over and took her hand, running his thumb across her knuckles. "I'm sorry. Let's just pretend I had to leave for a fire. So, you're holding my backpack and clothes hostage, huh? What do I need to do to get them back?"

She pulled the key to the B&B out of her back pocket. "Take the key back."

He snatched it out of her hand so fast she laughed. "There should be something else, that was too easy."

She tapped her lip as she thought about it, which made his gaze lock on her lips. He wanted to ravish her right here in the middle of the banquet hall, but he didn't think Amber would be too keen on the idea. Plus, they had a whole fricken list of other things they had to do today. "How about tomorrow you come over to my place and I'll fix you dinner. I'll get someone to take my shift at the bar and it's your mom's book club night. So, we can have the whole evening to ourselves."

A wicked light filled her eyes and she nodded slowly. "I think that sounds like a marvelous idea."

He didn't have a clue what she was thinking but he was totally on board with whatever it was. His body was humming from the look in her eyes, alone. He shook his head and cleared his throat. "Stop that and eat your lunch, we have lots of things we have to do today, so we can play tomorrow."

She laughed a deep throated wicked laugh and his whole body quivered in anticipation.

CHAPTER 25

Terry arrived the next morning, Greg had gotten a text asking if he had time to help unload the wood Terry had picked up on his travels. Greg told him of course, and that he would meet him at Terry's house.

Greg still didn't know exactly what he was going to say to Terry about Sandy and himself but decided he would play it by ear. If need be, he would be ready to execute a strategic retreat, by making up some excuse about the fundraiser. Since Terry had been gone all summer, he wouldn't know if it was true or false.

Greg got to Terry's first, so he waited in his truck for his friend. Terry drove up and backed his truck up to his workshop. The truck was piled high with lumber. Greg saw cherry wood, oak, maple and cedar. He assumed there was pine and a few other varieties lower in the bed.

Terry got out of his truck and looked like he was furious. Greg had no idea what could have pissed Terry off unless he'd heard news about his relationship with Sandy.

"Hey buddy, you don't look very happy. I know it's a

change, but you'll get used to it and it's got an expiration date."

"Dammit Greg, how did you know I bumped into that damn photographer at the dock? Did Sandy tell you she was going to be here for the fundraiser and the whole next week?"

Photographer? What was Terry going on about? Okay, changing gears. "No Sandy didn't mention it. Why does it piss you off so bad?"

"I don't trust her. Why do we need another damn coffee table book about our valley anyway? Rachel already did one, who needs two for cripes sake?"

Oh, that photographer. Greg wanted to smirk, he was pretty sure there was something else going on in his friend's mind, about the photographer, than some book. But he decided to leave it alone and let Terry fume.

"Let's get this truck unloaded. Don't worry about the photographer. I think she's irritating you because you're hungry. You always get here starving. Did you have breakfast this morning?"

"No. I was too busy moving the lumber from the semi to my truck. I figured I could eat when I got here. But that has nothing to do with the photographer. And I'm not hangry."

Greg just lifted an eyebrow.

Terry chuckled, "All right, maybe I am a little hangry. Let's do this and head over to Amber's for some lunch."

They made quick work of unloading the truck and drove together to the café. Terry greeted Amber and collapsed into a booth. They ordered and sat back to catch up on all the happenings.

Terry asked, "So how have my girls been, you've been taking care of them, right?"

Greg tensed for a second and then remembered he'd promised Terry to look after his family. "Your mom is doing great, she's up and running the B&B again just fine. Sandy is still helping out with breakfast and a few other chores, but she's also been working with me a lot on the fundraiser. She's really organized, and I think she'll be the one to make it a success. I think I would have failed on my own."

Terry rolled his eyes. "I doubt that Greg. Maybe Sandy has made it easier or even more profitable, but you would have done fine on your own. By the way I'm kind of insulted you didn't ask me for a contribution to your auction."

"I figured everything you had ready was on the truck."

"Not quite. I've got one blanket chest I was making that I didn't get finished in time to go on the truck. If I worked on it the next couple of days, you could put it in the auction."

"That would be awesome and greatly appreciated, but don't you need some down time after your trip?"

"What I've got left to do is down time, some sanding, some varnish. Consider it yours. Any news on the Janet front?"

Greg shook his head. "Sandy tried to get Janet to open up but that didn't go any further than it does when you or your mom try. Sandy was pretty frustrated by the whole thing."

"Yeah, I couldn't agree more. It pisses me off that Janet puts up with his shit."

"Some people let assholes get away with too much. Anyway, did you hear about Steve stealing Sandy's laptop?"

"Mom mentioned it when I called her. What in the hell was he thinking?"

"No clue. But he'll have some time to figure it out. Sandy's game company is going after him big time. To make a statement, I think."

Terry nodded. "Probably, just letting everyone know they won't tolerate theft or sabotage."

The waitress brought their lunch over. Terry crowed, "Finally, food!"

Greg laughed as his friend started shoveling his lunch in his mouth. Greg never could figure out how someone could forget to eat, but Terry seemed to do it often. As they ate Terry told Greg about his drive across the country to deliver his hand-crafted furniture.

Terry sat back when there wasn't a crumb left on his plate. "So, tell me about the fires."

While Terry relaxed and sipped his coffee, Greg told him all about the fires.

Terry listened intently. "Nolan checked with all of our junior firebugs?"

Yeah, most of those kids have outgrown their love of fire. None of them are considered to have pyromaniac tendencies, anymore. And they had alibis."

"Good to know. But if it's not one of the locals, then who could it be."

"No clue but Nolan's got men at the landing dock and the upper road, checking everyone who's leaving. The main issue is that it was so far in between incidents. Most people don't vacation that long. Nolan's checking the ferry logs for anyone that came in that way and is still here. But if they drove over the road we wouldn't know, especially if they're camping."

Terry rubbed his chin. "But if they drove in, they'll have to drive out or take the barge. So those people would be easier to catch."

Greg nodded, as he thought about that. When the waitress came up and asked if they wanted anything else, Terry ordered a piece of Amber's chocolate French silk pie. It was a favorite in the town and one of the only things she still cooked, now that she owned and ran the restaurant. Everyone teased her that she put some kind of aphrodisiac into it and had hooked the author Jeremy Scott with it.

The waitress went off to get the pie and Terry said, "Unless they hiked in."

"Shit. But if they hiked in, they probably wouldn't have been able to carry that much kerosene for two fires. One sure, but not two."

Terry said, "So they would have had to buy some here in town or in a neighboring town."

"Yeah, might be the reason for the long separation between the fires."

"We're just making shit up now." Terry said as the waitress put down a huge slice of pie, filled his coffee, and gave Terry a clean fork.

Greg grinned. "We are. I'm sure Nolan and his crew have thought this all through."

"Fuck, that woman is like a bad penny."

Greg followed Terry's gaze to the pretty photographer, who'd apparently just walked in the door. As he watched her scan the room, he saw the instant her eyes set on Terry and a purely evil expression crossed her face. She waved off the hostess and made a beeline for their table.

Greg decided this was the time for that previously mention strategic retreat, and he was about to throw his best friend under the bus when he did. He stood as she approached. "Deborah, isn't it? Nice to see you again." He shook her hand.

"Yes, thank you, Greg. It's nice to be back. I was wondering if I could join you two for a moment."

"Oh, sure, please have a seat." He gestured toward his side of the booth and she slid in. "However, I've got a meeting with Sandy in a few minutes to work on the fundraiser. It's this weekend you know. So, while I would love to stay and chat. I'm afraid I'll have to leave you in the company of Terry."

Deborah smiled sweetly at him and didn't look the least

bit fazed at him leaving. She was clearly here to needle Terry. Terry on the other hand was glaring daggers at him. He just saluted and said, "I'll see you later, bro. Deborah."

Before he made it to the front door the two were arguing. Greg congratulated himself on getting away from Terry, so he could cook for Sandy and none were the wiser.

SANDY NEEDED to keep herself occupied. She'd already done everything she could think of at the B&B, to the point where her mom had shooed her away. She was supposed to call her team in an hour. But that hour seemed very far away. She didn't know what to do to occupy herself.

The real problem was that she was going over to Greg's tonight and she couldn't wait. She'd been thinking about their night together for hours. Somehow it seemed more special because he was taking the night off to spend it with her. And cooking dinner. It felt like a real date rather than just a hook up. She'd even decided to wear a dress and sexy underwear that matched, and sky-high heels with peek-a-boo toes. Not at all her normal apparel.

But that was hours away and she had to do something else or she might go mad. She laid back on the bed trying to think of something that might interest her and keep her attention, when a thought caught her mind.

Sandy leaped up and opened her laptop. She'd forgotten weeks ago that she wanted to check on Steve's older brother Edward. If he worked at her company that might be the reason Steve had thought they were going to come out with a new game. By now everyone in the company knew about the sabotage, but they'd kept it very hush hush outside the company, so the theory was that the only other people that would know about it would be the people who actually orchestrated it.

She got into the company mail program and searched for Edward Jameson. Nope he wasn't in there. And wasn't that interesting? Next, she went on social media and did a search there. Only a dozen people came up with that name. Eight were clearly out of Washington. The other four she would have to look closer at. It took her only a few minutes to weed out two more. But the last two had more secure profiles. No information was open to the public. Drat.

Maybe she should try Steve's profile instead. Surely, he was friends with his own brother. She went into Steve's profile and since she was friends with him, she could access almost everything. There was an Edward Jameson as one of his friends, but the account was still locked to her and she didn't see any real correspondence between them. Only likes and happy birthday messages. Double drat.

She started to close her laptop when something else occurred to her. Steve had stolen her laptop thinking he could get into it because he knew her old password. He'd tried various combinations of that high school password before the security program had triggered.

She hadn't used that old password in over fifteen years. But Steve thought she might still use it. So, was it possible that he still used his high school password? She pulled back up his profile and looked at the alias he'd used. It was the high school login they had had. The only difference was that he'd put their year of graduation at the end.

She logged out of her social media account and typed in his email, along with his high school password. The first time it didn't work, but when she added the graduation year to the end, it opened right up. She didn't need to do a lot of digging, but she wanted to see if Edward listed who he worked for in Seattle.

She clicked on his friends list, found Edward and clicked on his profile. Sure enough, he did have his company listed right under his name and picture. She wasn't sure whether to be elated or pissed when she saw it was one of their top competitors. And the one game company that had rumors going around as to their ethics, or lack thereof. She decided to look at one other thing, and that was Steve's private message account to see if there were any conversations with Edward.

What she found made her blood run cold. But she took screen shots of it all and saved them to her computer. Next, she composed an email and sent it all to the managers in charge of security breaches, and her own manager.

Sandy's hands were shaking when she joined her team meeting. Before she could say a dozen words her phone rang, her email pinged and a skype request came up. "Sorry guys, I think I'll have to postpone our meeting until tomorrow. Go ahead and work on what you've got. I can look it over tomorrow when we get back online."

She clicked over to the second skype session and answered her phone. She spent the next two hours talking to the security people, the investigators and her own bosses. Yes, she'd done something illegal by breaking into Steve's profile, but since she knew the password and they were friends, no one could prove he hadn't given her his password. He had, in fact, given it to her, fifteen years ago.

It looked like Steve hadn't been in on the actual sabotage, but Edward had definitely known about it. Whether he'd been an accomplice or not, remained to be seen. But he'd certainly known about it. He'd told Steve not to count on the game being out in December and if it did go to market there would be some very interesting graphics to come up. Edward had even told Steve a couple of sequences to follow. So,

Edward at the very least was going to go to jail. Maybe he and his brother could be roommates.

By the time she finally got off the phone from talking to every person involved she was going to be late to Greg's house. She texted him to say she'd been delayed and would tell him all about it when she got there.

Sandy was terribly disappointed that she wouldn't have time for all the primping she'd planned to do. Greg was going to get her in the clothes she'd had on all day, but she knew he would understand. And she wanted to be with him now, instead of being even later, so she could change clothes.

She called out a goodbye to her mom and the book club as she walked out the door and got in her car.

CHAPTER 26

Greg was surprised to hear that Sandy was going to be late for their dinner date. He wondered what had happened. She'd sounded both keyed up and exhausted. It was a strange combination. He turned down the heat on the dinner that was in the oven and poured her a glass of wine. The dinner would keep for a while and she could tell him whatever it was that had delayed her.

He saw her drive up so went to open the door. He was a little surprised to see her in the clothes she'd had on this morning but decided whatever had delayed her was a bigger deal than he'd first thought.

Sandy looked him over and wilted. "Oh, you look so nice. I was planning to look nice too. I had everything planned out. And now look at me, I'm still in my morning work clothes. This bites."

She looked so defeated, but at the same time beautiful. He pulled her in his arms and kissed her softly to start with, but the heat and passion grew until they were panting. "I think you look lovely. And you're here in my arms, so that's all that matters. You can dress up another time. Besides who says you're going to be in your clothes that long, anyway."

She laughed and laid her head on his shoulder. "Thanks, it's been a crazy afternoon."

Greg drew her over to his couch and guided her to sit, then he handed her the wine glass and sat beside her. "Tell me what happened."

"It was rather clever of me. I was waiting for the online meeting with my team and was restless, because after the online meeting, I was going to start getting ready for our date."

She sighed and started to look sad again, so he prompted her to continue with a wave of his hand. "Mom had literally shoved me out of the kitchen, she said I was driving her crazy with all my energy. I guess I was a little keyed up about coming over. Anyway, I went to my room and then could find nothing that I could settle on. Then, I thought about Steve and why he was so adamant we were building a new game. I'd forgotten to tell my boss or anyone about my suspicions. Which was to wonder if Steve had somehow heard about our sabotage."

She continued with her story and Greg had to admit she had been clever, very clever. But as she talked about having to answer the same questions over and over again, when what she'd really wanted to be doing was getting ready for their date, he could see the frustration she'd felt.

He held her hand and rubbed a thumb over her knuckles. "I know you were frustrated but giving the investigators the information to possibly track down the people behind the corporate espionage, was a more important use of your time than looking pretty for me."

"I'm not sure you would agree with that if you'd seen what I was planning to wear under the pretty dress."

His mind went down a very dirty path, imagining everything from slutty underwear to nothing at all. He cleared his throat. "Maybe you can save it for next time."

"Will there be a next time?"

"Hell yes, there will be. If you've got something special in mind, I'll make damn sure there's a next time."

She smiled a siren's smile. "I'll save it for you then."

He wanted to carry her off caveman style and have his way with her, but he also needed to feed her and take care of her, just a little. She wouldn't accept a lot, but he could slide a little under her radar, if he was careful and sneaky.

"I'll be looking forward to it. But for right now I have food waiting in the oven to be eaten, so if you would come with me, my sweet, I will give you sustenance after your long afternoon of talking and talking and talking."

Sandy smiled at his silliness but gave him her hand as he held his out to her. As he pulled her up, she pushed in close, so their bodies were touching. "I have other hungers I hope you plan to fill."

He groaned at the expression on her face and then pulled back, so she wasn't plastered to him. "I'll be happy to take care of all your hungers. But food first, so you have enough fuel for the rest of them."

She sighed and tried to look sad. "I think I'd rather start on some of the others, but if you insist."

He laughed and dragged her to the kitchen before he pulled her down on the couch to give her what she was clearly asking for. "Food first."

Sandy followed Greg into the kitchen where he had a fancy table set with real dishes, linen napkins, candles, and flowers. Her breath backed up in her throat as she viewed the lovely table he'd set. She had no idea he would do something like this. She'd been expecting plastic dishes and maybe a grilled steak with a baked potato.

Now that she'd seen the table, she didn't know what to expect. He pulled out her chair and helped her sit. Then he refilled her wine glass and put an antipasto plate on the table. It could have been served at a five-star restaurant. It was beautifully arranged with lots of little snacks. He next set some bread and oil and vinegar on the table. He sat across from her and they sampled his appetizers. The man was pulling out all the stops and she felt a little overwhelmed and completely underdressed.

She yanked at the shirt she had on in frustration. He took her hand and ran a thumb over the knuckles, which sent tingles racing along her nerves. "You look beautiful, now stop worrying and enjoy yourself. Do you want me to go put on scruffy sweats and a t-shirt with holes and stains on it? That would make you more dressed up than I am."

She laughed, she didn't want him to change his clothes, he looked magnificent. Well unless it was to get naked, she could be onboard for that.

He apparently could read her face because he shifted in his seat. "Stop that, you're killing me." Then he jumped up and went over to the oven.

He retrieved something that smelled wonderful. The room filled with the rich aroma of red sauce and sausage. He set the dish of stuffed shells on the table. It looked like there were different ingredients in each shell. Some were a ricotta cheese mixture with spinach or something, and some were filled with sausage. Some looked like both the ricotta mixture and sausage had been combined. The shells sat on a bed of tomato sauce and more cheese. The top of the shells were covered in mozzarella.

Her mouth started watering and she realized she was hungrier than she'd thought. Next, he pulled out a loaf of garlic bread that filled the room with butter and garlic scents. And last was a fancy dish of vegetables covered in a sauce with bread crumbs on top.

They would never be able to eat even half the food he made, and it all looked too delicious to pass up.

"Did you really prepare all this yourself?"

He put one of each shell on her plate, a slice of bread and a few vegetables. "I did it all, except I bought the bread from Samantha."

"Well, of course."

"I actually do know how to make bread from scratch. I didn't have time because your brother got to town, and I spent the morning with him."

She felt herself tense. "Terry's back and you spent the morning with him?"

"I did, but you and I never came up in conversation, so he got no information from me."

She nodded and then remembered what else he'd said in that statement. She cut into one of the shells. "You were going to make bread from scratch? Seriously?"

He shrugged one shoulder. "I had thought about it, but it didn't work out."

"Wow."

"You're not the only one who can bake, although my breakfast is not nearly as fancy as yours is. If I don't eat at the B&B it's cereal or maybe an egg and toast. Getting all that cooking done before breakfast is simply not happening. I have to be awake to cook, not stumbling around like a zombie."

She laughed. "So, what did you and Terry talk about?" She took a bite of one of the sausage stuffed shells and moaned, as the flavors burst on her tongue.

He sat there with his mouth open like he was going to answer but was frozen.

"Greg? You and Terry?"

He shook his head like he was coming out of a trance. "Your moan short circuited my brain. No more sex noises." He waved his fork at her. "We talked about Terry's trip, and the fundraiser, and the fires. He was kind of insulted we didn't ask him for an auction donation."

"But…."

"Yeah, I know. I told him we didn't think he had anything left, and he informed me he had a blanket chest almost done, that would be ready for the auction."

She raised her brows. "All righty then, we can certainly find room to put that in the auction. Do you think silent or live?"

"It would be easier live, since we wouldn't have to rearrange anything, just put it up on stage."

She nodded. "I like the way you think." She took a forkful of the vegetables and realized they were as delicious as the shells. "Oh my God, Greg these are to die for."

He was clearly pleased. "They are a favorite of mine."

"I can see why. This entire meal is delicious, but you made enough food for an army."

He grinned. "Leftovers. Or maybe a midnight snack, after we handle some of your other hungers."

This time *she* squirmed in her chair at the look he was giving her. "Eat." She pointed her fork at him, and a tiny bit of broccoli flew off of it and smacked him in the nose.

One eyebrow flew up as he wiped the broccoli off his face. "Are you starting a food fight with my delicious labor of love?"

She laughed at his expression. "No, it was an accident."

"I'm not sure I believe you. I might have to get even with the dessert later. I think tiramisu-flavored Sandy might be just the ticket."

Oh, good lord, the man was heating her up. She grabbed

her ice water like it was a lifeline and drank deep, but it didn't cool her off one little bit. In fact, she was a little surprised it didn't turn to steam when her hand touched the glass.

"Now stop that. You're the one that said we had to eat dinner first. So, eat your dinner, Jones."

He chuckled as she said his last name, like that was going to deter him in the least. Which if she was honest with herself was fine with her. But two could play at his game so she twirled her wine glass and took a sip.

"You know that tiramisu might be tasty on certain parts of your anatomy, too." She put her wine glass down and ran her finger over the rim and then put that finger into her mouth and sucked on it for a second.

His eyes heated, and she was sure he was seconds from dragging her across the table and knocking the food to the floor. She didn't want to waste all that delicious food, so she dialed back the seduction in her gaze and took an innocent bite of another stuffed shell.

He just sat there for another minute or two and she could see him working to calm down. He finally took a fork full of food for himself, but right before he put it in his mouth he said, "You're going to pay for that later, young lady."

She waited until he swallowed to say, "I certainly hope so, Greg."

He laughed, and they went back to enjoying the meal. But there was a slight undertone of banked tension humming in the air.

CHAPTER 27

Greg's whole body felt like a live wire. Sandy had every molecule vibrating with excitement. He wanted her, and if she hadn't dialed it down a little, he wasn't sure he wouldn't have dragged her off caveman style to the first available flat surface. Or a wall would have worked. He'd thought about the table but it was covered in hot dishes and that wouldn't have been pleasant. The counter might have been.

He'd fought to get himself under control and stay in his chair, but she'd tempted him beyond what he thought he could handle. Finally, they were back to eating and making small talk. But she'd had him on a razor's edge of lust so powerful, he hadn't been sure of his own strength to stop it.

The woman made him crazy in the best possible way. He loved having her sitting across from him chatting and eating. He was glad she'd finally gotten over her unease about being late, and not getting to primp for him. She could wear a damn gunny sack and he'd still think she was beautiful.

He was sure he could sit across the table from her for the rest of his life and be perfectly happy. It was too damn bad she lived two hours away. It wasn't that far, but it was if he wanted to keep running his bar.

Sandy broke into his thoughts. "So where did you learn to cook like this anyway?"

"While I was in college, I worked at an Italian restaurant. Since I was there for five years, I worked my way up to sous chef, and the chef showed me how to whip up easy dishes like this." He pointed to the shells. "We also baked our own bread."

She'd been thinking about him dropping out of college when he'd decided not to stay in law. "Why did you drop out of college instead of changing focus and getting a different degree?"

He didn't really like talking about that decision, so he frowned for a minute.

"Oh sorry, I shouldn't have asked. It's none of my business."

"No, it's not that. I don't mind telling you. It was right before summer vacation and I was supposed to go back to the law firm to intern again for the summer, but the idea of doing that made me physically sick. So, I lied to them and told them I needed to come here for the summer. Anyway, when I got back here, I went to work at the bar, only this time I didn't have to work in the back. I could be out front, because I'd finally turned legal. You remember I worked there when I was in high school."

She nodded.

"When Sarah and Jimmy decided to retire to Phoenix, they made me an offer I couldn't refuse, so I bought the bar from them. Which made it easy to drop out of college."

"I'm glad you didn't sell your soul for the money and prestige of working for that high-dollar law firm. Your being here in town is a blessing to everyone that lives in Chedwick. You more than give back."

Greg didn't want to get choked up, so he tried to think how to express what the town and the people in it meant to him. "This place... they all had my back growing up. Whether I deserved it or not. The town and the people in it made me the man I am today. Plus, I can look at myself in the mirror and not feel shame. Interning for that law firm, I didn't feel that way. I couldn't look myself in the eye. I had to get away."

"I'm glad you realized that early on."

His breath whooshed out on a laugh. "You and me both. Can you imagine the debt I'd have built up, only to find out I didn't have a heart for the job? Five years was bad enough."

"Yeah, I hear you. Accumulating the debt is an investment, *if* you can use the education to pay for it later. When you can't, it's just not worth it."

"Exactly."

He looked at their plates which were mostly empty. "I'm done eating, did you want more?"

"God no, I'm stuffed to the gills. All that horsing around we planned is going to have to wait until some of that wonderful food digests. It was delicious, Greg, thank you for making such a fantastic meal."

"I'm glad you enjoyed it. I love to cook. Cooking for you, made it extra special."

She blushed, and he loved putting the color in her cheeks. She was so beautiful, it hurt to look at her, and at the same time that's all he wanted to do. She stood and started gathering up the dishes.

"You don't need to do that, they can wait."

"No, it will help digest the food to move around a bit. I'll rinse the dishes, you put the food away."

"If you insist. Do you want me to make you a doggy bag?"

"No, if Terry is back, he'll find it and eat it."

Greg shrugged and started covering the leftovers. Some of the baking dishes had lids, so he snapped those on and put them in the fridge. "He should be busy working on the blanket chest, but you're probably right. He'll be around mooching breakfast most likely. Although I didn't tell you the best part of my lunch with him."

"Tell me."

He gave her a sly look. "That photographer is back."

"Yeah, she checked in this morning."

"Well, Terry and I had finished eating and he'd just gotten a huge piece of Amber's French silk pie, when Deborah walked in and came over to sit with us. I was finished, and wanted to get back here to start cooking, so I invited her to sit down and then left the two of them. They were arguing before I got out the door."

Sandy's eyes were filled with mirth. "You didn't."

"I did."

She laughed. "That's just evil."

"It is, and I loved every second of it. Plus, it gave me a clean getaway."

She shook her finger at him after she put the last of the dishes into the dishwasher. "He'll try to get even, you know."

Greg knew that was true, but he'd had too much fun trapping Terry with the photographer to care about that. "Yeah, but he can't stop the pleasure I had today."

"You might want to sleep with one eye open."

"Naw, he'll do it in broad daylight. Terry's not much for sneaking around in the night. Unless it's for a fireman's prank."

"True, he's a bed baby. By the way, I got to see the tire marks you put on the back of Kyle's bunker coat."

He held up his hands. "Not me."

"Well one of you, anyway. What did Kyle think?"

Greg chuckled as he thought about Kyle's reaction. "He was just glad we didn't pull out every one of his real estate signs and put them in his yard. That's what he thought we'd do. I think we gave him insomnia for a few nights, until he found the tire tracks."

"They glow in the dark, don't they?"

He put some cling wrap over the antipasto plate. "No, but they are made of reflector tape, so when light hits them, they stand out, for sure."

She waved the bread knife at him. "So, he won't be getting run down in the street anytime soon."

"Nope, that's for certain."

"So, a practical prank."

"If you say so." Greg shook his head and chuckled at her enjoyment of their prank on Kyle. "Want to sit on the deck, or in the living room for a little while?"

"The deck, for sure. It's nice out tonight, not too cold. Besides you can keep me warm."

He gulped at the look she gave him, as fire shot through his body.

SANDY NOTICED Greg's reaction to her suggestion that he keep her warm. The statement had accomplished exactly what she'd wanted it to. She wanted to keep him interested and on the edge. Sandy didn't want some long drawn out love making session. She wanted it hard and intense and fast. She wanted to make him go berserk and take her, possess her. None of this making love business. This time she wanted primal, wild, animalistic sex. And to do that she needed to keep his engines revved, and him on the brink of losing control.

She was having a great time.

But now she needed to distract him with more talk because she was entirely too full to move to the bedroom. Yet. She walked out onto the deck, it was well built and huge.

Terry had mentioned that he and Greg were rebuilding it a few years ago. They had done an excellent job. There was a ginormous grill on one side and a hot tub on the other. In between were chairs and a table. Tiki lights ringed the area, but Greg hadn't lit them.

Sandy walked up to the railing at the back to look out over the mountains in the background. The sun had set but the sky was still lit up behind the mountains. The last rays were lighting up some drifting clouds with pink and gold.

"Deborah, the photographer, wants to take some pictures during the fundraiser. I told her I thought that would be fine."

It took Greg a minute to answer her. She guessed he was changing gears from sex to normal life. He stood behind her with both arms wrapped around her to join in front. He said gruffly, "She does know that this is the first time we're doing it, doesn't she? It's not like we have a fundraiser every year and it's always part of our late summer, early fall, activities."

Sandy wriggled back into him. "Yeah. I mentioned that to her. She's not sure the pictures will be used anywhere, or in the book she's working on, but she thought it would be fun."

"I assume she knows she can't use those pictures anywhere without the consent of the people in them."

Sandy shrugged. "She's a professional, so I imagine she knows. Although I do think her forte is landscapes, rather than people. I can mention it to her when I see her next. Since she's staying with us, that will probably be tomorrow."

"If you get the chance go ahead and mention it. We don't need any misunderstandings. I wonder how your brother will react to her being around all weekend."

She thought about that and then laughed. "That will be an interesting thing to watch. Maybe we should bring a camera to capture it."

"Our phones will work without being too obvious."

"True."

Greg shuffled his feet. "You know, I hate to admit it, but I'm still a little nervous about this whole thing."

Sandy turned out of his arms, so she could see his face. "The fundraiser or some piece of it?"

"All of it. There are so many different things going on. How can only the two of us keep track of everything. Even just the parade seems like a nightmare. Let alone the booths and food on Saturday. Then Sunday is the relay race early, and the auction and dinner. It kind of makes me sick to think about all of it."

Sandy smiled at the big strong man in front of her, who was worried about a parade. He could confidently manage an entire crew on a fire, where lives were at stake, but a fundraiser was making him crazy. "So, if this was a fire, how would you handle it?

"That's easy. I give the squad captains their orders. They carry them out and I simply oversee the operations and trouble-shoot."

She nodded. "That's exactly what you'll do this weekend. We've got competent people helping. Amber is certainly capable of feeding people. Jeremy is handling the relay. Sheila is a great coordinator and we've asked her to help with the auctions. Chris's crew is handling the amusement park. You asking Mary Ann to help with the craft booths was a stroke of genius, she'll do a great job on that. As long as the baby waits until it's over, but I heard she has Tammy as her backup. They've been working at the art gallery together for several years, so even if the baby decides to come early it's covered. Those are the major pieces. The parade is only lining everyone up in order and we sent them their numbers in line already, so that should be fine, too."

"I hope you're right. It seems so big. But I guess if I look at the individual pieces, it doesn't seem so bad."

Sandy squeezed his hand. "And there are a lot of people in town that have your back. We all just need to have fun and give the tourists a good time, so they open their wallets, or in reality, zip those credit cards through the readers. Now enough of this fretting and stalling. It's time to make good on your promises, take me to bed."

"I can do that." He hoisted her over his shoulder in a firemen's carry, she laughed and pinched his butt, since it was right there in front of her face.

CHAPTER 28

Sandy expected to be dumped onto his bed, but she was surprised when he set her back on her feet. She pushed the hair out of her face and felt her body still as she took in the scene of seduction, he'd transformed his room into. He had flameless candles set all around the room and he was lighting real ones. There were rose petals on the bed and a bottle of Champagne chilling next to a box of chocolate-covered cherries. It was totally cliché and she loved every bit of it.

He finished lighting the other candles and touched a button on his phone that had soft music playing out of blue tooth speakers on both sides of the bed.

He looked up with a sheepish expression. "Too much?"

She shook her head and walked over to him. "Not in the least, Greg. It's perfect."

"Not too cheesy?" Now that she was closer to him, she could see that his ears were a bit pink. How could this self-confident man so underestimate himself? It surprised her every time.

"It's perfect. I just wish I had my sundress and sexy underwear on to match."

Greg put his hands on both sides of her face. "Sandy, you could be covered in mud and a burlap sack, and I would still think you looked perfect." He lowered his head and kissed her in a slow deliberate manner that raised her temperature. Her body responded, and her nipples reached out for him.

She'd planned on a hard, fast, out of control, sexual adventure, but he was clearly wanting to romance her. She couldn't bring herself to disappoint him, so she sank into the romance and let him lead the way.

He pulled out the hair tie and ran his fingers through the strands, while he kissed her face. Little loving kisses on every part, cheeks, chin, eyes, nose, and forehead. Going back often to her lips, drawing her deeper with each kiss.

Greg moved his mouth to her neck, moving up and down from her shoulders to her ears, where he nipped her earlobe, and she shivered. Sandy tilted her head to give him better access. A slow but sure fire was building in her veins. She wanted skin beneath her fingers, so she started unbuttoning his shirt, which caused him to do the same with hers. As each inch of her skin was revealed, he kissed it.

He had a t-shirt on under his shirt, so even after she pushed the outer layer off, she had no skin. She growled low in her throat.

Greg was kissing the tops of her breasts but stopped at the sound and looked up. "Problem?"

"I want skin and you have on too many clothes," she said with a petulant tone, that even she thought sounded ridiculous.

He grinned and yanked his t-shirt over his head. "Better?"

"Much."

"Mind if I get back to what I was doing?"

Sandy waved a hand at her front. "Carry on."

Before he returned to kissing her, he unhooked her bra and dropped it on the floor where there was starting to be a pile of clothes. He kissed her lips and said, "Totally worth the interruption."

When his lips met with her hot flesh, she moaned. He took one nipple into his mouth and suckled. She clutched his head and held him there, it felt so darn good. She let up enough for him to move to the other breast and repeat. When he'd thoroughly loved both of them, she let him move on, he chuckled against her skin which caused more shivers to race through her body.

His kisses continued down her torso and he nibbled the skin above her waistband as he unzipped her jeans. He pushed them and her panties down her legs, she wasn't sure she could stand much longer, her legs had turned to jelly. She held on to his shoulders as he helped her step out of her jeans.

Her legs wobbled as she fought to stay standing. "Greg."

"I know sweetheart, let's get you over to the bed so you can sit, or lay down if you prefer." He pulled her over and sat her on the edge of the bed. Then he knelt in front of her and hooked her legs over his shoulders.

She shuddered at the thought of what he was planning to do next. "Greg."

"I know baby, just relax and enjoy. So pretty."

She didn't think the part of her anatomy he was looking at was the least bit pretty, but she didn't have the strength to argue. She felt a puff of cool air and then his warm mouth was on her, and that was the last coherent thought she had.

GREG WAS ENTHRALLED with the pleasure he was bringing to Sandy. He loved to hear her moans and sighs, and when she screamed his name at her climax it made him feel like a god. He couldn't get enough of her. He couldn't give her enough pleasure. He wanted to continue for hours, all night even. But he knew she wouldn't allow that, so he slid her up fully onto the bed and dropped his clothes to join her.

He laid on his side next to her exhausted body and watched as she came back to herself. She was so beautiful; her body was perfect for him. Exactly the size and shape he thought was the most gorgeous of all creation. He loved her, more than anything or anyone. He wanted to tell her. Would she want to hear the words? Would she run away from them? From him? He was too afraid to risk it, so he kept his mouth shut. But his heart and mind pounded with the knowledge. Maybe he would risk it after the fundraiser.

When she had recovered, she smiled into his eyes and then ran a hand down his chest, and took hold of his straining cock. His eyes crossed in pleasure, as she stroked him.

Sandy cleared her throat. "So, I assume you have a condom handy."

"I do."

"Well what are you waiting for? An invitation?"

"Just giving you some time."

"Thank you. I was a little wrung out. In the best possible way. You were very diligent. But I'm ready to continue to phase two." She squeezed him and flicked her thumb across the tip.

Greg thought he might have a heart attack. He gritted his teeth against the pleasure and ground out. "I'll get the condom."

She squeezed him one more time before letting go, so he could reach for a condom.

When he had it in his hand she said, "Let me help."

He nearly groaned. He didn't think he could handle her

'helping'. He didn't want to blast off prematurely and he was definitely on the edge. But he handed her the condom and firmly told himself to man up and take it.

He clenched his jaw and fists, as she very much enjoyed rolling the condom on his straining flesh. When she was finally finished he couldn't take any more, so he flipped her over onto her back and fit himself between her legs. She took hold of him and guided him inside her. Then Sandy wrapped her legs around his waist and he slid in deeper. She gripped his arms and urged him to move.

He wanted to take it slow and easy, but she squeezed him with her inner muscles and he couldn't hold back. All finesse was gone, and he started pounding into her.

She met him stroke for stroke and urged him on verbally. "Harder, Greg. Faster. More."

He had no control and he let her drag him into the heat and the flames. Burning as they joined in the frenzy of their bodies' desires.

She stiffened and said, "Now, Greg, come with me."

He had no choice as her body convulsed and milked his.

He collapsed on her and when he was able, he rolled onto his back, drawing her with him, so she was half on top of him and half on the bed. They both lay there exhausted and panting while their bodies cooled.

His heart urged him again to tell her, just tell her he loved her. He wanted to. Should he do it? He decided to risk it. But it was too late, she was asleep, her body had softened, and her breathing was deep and relaxed. He whispered it to her anyway, "I love you, Sandy darlin'. I'm so in love with you it hurts. I want to be with you forever."

Sandy slept on, completely unaware he'd told her his deepest secret. At least he'd admitted it to himself and said it out loud. Maybe after the fundraiser he could tell her again and she would be awake this time.

CHAPTER 29

As it turned out the hardest part of the whole weekend was the parade. Since neither Greg nor Sandy had ever planned a parade before, they had no idea what they were setting themselves up for. But the moment people started lining up, the complaints came rolling in.

The tiny twirlers were behind the horses. And horses poop. So, they moved the horses to the end of the parade. And quickly found a couple of volunteers to be pooper scoopers.

The firetruck sirens would drown out the school marching band. They moved the firetrucks to after the pooper scoopers to signal the end of the parade. And then they realized they had all the music bunched together, so they spaced the different groups out over the parade length.

The girl scouts didn't want to walk that far and asked if they could trade off girls walking with girls riding, but they hadn't made a float, so they just wanted to drive a car. Sandy found someone with a decorated pickup truck who volunteered to let the girls ride in the back of the truck, as long as they didn't mind being in a truck set up to advertise the barber shop.

The republican politicians and the democratic ones didn't want to be together. So, they decided to move one set to later in the parade, and of course, they were ticked off that they were second. Greg finally told both sets that if they couldn't be civil, they would be banned from the parade completely. Since they were not from town, but were there on a state or national campaign, he really didn't care if they liked it. Basically, it was shut up or get out, and no, they wouldn't get a refund of their parade entry fee.

Then one of the mothers came to complain that she didn't want the parade participants to throw candy, and couldn't they have a healthier alternative? When Greg looked at the woman like he was going to kill her right there on main street, Sandy pulled the woman to the side to explain that the participants got to choose what they wanted to hand out. But she really didn't see a way for people to toss apples or tofu.

The woman left in a huff saying, "Granola bars would be easy."

Sandy shook her head and mumbled under her breath, "But very expensive."

When she got back over to where Greg was, he said, "And you thought I was being silly worrying about the parade."

Sandy held up her hands in surrender. "I was wrong, very, very wrong."

"Do you think this is a foreshadowing of the entire weekend?"

"No, not at all, we had no idea that planning a parade was this complicated. We did not make that same mistake with the rest of the activities and planned them much better than we did the parade."

Greg's shoulders relaxed and the tight expression on his

face eased. "You're right, we did take more care with the rest. We thought the parade was simple. We know better now."

"We do."

"Okay then let's get this show on the road. Literally. I saw a lot of people lining the walks." He signaled to the people carrying the banner to start the parade and it was off.

From there on out things went relatively smoothly. The Grange carried the flags and one of the town's garage bands played the Star-Spangled Banner so well, that everyone was shocked at their musical ability. He was proud of the kids, and figured they'd just launched their career, at least here in town.

The drum major for the high school marching band got nervous and had to take a quick pit stop, the band was worried he wouldn't be back in time, but he made it within a split second, and although he looked a little green, he proudly led the band down the street playing their school song.

One of the tiny twirlers dropped her baton, it rolled into the gutter and got dirty. She couldn't possibly use it dirty, so she cried and had to be carried the rest of the parade.

The king and queen of the parade got visited by the town peacock who decided his place was on the front hood of their car. Several people tried to shoo him off, but he wasn't going anywhere and screeched at anyone who tried to make him move. Sandy and Greg decided he was giving his approval to the fundraiser and took it as an omen for good things to happen. The driver had a heck of a time trying to see around the bird. The king and queen were virtually ignored in favor of the bird, and they didn't see anything wrong with that.

The horses didn't much care for the air horns, and skittered each time they went off, so Greg radioed to the trucks to only use the sirens. Which kept the horses from charging off, but the kids along the parade route were disappointed when they pumped their arms, and nothing happened. The firefighters handing out candy made sure each one of the kids got an official junior firefighter badge, that Greg hoped would soothe their feelings. Maybe the horses and the fire trucks should have been spread out a little more.

When the parade finally ended both Sandy and Greg collapsed on the first flat surface. Sandy felt like she'd been through the wringer, and she'd never seen Greg so discombobulated.

He said, "Thank God, that's over."

"I couldn't agree more. Let's never have a parade again."

"Well, if somebody wants one, they can find someone else to plan the darn thing. Because I sure as hell am not going to."

Sandy sighed and put her head on his shoulder, she couldn't hold it up any longer. She felt wrung out and they had two more full days of activities left. She had to believe it would be better, or she might be tempted to run out of town this very second.

Greg sighed like the world was on his shoulders. "I suppose we need to go see if the booths are ready."

Sandy looked at the empty street. "If they aren't, it's too late. Everyone is either at the booths or the amusement park."

They both sat there for a few minutes enjoying the quiet. Sandy linked one arm through his and sighed. Then she slapped her other hand on her knee and said, "Okay, let's get over there, just in case we're needed."

Greg sighed one more time and stood pulling her up with him. "Yep, let's get 'er done."

Sandy laughed, and they walked slowly toward the park and dock, where the booths were set up.

~

Greg felt enormous relief when they found out the booths were fine, as was the amusement park. So, he and Sandy went over to the auction to take one last look. They found Terry there, with the blanket chest he was donating.

Sandy said, "Oh Terry, that one is gorgeous."

Terry grinned. "I like it. I kind of had a wild hair and wanted to try this design. It's got three different woods on the outside to make the pattern, and is lined with cedar."

Sandy walked around it. "It looks like cherry, mahogany, and pine. Is that right?"

Terry nodded. "Very good Sis, that's exactly what it is."

Greg watched her open the lid and take a deep breath as the smell of fresh cedar filled the room. He could tell she really loved that chest, and he was determined to win it for her. She certainly could bid on it herself, but he knew she probably wouldn't, thinking someone else should have it. Greg knew she already had one of Terry's first blanket chests, but it wasn't lined with cedar and was very plain compared to this one. Terry had really outdone himself on it.

Sandy turned to Terry with her eyes aglow. "Terry, it's beautiful. Someone will love it."

Greg hid a smirk as he thought, "Yeah you will, Sandy."

Terry walked down the line of items that would be part of the live auction. "You've got some great things here. The glass sculptures from Lucille and Nolan will bring in a pretty penny, maybe even a million dollars. That will buy a lot of helicopter flights into the hospital in Chelan."

Sandy said, "Especially after Gus matches it."

"At over thirty K a pop, a million dollars is only about thirty flights. I would like to see this fundraiser last at least five years, ten would be better," Greg said. He frowned as he thought about it. If they raised five million and Gus doubled it, that might last ten years. But five million was a lot of money to raise in a weekend.

Terry smirked, "Just tell everyone in town to be careful so they don't have to be airlifted to Chelan."

Greg sighed, "I wish it was that easy, my friend."

Sandy was the optimist of the group. "We've got some great auction items. That glass sculpture of Lucille's could easily bring in half a million, maybe more. And Nolan's is no slouch, he doesn't have Lucille's name, but his art is fantastic. And I think a full set of signed books of Jeremy's could get up there if we get a collector in town. I think it's going to do great."

Terry nodded, "Your full set of games signed by the programmers and designers could rank up there, too. If the people know what they're getting."

"That's the key to the whole thing. We won't know until we get started if we have the right people in the room," Greg said. "If we don't have people that know the value, we might not make squat."

They all nodded, silently contemplating that.

Sandy said, "I think we did well on advertising, so I'm hopeful."

Terry tugged on a strand of her hair. "You keep that hope going, Sis, we might need it."

Greg wanted her to be right. The town really needed this fundraiser to succeed. Everyone was putting their all into it, and he hoped he hadn't let them down in organizing it.

CHAPTER 30

Sandy was thrilled when the rest of the fundraiser went excellently. Even before they got to the auction it looked like they were going to have a million dollars raised. She didn't really know how that had happened, but she wasn't complaining.

When the dinner started up, they practically had to drag people away from the silent auction to feed them. People were hovering over the items they wanted and outbidding each other. A couple of people were literally running back and forth between items on opposite sides of the room.

Finally, Sheila, got up on the podium and said with an authoritative voice, "If you don't sit down right now you are going to miss out on the fantastic meal Amber has prepared. The silent auction will remain open after dinner. So, you'll have more time to fight for your favorites."

Everyone took their seats and started eating. Once they were sat down and relatively quiet Sandy went up to the podium. "I want to thank everyone for supporting this fundraiser and joining us here tonight for the auctions. While you dine you can peruse the information at your seats, on the auction items that will be bid on during the live auction. Immediately following the meal, we will let you come by the front and look over each of the items. Since some of them are fragile there will be no touching allowed."

Sandy pulled out an auction paddle and held it up. "Everyone got a sign to hold up when they registered at the door, so you can use that. We are also allowing you to text in bids, that will be displayed on the screen, by number. There are a few people who could not join us that will be using that method, but you are welcome to, as well. Plus, there are more pictures of each item on the website. The URL is in the handout. If you have any questions you can ask any one of us with the nametags." She held up her nametag and then pointed to several people who also had them on. "Again, thanks for supporting this very important fundraiser to save lives."

People nodded and went back to eating, but she heard a lot of page rustling as they looked through the brochure. Once the auction was over, they would have a few minutes to make a plea for donations to the cause, and then announce the silent auction winners.

Based on the frenzy she'd seen in the silent auction area her hopes soared. When the live auction started, Sandy watched it start slowly, and wondered if it was going to be a bust. The first two items barely reached their retail price, but they were smaller things, so she hoped it was just the nature of an auction. When the auctioneer picked up the full set of Jeremy's autographed children's books the bidding became livelier and stayed that way through the next few items, including the season passes to the Amusement park and the signed set of games her company had donated, each of them going for more than their purchase price. Of course, the signatures added to the value.

Next up was Lucille's glass sculpture, they'd thought

about making it the grand finale item, but decided that hyping people up early on, might be advantageous. Sandy was electrified when the final bid was one point two million dollars.

The next item up was her brother's blanket chest. She and her mom both bid on it until it hit above five hundred dollars. But the bidding didn't even slow down as a lot of people dropped out. There seemed to be two people duking it out over texts, one was number 404 and the other was 900. Sandy wondered about the nine hundred number. She didn't think they'd given out numbers above about six hundred.

Sandy looked around to ask Greg if he thought it was a legit number, but didn't see him anywhere. She chuckled to herself, when she decided he was fighting fires about the fundraiser, not real ones. The bidding between the two numbers topped a thousand dollars, and although she knew her brother was uber talented, she thought that was kind of excessive for a blanket chest. It hit fifteen hundred and she was worried Terry might faint.

When bidder nine hundred bid two thousand dollars, Deborah, the photographer, threw her phone down in disgust. Sandy realized Deborah was number four oh four. Terry obviously realized it at the same time, because his head snapped in her direction, and he stared in what looked like awe.

The bidding went on to the next item and Sandy assumed that maybe bidder nine hundred was one of Terry's customers. He'd let a few of them know he'd have a piece in the auction and that they could join in remotely.

The auction continued on with several other high-ticket items. Nolan's glass sculpture went for eight hundred thousand, Kristen was so proud of him she was glowing. Then a set of her jewelry went for two hundred thousand and Nolan practically had to keep her from falling off her chair in surprise. Sandy laughed as they whispered back and forth in joy.

She noticed Greg was back in the room, and wondered what he'd gotten caught up in. He didn't look upset though. In fact, he looked happy, maybe even pleased with himself.

When the live auction ended, pandemonium broke out in the room, as people ran to the silent auction area in order to put in final bids. Sandy went up to the auctioneer to have him announce the minutes remaining to bid, and he counted down the last twenty seconds. Sandy was shocked by the free for all that had erupted in the back area, and was worried they might need referees, or maybe a doctor in case bloodshed broke out. Then she noticed that the doctor was one of the crazy ones in the back and shook her head.

Greg came over and asked, "What's wrong?"

She pointed to the back of the room and muttered, "People are weird."

Greg laughed in a full booming way, that startled a few people sitting nearby, watching the craziness. When they looked at him in question he laughed again and repeated her comment. Since they weren't caught up in the chaos, everyone around her and Greg laughed and agreed.

The last ten seconds of the silent auction was counted down and the auctioneer boomed out, "Time's up! Pens down!"

Everyone dropped the pens like they were bombs, because he had warned them that anyone holding a pen at the end would have their name crossed out.

People shuffled back to their tables and the auctioneer took the cordless mic back to the silent auction area. There was a lot of shuffling of chairs, so people could watch easier.

The auctioneer said, "Now before I start reading off the winners, I want everyone to take an envelope out of the large one in the center of the table and one of the donation slips." More shuffling ensued.

"Now everyone take out your checkbook or credit card, and write down the largest donation you can handle, on the donation slip. You people that bought the glass sculptures I expect to see a lot of zeroes following the first number."

Everyone chuckled.

The auctioneer waited for a minute for the sound to subside. "Now I know you all realize this is an important fundraiser. Lives depend on it. Someone hurt in this town or in the mountains near here might not survive without the helicopter service to Chelan." Sandy was in shock when the man related a personal experience of a family member needing air transport and how they wouldn't have survived without it. When he said it was his son, there was a lot of sniffling. He finished with. "If you've got money to buy all this stuff, you've got money to save a life. Give generously."

Sandy had tears in her eyes and a heart swelled with pride, at what she and Greg had accomplished, with a lot of help, of course. They hadn't asked the auctioneer to do anything more than point out where the donation slips could be found, but him relating a personal incident made it more real to everyone, and she was sure he'd increased the donations.

Once the donations were back in the main envelope the fun continued as the auctioneer joked about the silent auction bidding and items. Several times when people lamented that they were disappointed not to win, the artisan who created it, offered to make a second item for the second-place person, if they also donated the winning amount.

Kristen had started it, when some woman was fussing about not winning the pendant Kristen had put in the silent auction. The woman was a tourist and did not realize she was sitting near enough for Kristen to hear her moaning and groaning about not winning.

Kristen finally turned to the woman and said, "If you will shut the hell up, I will gladly make you a similar piece if you pay the winning bid."

The woman blinked for a minute and then jumped out of her chair to give Kristen a hug and promised to pay. Sandy cringed, hoping Kristen didn't punch the woman. Kristen was not a hugger, and she barely tolerated people. The fact that she'd come to the auction at all, proved her devotion to the cause.

When Kristen said, "Just write the check and give me your address. I'll have it to you in about three weeks." Sandy breathed a sigh of relief. Kristen looked straight at Sandy and rolled her eyes as if to say, "I wouldn't punch her. At least not in public." Sandy stifled the laugh that wanted to burst forth.

That encounter paved the way for other people to follow suit, which doubled profit on a lot of the silent auction items. Greg winked at her and she grinned back at him. She didn't think either one of them had been able to keep a running account of how much had been bid, so they had no idea where they were on the scale of things. But a lot of items had gone better than they'd expected so it was a happy moment.

When all the prizes had been claimed and checks and credit cards had been run, people started leaving with their treasures. They planned to put all the money in a safe at the town bank tonight and start the tally tomorrow afternoon. They'd talked about doing it tonight, because everyone was antsy to see what they made, but they also knew this event was going to run late, and it would be better to start fresh tomorrow. Sandy knew all the money from yesterday was already in the bank vault, and the bank officials had gathered up everything tonight into big bags, sealed them and took them back to the bank.

Sandy looked around at the nearly empty room and was glad they'd hired a cleaning crew. She was surprised to see Terry's blanket chest left on the stage. She didn't see Terry anywhere, so he wasn't taking it with him to ship. She pointed to it and asked Greg, "Did we get scammed on that? I didn't think we had that many bidders, to use the number nine hundred."

Greg shook his head. "No, we didn't get scammed, and no we didn't have that many bidders."

He didn't say anything else as he walked over to it and hefted it down off the stage onto a dolly she hadn't seen on the floor. He started rolling it out of the mostly vacant room, so she followed him, calling good night to Amber and a couple of her staff members, still moving the food.

Sandy was surprised when Greg loaded the chest and the dolly into his truck and wrapped the chest in one of the moving blankets Terry used to transport his furniture.

She decided that Greg had volunteered to deliver it to the buyer, so when he motioned for her to get in the truck she did. She'd ridden with him this afternoon, when they'd gone early to the banquet room, to check to make sure everything was ready and in place.

Only he didn't go anywhere except straight to her house. She didn't think he would really leave the chest in the truck, so when he lifted it out of the bed, and onto the dolly she decided he was going to deliver it in the morning, and leave it at the B&B until he got the chance.

Sandy was happy he planned to stay for a while, she knew for a fact they could both use some stress release. It had been a long damn weekend and she knew they'd raised at least three or four million. Which was a success in her book.

When Greg hauled the blanket chest up into her room, she thought it was kind of overkill to have to guard it all night, but she was too tired to argue. She wanted to be horizontal and naked with the man and that's all the energy she had left.

Greg pulled the straps off the dolly and the moving blanket off the chest and then turned with a grin and asked her where she wanted it. She just stared at him, not really understanding the question. She tipped her head and asked, "What?"

Greg's grin grew, and he said slowly and carefully, "Where do you want your new blanket chest, Sandy?"

"My blanket chest?" she asked, still not quite understanding.

He nodded. "Your. Blanket chest."

Finally, the light dawned and if they hadn't been in her mother's B&B filled to the rafters with guests, she would have screeched. Instead she whispered, "You bought the blanket chest? You were number nine hundred?"

Greg nodded. "I was."

"You spent two thousand dollars to buy a piece of furniture that my brother made? You could have talked him into making me a new one for a quarter of that price."

"I was going to give that much anyway. I figured why not win you the blanket chest, in the meantime. You clearly loved it when you saw it."

"I did, but…."

"No buts. Now where do you want it?"

Sandy didn't know what to do first, kiss the man or find a place for her gorgeous new chest. So, she quickly did both. First, she gave him a smacking kiss, and then she showed him where to put the chest. When he had it perfectly positioned, she ran her hands lovingly over it, and then leaped into the man's arms.

~

Greg was damned glad he had good reflexes. One minute she was petting the gift, and the next she'd launched herself into his arms. He caught her easily and she peppered his face with kisses. She'd wrapped her legs around his waist and her hands gripped his head.

He noticed after the tenth little kiss that his face was getting wet. He pulled back enough to see her face, and sure enough tears were streaming down her cheeks. "Sandy?"

She sobbed out, "No it's all right, they're happy tears. No one has ever done anything like that for me before."

"Surely Terry or your mom…"

"Of course, they have, but not anyone who wasn't family. Thank you, thank you, thank you."

"Oh, Sandy, sweetheart, I was excited about the idea of winning something you would love. With the added advantage that you will think of me each time you see it."

Her laugh had a watery sound and the tears kept flowing, but the joy on her face told the whole tale. Greg felt like superman to be able to give her such pleasure. He'd waited a long time to be in this position with her and he wasn't about to waste one second. Or any possible opportunity to show her how much she meant to him.

His heart burned to tell her how much he loved her. Fuck, if he wasn't positive she'd run like hell, he'd ask her to marry him. But he knew she wasn't ready for that. Plus, he didn't want there to be strings attached to the blanket chest, or any hint that there might be some. So, he kept his big mouth shut. He would tell her eventually, but not tonight.

Sandy dragged at his clothes. He'd worn a dress shirt to the dinner and auction tonight and even a tie. She was yanking on the tie and fumbling with the buttons on his shirt. "Off, off, off. I want skin. Now. I want you inside me. I want to make love fast and furious. No holding back, no slow build up. Fast and hard and all consuming."

That wasn't his normal MO, but he wasn't about to disappoint the lady. So, as she dragged his clothes off, he returned the favor. Between the two sets of clothes he thought the only casualty was one button on his shirt cuff.

She grabbed his hand and dragged him to the bed and pushed him onto his back. "I'm in charge, and on top, so you just get ready to be ravished.

He laughed and spread his arms wide. "Be my guest."

She yanked a condom out of her bedside stand and after giving his cock one long lick, that made it twitch and strain towards her even more, she rolled the condom on and climbed onto him. Impaling herself with a great look of satisfaction as she did so.

He clutched at the bed sheets as she pleasured herself and him. When he got his body calmed down enough, he took hold of her breasts and squeezed them, pinching her nipples which caused her inner muscles to clench on him.

He reached one hand down between them to the tight bundle of nerves and rubbed it in concert with her movements. Which caused her to speed up the nearly frantic action of her body. He felt her start to gather and let his control slip. She ground down on him one last time and came with an explosion that would have woken the entire house, if she hadn't clapped her hand over her mouth, to capture the sound.

His body pumped into hers one final time and he joined her in the flames.

She slumped down on him, completely spent.

He held her close and marveled at what had just happened. He'd never in his life had such a frantic coupling. It was the most magnificent experience he'd ever had.

As he thought about it, his body was aroused again, and he realized Sandy wasn't asleep when she looked sleepily up at him.

"Seriously?"

"It's not my fault, that was the most amazing sexual escapade, ever. Just thinking about it is making me hard."

She smiled a sexy smile. "Well, let's see if we can repeat that."

He wasn't about to complain, but they didn't get much sleep as Sandy continued to try to wear him out.

CHAPTER 31

Greg went down with Sandy to get the breakfast going. Since he'd kept her awake half the night, he figured it was fair that he help her with the early morning chores. They were hand in hand and chuckling when they walked into the kitchen. One of the lights was on, so he assumed Carol was up.

He was surprised to see Terry sitting at the counter, a cup of coffee was clenched in his fists and he was clearly pissed. Sandy dropped Greg's hand the moment she saw her brother.

Terry pointed at the two of them and growled out, "What the fuck is this all about?"

Sandy looked flustered and didn't speak so Greg pointed between himself and Sandy, then said, "This, is none of your business."

"The hell it isn't. That's my sister you're clearly fucking with."

Greg said, "Watch your mouth Terry. Do not insult your sister."

Terry frowned. "I'm not insulting her, but you, my supposedly best friend, yeah, I might be insulting you."

"I am your best friend. However, Sandy, and I are adults and if we want to spend time together we will. I repeat, it's none of your business."

"Well it sure is a damn big surprise to me."

Sandy finally found her voice and said, "You've been out of town all summer, Terry. It's been a gradual thing."

"I've been back nearly a week, and no one mentioned a thing to me."

Greg was getting tired of this. "What was I supposed to do? The minute you hit town, run over and tell you like we were some teenaged girls with our first crush." He heard Sandy suck in a breath, so he continued on, "Or even worse teenaged boys in the locker room boasting about which base we got to?"

"Fuck you, Greg. Of course, that's not what I wanted. But not to be blindsided by seeing your truck parked out front all night, might have been good."

"Well clearly you were arriving here in the early morning and I doubt it was to make coffee."

"That's none of your business."

Greg lifted an eyebrow at the irony of that statement.

"It's completely different, you are supposed to be my best friend, and this is my sister."

Greg got deadly quiet. "Yes, she is and she's a lovely woman. I've been honored she wanted to spend time with me, both in and out of the bedroom. If you don't like that, then that's just too damned bad."

"So that's why you bought my blanket chest? To bribe her into your bed."

Sandy gasped, Greg stalked over to his ex-best friend and grabbed him by the front of the shirt. In a low voice he said,

"You fucking know better. Now apologize to your sister, before I kick your ass."

Terry stiffened, and Greg wondered if they were going to have to take this outside and settle it. Then the expression on his face changed to chagrin and he looked at his sister. "I'm sorry Sis, that was uncalled for. Greg wouldn't treat any woman like that, especially you."

Sandy looked broken, but she nodded her head. "I know, Terry. Greg is an honorable man and I chose to be his lover several weeks ago."

She sucked in a deep breath and squared her shoulders. "He wanted to tell you as soon as you hit town and I asked him not to. I didn't want to have to explain it, and since I'm only going to be here a few more days, I didn't think it was necessary."

Now Greg felt broken. Her imminent departure fractured something inside of him. He had deliberately avoided thinking about her going back to Seattle, but her ease in saying the words to Terry broke his heart. She didn't seem the least bit sad about leaving him. He knew he would never recover.

But rather than let that show he slapped a smile on his face and turned to Sandy.

"I think I'll go on home and leave you to talk things out with your brother." He gave one more sharp look to Terry telling him silently not to hurt his sister. Terry gave him a slight nod and Greg walked out the door. When he was halfway home, he realized he'd left the damn dolly and the furniture blanket and his tie and dress shirt in Sandy's room. Fuck it, he would get it later, maybe after Sandy went back to Seattle.

~

SANDY GLARED at her brother who'd just chased off Greg. Although it didn't actually seem like Greg had been intimidated by Terry. In fact, he'd confronted him and told him to back off. So why he'd left, Sandy couldn't quite figure out.

Sandy turned on her brother, since she couldn't go racing after Greg. "Since when are you the keeper of my sex life?"

"Sandy…"

She shook her finger at the idiot. "I will fuck every man in this town if I want to. It is none of your God damned business."

"Sandy…"

She put her hands on her hips. "I cannot believe you treated your best friend like some kind of pervert. What in the holy hell is wrong with you?"

"Sandy…"

She tossed her hair. "No. I don't even want to hear it. I have work to do, that Greg was going to help me with and now you've chased him off, so I need to get busy. Just go find someone else to be an ass to. I have people to feed." She turned her back on her brother to march over to the fridge.

Terry said, "I'll leave, but it wasn't me that chased Greg off. Your plan to blithely return to Seattle is what put the hurt in his eyes. Not me."

She whipped back around. "What?"

"You heard me. Greg wasn't the least bit intimidated by me… Just think about it."

She crossed her arms. "I've got work to do."

"Think about it." Then he got up and left her alone.

She didn't want to think about it, but that's exactly what she did. She nearly messed up the biscuits she was making, she was so busy thinking about it. The coffee ended up being too strong and she guessed she must have lost track of the amount she'd put in. The guests had to ask for butter, since she'd forgotten to put it out, along with the cream everyone needed for the too strong coffee.

Breakfast was a mess as she thought about what Terry had said. Her mom finally pushed her out of the room, so she didn't do anything else wrong. Carol patted Sandy on the hand and told her to go get some rest, she deserved it after working so hard on the fundraiser.

Sandy grabbed that excuse like a lifeline and went to her room. Where her beautiful new chest was. Which only made her think even more.

Had she really hurt Greg by mentioning she would be going back to Seattle? It wasn't like it was across the country it was only a three-hour drive. They could meet in Leavenworth if they wanted to. Or she could come back and work remotely, sometimes.

His dress shirt and tie were tossed across a chair where she'd dragged it off of him. He'd gone home in a t-shirt. The dolly and furniture blanket were still in the room. She supposed those were Terry's, but she knew Greg wouldn't have left them on purpose. Maybe she *had* hurt his feelings. But she hadn't said anything that wasn't true.

She had hours before they were supposed to go to the bank to help count up the fundraiser profits. Sandy thought about going by to see Barbara, but with the new baby she wasn't certain what their schedule was like yet. She wouldn't want to wake them if they were all taking a nap.

She decided to drive by her sister's to see if Brett was still in town. If he was, she would keep on driving, if he wasn't maybe she could stop by and have a chat with her sister.

When she turned the corner to her sister's street, she saw flashing lights in front of Janet's house. With her heart in her throat, she mostly parked and jumped out to run down to the house. As she got closer, she saw police cars, the town's ambulance, and both Terry and Greg's trucks. She looked for them and spotted Greg, so she ran up to where he was helping to keep the crowd from gathering.

She wheezed out, "What happened?"

Greg took her hand. "Janet finally called the cops on the bastard and he's going to jail."

"But why?"

He squeezed her hand and said quietly, so that no one else could hear, "It's my understanding he hit Gerald."

She hissed, "What? Oh, that asshole! Is Gerald okay?"

"The doc is in there with them, and so is Terry and the cops. They haven't rushed Gerald out to the clinic or for a flight to Chelan, so I have to believe he's all right."

"How did you know?"

"Terry and I both heard it on the radio and came straight here. They didn't tone it, just called for backup assistance from anyone nearby. We can help with crowd control and let the police do their job."

Scott Davidson and Jeremy Scott drove up and Greg gave them assignments. Which left him free to be with Sandy.

She was shaking when she asked, "Should I call mom?"

"Let's go up and see if Gerald's okay first. You don't want to scare her if it's not needed."

They got almost to the door when they saw the police coming out with Brett in custody, so they stepped back.

Brett saw them and went ballistic, he jerked out of the officers' hands and barreled toward her screaming, "You fucking bitch, how dare you waltz in here from Seattle and tell my wife, MY WIFE, that she doesn't have to put up with me. That she can just leave and take the kids. Well let me tell you missy, over my dead body. I will fucking kill her dead, before I let her leave me, and take away my kids."

Greg had pushed her behind him and taken the brunt of the shoulder Brett had tried to aim at her head. Greg shook off the attack and helped the officers restrain the crazed man.

Spittle was flying as he continued to scream at her about putting crazy ideas into his wife's head, and Sandy better watch her back, because he would be coming for her, and she wouldn't even know what hit her.

Sandy stared at him in silence while he spouted threats in front of over a dozen witnesses including, police, firefighters and neighbors. Even if Janet backed down on pressing charges, both Greg and Sandy would follow through. The man was going to jail.

After they got Brett into the police car and on his way to jail, the doctor and EMTs brought both Janet and Gerald out to transport to the clinic. It looked like Gerald had a broken arm and a few bruises. Janet was a bloody mess on the gurney and Sandy's heart clutched at the sight.

She rushed over to Janet. "I'm so sorry."

Janet peeked up through almost completely swollen shut eyes. She smiled a tiny smile and whispered, "No don't be. It's over. He's going to jail, and I'll be free. I won't take him back, this was the last straw."

Janet then turned her attention to Greg. "I'll need a good lawyer."

Greg nodded. "I'll get you the best. Brett will be in jail a long, long time."

Janet sighed and closed her eyes as they loaded her into the ambulance. Sandy's heart was breaking at the thought of her sweet sister at the hands of that horrible excuse for a man. She didn't know whether to cry or scream in fury.

Greg put his arm around Sandy and held her, as the ambulance went off to treat her sister and nephew.

Terry came out next, with Carrie on his hip. She had a backpack, a blanket and a stuffed animal. Terry said, "I thought she could stay with you and mom."

Sandy slapped a smile on her face for the little girl. Fortunately, it didn't look like she'd been touched by Brett. "Absolutely, we can have a slumber party. Would you like to have a slumber party with me and Nana, Carrie?"

Carrie nodded hesitantly. "I would, but daddy doesn't like you and Nana very much. He gets really mad if mama talks about you. Will he be mad and hit mama if I come stay with you?"

Sandy's heart broke for the little girl. "No sweetheart, daddy won't know, or be around much for a long time."

Carrie asked, "He's going to work for a long time?"

Sandy didn't know what to say, or what Janet wanted the little girl to know, so she just nodded her head.

Terry tossed Greg a set of keys. "Greg, could you take Carrie to go get her car seat?"

Greg didn't hesitate, both he and Sandy could tell Terry wanted to talk to his sister out of the hearing of the little girl. "Sure, come with Uncle Greg, Cutie Pie, and we'll go get your car seat so you can go with Auntie Sandy."

"Okay, Uncle Greg, it is kinda hard to get out of the car."

When Greg and the little girl were out of hearing, Terry said, "She missed the whole thing, she was upstairs in her room watching a movie with the door shut."

"Thank God."

"Right!"

"Anyway, Brett was slapping Janet around and she knocked a lamp over which Gerald heard. He'd been up in his room too, but apparently came down to try to defend Janet. Brett got a little crazed about the boy backing up his mother, and grabbed his arm then knocked him into a wall."

"That bastard."

"Yeah. That apparently opened Janet's eyes and she called the cops. Then Brett went batshit crazy, punching Janet, throwing food, and breaking everything he could get his hands on. The place is torn up inside, so I didn't want Carrie to see it. I'll get Greg to help me clean up the mess, so they can all come home to a nice house. Janet refused transport to Chelan, so the doc is going to run some x-rays and make sure she'll be okay. The doc says they'll want to keep Janet a couple of days, so I thought the kids could stay with you. He also said they'd keep Gerald for an hour or two, they want to take x-rays to see if his arm is broken or just sprained."

Sandy knew the doc was going to be busy with the two of them for the next couple of hours. She hoped the boy's arm was only sprained.

"Once Greg and I get the place cleaned up, I'll grab some clothes for Gerald and pick him up from the clinic and bring him to you. Can you postpone your trip back to Seattle for a few days?

"Yes, that's not a problem I'll stay as long as Janet needs help. We'll make room for the kids. A lot of people that came in for the fundraiser will be leaving today so it will be fine."

Terry ran a hand down his face. "I forgot about the place being full."

"It's no problem, they can always bunk down in my room if needed."

Terry rubbed the back of his neck. "You could probably stay here at the house with the kids."

"No, I think it would be better for them at the B&B and then they can come back home when Janet's here with them."

"Yeah, that's what I thought, too. Here come Greg and Carrie."

Terry said to Greg, "Can you help get the car seat into Sandy's car and then come back here to help me with something?"

Greg nodded affably, but his eyes were hooded. Sandy hoped the two of them could get past this, she didn't want to be the cause of their twenty-eight-year friendship being broken.

~

Greg didn't know what Terry 'needed help' with but he'd see it through. He didn't plan to give up on their friendship, but he wasn't going to let Terry dictate who he could or could not date, either.

He secured the car seat, it practically took an engineering degree to get it in and out of a car. Carrie had chattered on about how she would be able to graduate to a booster seat as soon as she weighed a few more pounds. She said she was old enough but too skinny. Her mom had told her maybe they should put rocks in her pockets when they were in the car.

Carrie had thought that was very funny. She'd said daddy didn't think it was funny and had told her mom to stop filling her head with nonsense. But Carrie knew her mom was joking, so she didn't understand why her daddy had gotten mad.

Greg hadn't known what to say, so he had only said that some people didn't have much of a sense of humor. Carrie had nodded sagely and said that she thought her daddy must be one of those people because he'd often said things weren't funny.

Greg snapped the little girl into her car seat, kissed her on the forehead, and went around to the front of the car where Sandy was. "You going to be okay?"

"Yeah, mom and I can take care of the kiddos. I'm going to stick close while Janet needs help."

His heart raced. "Not going back to Seattle?"

"Not now, for sure. Depending on how beat up she is, she might need some help."

He nodded. "Sad, but true. Let me know if there is

anything I can do. Oh, and I'll call the bank and let them know we won't be there to help with the counting."

"I totally forgot about that, I hope Janet doesn't need the funds."

"I hope so too. But at least we have them, now."

Sandy wanted to cry, but instead she touched his shoulder and he winced. "Are you hurt? From Brett?"

"Only a bruise, don't worry."

She shook her finger at him. "You get to the doctor if you need to."

"I will."

"You better." She gave him a small peck on the lips and got into her car.

Greg walked down the street to where Terry was standing there staring at him. "Don't start."

"I have no intention of it. I was out of line."

Greg felt the stiffness flow out of his shoulders and neck. "You know I've been crazy about her since fourth grade."

Terry nodded. "I do, and I'm sorry I was a dick about it. I couldn't pick a better man for my sister. I was mostly just pissed you didn't tell me."

"I know, and I should have. So, are we good?"

Terry said, "Almost."

Then he pushed on the same shoulder Sandy had and Greg nearly passed out from the pain that shot through it.

"What happened?"

"Brett was coming at Sandy with his shoulder, when he broke free of the officers."

"Damn it. Thanks for taking the hit, that guy is not little. He might have cracked something."

"It's fine. But if he'd hit Sandy…"

Terry rubbed his chest. "Yeah, two sisters in the hospital from the same guy. Fucker." Terry slapped a fist into his hand.

"She's good, and so am I."

"We'll see if it's fine. We need to clean up the mess—Brett the prick—left inside. One of the cops took plenty of pictures and some blood samples, so they could release the house for cleanup. When we get the broken stuff thrown away and the blood cleaned up, we can grab some clothes for Gerald. Then we'll go by the clinic and you can get x-rays with the rest of the family."

Greg didn't want to admit he might need them, but the truth was it hurt like a mother, so he'd let Terry think he was bullying him into it.

CHAPTER 32

Sandy drove Carrie to her mom's house. "So, Carrie, you and Gerald are going to spend the night with me tonight. Do you want your own room, or shall we have a slumber party in my room?"

"We have slumber parties with mommy sometimes, but not when daddy is home. Daddy says we have to sleep in our own rooms. He says mommy's job is to take care of his needs. I don't know what he means by that, but sometimes mommy and daddy make weird sounds at night and I get scared. Gerald lets me come to his room and sleep with him."

"He's a good big brother." Sandy didn't know whether to ask Carrie about the sounds or if she was better off not knowing. Then again would it be good for Carrie to talk about it? Sandy had no idea, she was at a total loss on what to say or do.

"I think a slumber party would be fun if daddy isn't coming."

"No daddy is busy tonight, he won't be here." For a long time if Sandy had anything to say about it.

"Then let's have a slumber party. Nana has sleeping bags, she's let us sleep in before."

This was news to Sandy, she'd not known the kids had ever spent the night away from home.

"When did you spend the night at Nana's?"

"One night when daddy came home from his job, he took us over to stay with Nana. He said he and mommy were going to be busy."

"Busy?"

"Yeah. He said he was going to teach mommy some new things. But I don't think he got to teach mommy anything because she got sick. She had to stay in bed for two days. And when she did get up, she walked funny like her tummy hurt or maybe like she had to go potty. And she had red marks on her arms like when I put a rubber band on mine and it gets kinda red, only mommy's were much bigger."

Sandy felt like she was going to throw up. What had that bastard done to her sister?

Carrie didn't notice her silence and continued with her story. "When daddy went to work he pinched mommy on her booby, and said he would be looking forward to teaching her other fun things. Mommy threw up after daddy left. She said it was from eating something bad, but mommy hadn't eaten anything."

Sandy was so glad that Carrie had no idea what had really gone on and wondered what Gerald had thought. She cleared the knot from her throat. "What did Gerald say about mommy being sick?"

"He wasn't there, it was only me. Gerald went to scout camp after we stayed with Nana."

Sandy was partly horrified that Carrie had been left alone with that monster and partly glad Gerald hadn't seen his mother. He was four years older than Carrie and might have understood more.

"We didn't get to come back to Nana's after that because Nana said that she was too full of customers. Daddy just laughed and told mommy he was a very patient man. He said maybe we could go visit Grandma and Grandpa for a whole week this summer. But then Nana fell down and you came, so we didn't go.

"I didn't mind though, because Grandpa is kind of grumpy and Grandma is kind of weird. I don't know them very well to stay a whole week. Daddy said it would be a fun family vacation, but that he and mommy would be busy a lot of the time. He told mommy there was a fun room for just the two of them to use. Mommy didn't look very excited about the fun room though."

Sandy thought she might be sick at the thoughts of what Brett had been planning to do to her sister. She was glad when they pulled up in front of her mother's house, so Carrie had something else to think about.

She walked in and Carrie made a beeline for the kitchen and Sandy could hear her squealing as the two of them connected. Sandy hurried into the room, so her mom wouldn't be alarmed. "Carrie is going to stay with us tonight and so is Gerald. Maybe two nights. Janet is at the clinic with Gerald."

"Auntie Sandy said we can have a sleepover."

Carol looked at Sandy for a long moment and then down at her granddaughter. "Goody. You remember where I keep the sleeping bags, don't you? Can you go grab one at a time and take it up to Sandy's room?"

"I can. I'm a big girl. I'll try to unroll them and make them look like beds, too." She took her blanket and stuffed animal from Sandy. "I'll take these too. I can get my clothes later."

When the little girl was out of hearing range Carol asked, "What happened?"

"My understanding is that Brett was using Janet as a

punching bag, and Gerald tried to intercede, and got knocked around a bit. That made Janet finally see the light and she called the police. Fortunately, Carrie was in her room watching a movie and missed the whole thing. Terry is going to the clinic to check on Janet and Gerald. He'll bring Gerald here when they release him."

Her mom said, "Do you think Janet will finally follow through on it?"

She nodded. "I do, apparently she'd told him she didn't have to live like that. Because he was screaming at me for putting false ideas in her head. He was threatening that he would kill her before he let her take his kids away. The whole neighborhood heard him. And he shoulder-checked Greg. Brett was aiming for me, but Greg pulled me behind him. Brett would have laid me flat. As it is, Greg winced when I touched his shoulder, so he might be hurt too."

"Well it's about time Janet saw the light."

"Carrie told me a horrific story. She said she and Gerald came to spend the night with you."

"They did, and after that, Janet called and asked me to tell him I was too full and couldn't watch them. It about broke my heart to not let them come over, but I feared for Janet. She'd sounded half dead when she called."

"Yeah, Carrie's descriptions scared the crap out of me. I'm glad that bastard is going to jail. Maybe he'll be in there a long time."

Carol huffed out a breath. "We'll be lucky if he's in for two or three years. Wife abusers have to nearly kill someone, before they are even kept for seven years."

"Are you kidding?"

"Nope, I wish I was." Carol shook her head in frustration.

But then Carrie bounded into the room. "I got the sleeping bags to the room and one is mostly flat, but the other one has a knot I can't untie. Can you help me Auntie Sandy?"

Sandy took the little girl's hand. "I can. Let's go up and see if we can get that knot to behave itself."

"Daddy says—"

"You know what Carrie, let's not worry about what daddy says right now. Let's have a daddy-free hour."

"That's silly, Auntie Sandy. But it might be kind of fun, if we can do all the things daddy says are bad."

"We can do that, as long as nothing is dangerous."

Carrie laughed. "I don't like dangerous stuff, Auntie Sandy."

"Then we're good. What do you want to do first?"

GREG HELPED Terry straighten up the house and sweep up all the glass. His shoulder was killing him, but he didn't want Janet to come home to this disaster, so he sucked it up and worked side by side with his friend. They loaded the dishwasher, and vacuumed the floors, and cleaned up the food it looked like Brett had thrown around in a temper tantrum. They also cleaned up blood. More blood than he wanted to see, since it was probably all Janet's.

They went up to the bedrooms and gathered clothes and some toys for Gerald and a few more things for Carrie. Greg started down the hall toward the stairs but noticed Terry had gone in the opposite direction. He heard Terry swear and turned to look back at his friend, who was standing in the door of his sister's room.

"God damn him. I am going to kill that bastard."

Greg turned and went to the door, what he saw made his stomach turn. The bed sheets had blood on them mixed in with semen. It looked like a horror flick. Terry took pictures with his phone, just in case, and then the two men started stripping the bed without saying a word. Terry found a large trash bag and threw the sheets and some other things he'd found on the floor into the bag.

They didn't discuss it, they just threw it all in a bag. Greg put the bag in his truck and Terry took all the kid's belongings in his. They drove to the clinic where the doctor met them, next to the doctor was Nolan, both men were kind of gray in color.

Nolan cleared his throat. "Your sister…."

Terry said, "Yeah, we brought the sheets from the bed and some other things I found. It's in a black trash bag in Greg's truck."

Nolan nodded, "I'll keep that as evidence. Did you guys have on gloves?"

Greg answered, "As a matter of fact we did. It's standard procedure in fire investigation so we didn't even think about it when we went in to clean up."

"Good. As of right now, I gave you instructions to clean up the house. You didn't by any chance take pictures."

Terry grimaced. "I took a few. Again, kind of standard procedure."

Nolan gave him a fierce smile. "Excellent, that fucker is going to spend as much time in jail as I can possibly manage." He looked at Greg, "Don't you have some ruthless lawyer friends?"

Greg was never so glad to have spent time with that law firm as he was at this moment. "As a matter of fact, I do. I'll get Janet the meanest one of the bunch."

"Perfect, let's see if we can get Brett more than a slap on the wrist."

The doctor spoke up, "I'm going to keep Janet for at least two days, maybe three, depending on how she does. Gerald has a slight fracture, so I put him in a cast, he'll only need it a few weeks. He can go with you now."

Terry said, "Can I see Janet?"

The doctor shrugged. "You can go in, but I gave her a sedative and she's sleeping. But if you want to see her you may."

Terry motioned to Greg. "Doc, you need to check out his shoulder or collar bone. He's favoring it and about passes out if anyone touches it."

Greg didn't even try to protest, the small amount of work they'd done at Janet's had about done him in, and pain was pounding through his body. He'd be a fool not to have it looked at, and he was no fool.

"I should give all of you some kind of discount. At least Janet and Gerald's will be on Brett's company policy. Come on Greg, let's go take some pictures of your shoulder."

Greg heard Nolan directing Terry to Janet's room and where Gerald was with the nurse. He said they were drawing pictures of Tsilly on the cast.

CHAPTER 33

Fortunately, Greg's shoulder was only strained and bruised. Gerald seemed to be fine with his cast. Janet on the other hand wasn't doing so well. Brett had gone ballistic on her, it was by far the worst abuse he'd ever heaped on her. Sandy visited Janet often, she felt that some of the abuse had been from the words she'd used, trying to convince her sister to leave the jerk. Neither Sandy nor Janet had thought he would get as crazy as he did.

Greg had spoken to a lawyer he knew, that would take Janet's case, to try to get Brett put into jail for a significant amount of time. Janet never reporting him before, wouldn't help the case. But Brett had done enough damage both to Janet and the house, that he thought they had a good case. He also told Janet he would make sure the divorce was added into the mix. She did not need grounds to divorce him, but she certainly had them. Washington state had a ninety day 'cooling off' period, but then the divorce would go through.

Sandy had just finished telling Janet that they had raised seven point three million dollars during the fundraiser. Gus was matching that and rounding it up to fifteen million.

Janet had been happy to hear the news, even though she was sorry she couldn't participate, due to Brett being home.

Sandy said, "Well, soon you'll be able to do whatever *you* want to do, whenever *you* want to do it."

Janet smiled, when they were interrupted by a knock on the door. The lawyer had come to the clinic to talk to Janet. Lawyers didn't normally make house calls and especially not from Seattle, so Sandy knew Greg had pulled some major strings.

"Mrs. Grimm, my name is Mr. Franklin Jade, from Williams, Jade and Klout. I've been hired to represent you in the prosecution of your husband for abuse and a few other things. As well as a divorce." He looked from Janet to Sandy. "Is this a good time to talk?"

Janet nodded.

Sandy said, "I can step outside for a while or come back later."

Janet took her hand. "Stay, take notes, so I don't forget."

Sandy looked at the lawyer. "Is that all right?"

Mr. Jade answered, "As long as Mrs. Grimm is willing to speak candidly in front of you. I am going to need specifics to make a strong case against Mr. Grimm."

Janet sat up a little further in the bed, even though it looked like it was painful. "Call me Janet. I'm not keeping his name. This is my sister, Sandy, and she's the person I trust the most, besides my mom and my brother, Terry."

"Very good. Let us proceed then, Janet."

Sandy took notes and helped whenever she could. She'd told what happened when the police had taken Brett in custody, and given names of the people who'd heard his threats.

When the lawyer had left, and her sister had been given a sedative to help with the pain, Sandy walked out of the hospital room and directly to the bathroom, where she threw up. What her sister had gone through at the hands of that bastard had made her sick. She'd forced it down while the lawyer had been there, but...

When there was nothing left in her stomach, she washed her face and then with trembling hands called Greg.

"Hello, beautiful. What can I do for you?"

"G-Greg."

His voice changed in an instant from flirty to concerned. "Sandy, what's wrong?"

"C-Can you come g-get me from the h-hospital. I d-don't think I should drive r-right now."

"I'll be right there. Your brother is with me."

"F-fine. He can come too."

By the time Sandy made it to the door of the hospital both Greg and Terry were rushing in. How they'd made it there and parked before she could get to the door, was beyond her.

She walked straight into Greg's arms. "G-get me out of h-here."

Greg picked her up and quickly walked out the door with Terry following close behind. He got her to the truck, which was Terry's and they all slid in.

Just a few more minutes, she had to hold it together, until she was safe. Greg's house was the closest. "T-Terry take me to G-Greg's house. H-hurry."

GREG LOOKED over Sandy's head to Terry who nodded. Sandy was shaking like a leaf. He was damned glad Terry was driving so he could hold her. Greg was relieved to see Terry was taking this seriously and drove as fast as he could to Greg's house.

His shirt was getting wet as Sandy cried silent tears into

his shoulder. She was shuddering, and her skin was cold. Was she going into shock? They needed to get her where they could tend to her immediately. He grabbed a blanket Terry had in the backseat for hauling furniture and wrapped it around them. She could use his body temperature.

Terry tore up the street and charged into the driveway. Greg handed him the house keys. Terry rushed to the front door and Greg carried Sandy into the house. They laid her on the couch and raised her feet. Terry grabbed blankets out of the bedroom and brought them back. The moving blanket wasn't meant for warmth it was for padding.

"Hot water bottle, bathroom, under the sink."

Terry rushed off.

"Sandy, sweetheart, talk to me."

"I-it was horrible. That b-bastard."

Greg had no idea what she was talking about.

"I d-don't want him in j-jail. I want him dead."

Aw, the light dawned, Brett. She was talking about Brett.

Terry hurried in with a hot water bottle and a glass of water and handed them to Greg. "What happened, Sandy?"

"The lawyer, Mr. J-Jade came to talk to J-Janet. She wanted me to stay while he interviewed her."

Greg could hear the firmness begin to return to her voice and some of the tenseness in his gut started to loosen.

"So, I could take notes, because she's so doped up on pain meds, she was afraid she wouldn't remember. Mr. Jade was very thorough in his questioning."

Greg and Terry realized at the same time what had upset Sandy.

Greg said, "Dammit, and you had to listen."

"Fuck, I wish it had been me," Terry said.

Sandy let out a sound that was half chuckle, half sob. "Terry, you would have gone straight to the j-jail and killed him. Then you'd be the one facing trial."

"Tell us," Terry said.

She nodded, but first Greg handed her the water glass. "Have a few sips."

She drank dutifully and then started relating what she'd heard. When she got done talking, she was exhausted, and both of the men were gray.

Greg said, "You rest here for a few minutes. I'll go make you something to eat."

He tucked her in with a blanket and pillow and nodded to Terry to follow him into the kitchen.

Terry's fists were clenched so tight the knuckles were white.

Greg said, "I think she'll sleep for a few minutes, let's go out on the deck."

Terry nodded and followed Greg out the door. "That fucking bastard. If I'd had even an inkling of what he was doing, I would have dragged her away and beaten the shit out of him. Better yet, follow him out on the road, kill him, and bury his body in the desert. Or—"

"I hear you, buddy. Fuck. Why did she put up with that shit? We all thought he was knocking her around, but… but… I have no words."

Terry stalked back and forth on the deck. "Prison is too good for him. What if he only gets a slap on the wrist? I'll just wait until he gets out and then bury him in the desert."

"I called in Franklin Jade, because he'll do his very best to put that fucker away for as long as possible. Maybe we'll get lucky and someone will take him out in jail."

Terry hung his head. "How are we ever going to act normal around Janet? I want to wrap her in bubble wrap so nothing else can hurt her."

Greg shook his head. "That's probably why she didn't let on. She didn't want anyone to know. She was too ashamed."

"Dammit. You're probably right."

"Time for us to man up and use some of those acting skills she's been using for years." Greg shuddered at the thought of sweet Janet being tormented by that bastard.

Terry said, "Starting now, with Sandy. Let's get some food and more hydration into her."

Greg sighed. "Right. She had to hear it first hand and in all the gory detail. We only got the overview I'm sure."

"Don't remind me."

CHAPTER 34

Janet was released from the clinic a few days later but was in no hurry to return to her home. She was happy to let Sandy assist her with the kids. Since Carol had returned to her own room, they decided to put Janet up in the parlor, they hadn't yet returned the hospital bed, so Janet used it.

Sometimes the kids stayed in there with their mom, and sometimes they stayed in one of the guest rooms or with Sandy or Carol. They were having so much fun swapping between the different adults for sleepovers, and they also loved the little attic room that Carol had remodeled.

Since the summer season was over there were only a few guests. Deborah, the photographer, was staying at least two weeks to be able to capture all the fall foliage in the area. She'd mentioned that she might even decide to remain for Octoberfest and go see how the town of Leavenworth celebrated it. Leavenworth was made to look like a little German village and they did Octoberfest up good. It was only about an hour from the Chelan area, and on the way to Seattle.

Sandy and Carol were talking about breakfast plans for the next week when Janet came into the kitchen.

Sandy said, "I was about to bring you a tray. Are you feeling better?"

Carol pulled out a chair for her daughter to sit with them and went to pour a cup of coffee for her. "Here, sit with us."

Janet eased down onto the chair. "I am feeling better. I need to start getting up and around some. At least to take care of myself and the kids. Plus, I need to start making some decisions about my life."

Carol put the coffee on the table. "You've got time. There's no rush."

"I can't keep mooching off my family forever. I need to get a job and decide what I want to do about the house. I don't want to live there anymore. It's too tainted with bad memories for all of us. We need a new start."

Sandy nodded. "I can understand that. What have you been thinking?"

"I called the lawyer and told him to put into the divorce proceedings that we will sell the house and split the equity. Since we bought it during the recession, it should have some decent value, now that things are looking up here in town."

Carol said, "But that also means that any new property will have gone up in value."

"Yes, I know, but I don't want to buy anything right now. I was thinking I could have Kyle look for a rental. I need some time before I jump into anything long term."

Carol took Janet's hand. "You are welcome to stay here for the next few months. I don't have this place full until November. And even in November we could find you a room."

"Thanks mom, and I will take you up on that for a month or two, but I want to be out and on my own before

November rolls around. Although how quickly the divorce will be final might slow me down some. There is that ninety day waiting period."

Sandy counted it out and realized her sister wouldn't be free from that jerk until mid-November, at the earliest.

Carol said, "I'll sleep better with you in the house, at least until the divorce is final, or he's been sentenced to prison. Preferably both."

Sandy asked, "What are you thinking about a job?"

Janet smiled slyly, "I've been taking online classes. I have a business degree, with a specialization in accounting. The only thing left is the CPA exam and I could take clients."

Sandy was pleasantly surprised to hear this news. "Oh, Janet, that's terrific. You can take clients without a CPA, to do bookkeeping and things like that."

Janet grinned. "I know, and I have done a few things for a couple of people. Nothing big, and it's certainly not a living wage, but I've got a few thousand dollars in a separate savings account."

Carol laughed. "That's my girl."

Janet ducked her head. "The money isn't all from accounting. I've been doing some crafts, too. Brett always said it was foolishness, but people have bought them online."

Carol waved her hand. "Who cares what Brett thinks? What kind of crafts?"

"Trivets. You know how I love them. I started making them for myself. There was one I really liked, and it was so fun to make. I made a half dozen of them and then didn't know what to do with them. I decided to sell them online, just to get them out of the house, so Brett wouldn't get cranky. They sold so fast I was shocked. I wondered if they would sell if I upped the price to more than the cost of materials and shipping. So, I made more and increased the price.

They sold, too. I gradually added different designs and materials, and well, they keep selling so I keep making them."

Sandy gaped at her sister. "That's awesome. You should definitely take some over to Kristen to put in the gallery."

Janet said, "Do you really think so?"

Carol had pulled up the listing Janet had mentioned online. "Oh my, they are gorgeous, absolutely you should take some to Kristen."

Carol turned the phone around to show Sandy. "Oh, yes, dear little sister, those are amazing. How many do you have made up?"

"Maybe ten or fifteen of each design. So, around a hundred."

Sandy was shocked. "At the house?"

Janet shook her head. "No. I got a little storage unit to keep them in. I didn't trust Brett to not destroy them. Just because he could."

Carol beamed at her daughter even as her eyes filled with tears. "So, you got a degree, and have been selling those, and Brett didn't know a thing? I am so proud of you."

"Thanks mom. I was trying to get a nest egg, so I could eventually leave him. I knew you guys would help, but I wanted to do it on my own, as much as I could."

Sandy nodded. "It's good to do things for yourself, but it's good to take help sometimes too."

Carol wiped the tears from her eyes and cleared her throat. "I'll get you some breakfast."

Sandy could hardly wait to tell Greg, she was so proud of her sister. She and Greg had made plans for later tonight. They'd not spent much time together, with Sandy taking care of Janet and her kids. Carol had told Sandy to get out of the house and spend some time with Greg, since it was book club night, she said she and her friends were perfectly capable of handling things. Sandy hadn't argued, and Greg had taken the night off, too.

Now that Janet was up and wanting to take over, Sandy could see that she wasn't needed, and she would have to decide when to head back to Seattle and her life. She wasn't very excited about that prospect.

~

GREG WAS COOKING UP A STORM. Sandy was coming over tonight and he wanted to wow her again. They hadn't spent much time together since Janet and the kids had been at the B&B. They had talked on the phone daily, but that was all. Terry went over every morning supposedly to help around the B&B, but it was mostly to check on his little sister, so Greg had skipped the morning breakfast mooching.

Sandy coming over tonight was kind of spur of the moment, so he hadn't planned as carefully. But he could still whip up a decent meal.

He didn't however have time to get rose petals or Champagne like last time. He did manage to change the sheets on the bed and get out fresh towels for the morning.

He'd decided on Chicken Marsala for dinner tonight, since he had fresh mushrooms. Greg put the food in the oven to stay warm as the doorbell rang. He tossed the oven mitts on the counter and went to answer the door.

Once the door was open all his brain cells leaked out of his ears at the vision of loveliness standing on the porch. Greg was certain his mouth was hanging open and he was drooling.

Sandy raised her eyebrows. "Aren't you going to invite me in?"

He managed to move out of the doorway, but all he could say was "Mrumph."

Sandy walked into the house and twirled. "I take it you like my dress. It's the one I was going to wear the last time you cooked."

Greg knew he had to get his act together, he couldn't just stand around drooling all night. He shook his head like a wet dog. "I think it might take me a few minutes to get my brain working again. You look amazing." He leaned in to give her a kiss. "And you smell amazing, too. Are you trying to kill me?"

"Not at all, only wanted to show you my appreciation for your cooking."

"In that case I will cook, every night, and morning, and lunch time. We could take up the British fashion of afternoon tea. And maybe a midnight snack."

Sandy giggled at his foolishness. "That would make me fat and I wouldn't fit in the dress."

"No worries about that, because I would be happy to also give you plenty of exercise. If you know what I mean." He wagged his brows at her.

Sandy poked him in the stomach and walked toward the kitchen. "You are a silly man, Greg Jones."

Greg rubbed his stomach where she had poked him and muttered, "Not silly. Horny maybe, but not silly."

"I heard that."

He was thrilled to see she was in a joking mood. Greg had been wondering how she was feeling, being with her sister and the kids. He followed her into the kitchen, where she was sniffing the wine he had opened. Since the food already had wine in it, he'd picked a light bodied red wine that was a little fruity.

She held the bottle out for him to fill her a glass. "This is a little different."

"It will go well with the meal. So, you seem to be in a good mood."

"I am. Janet is feeling better and wants to start taking her life back. Oh, and wait until you hear what she told mom and me this morning."

When she was done telling him all about what Janet had said, he could understand her enthusiasm. He was glad to hear Janet had been plotting to escape, and not just accepting her fate at the hands of the monster she was married to.

Except for the fact that if Janet was back on her feet, how much longer would Sandy stay in town. He did not want to think about that. At all.

They had a wonderful dinner, Sandy talked and laughed and neither of them mentioned her leaving.

When they had eaten their fill and were ready to take things to the bedroom. He vowed to himself that he would cherish every moment he had.

It seemed like Sandy had the same idea in mind because their love making took on a kind of frantic note, with each of them trying to wring every bit of pleasure from the other one.

She'd worn underwear that had stolen his breath and made his heart pound. He'd wanted to imprint the vision on his brain to remember for all time. Or maybe keep them as a memento, maybe frame them.

She'd distracted him from those thoughts by taking them off and that was even better. She was so beautiful. He wanted to worship her, but they'd both been too frantic, too needy, to do much more then fall into bed and onto each other.

He craved the feel of her skin against his, it was so soft, and she smelled like heaven with just a touch of sex and sin woven in. It was her own personal scent that he wanted to bottle to keep forever.

They came together in a frenzy once, twice, a third time.

The third time as they lay tangled together, exhausted, slowly relaxing into sleep he'd not been able to stop his mouth from telling her that he loved her and never wanted to let her go.

He'd thought she was awake but when she didn't answer, he'd decided that he'd again missed his opportunity to tell her he loved her. Tomorrow morning, he would tell her, whether she wanted to hear it or not.

CHAPTER 35

She couldn't do it. He couldn't love her.

Sandy eased out of Greg's bed, long before the sun came up.

She hadn't slept, she'd laid perfectly still while Greg had dozed off, and then she'd worried for hours.

Their lives were in different places. They didn't have the same goals.

She quickly gathered her clothes and tiptoed down the hall to the bathroom.

He planned to stay here, and her life was in Seattle. That might work for a casual dating and sex relationship, but it wouldn't work for what Greg was looking for.

Sandy pulled on her clothes and snuck down the stairs to where her purse and shoes were.

He wanted permanence, and a family, and a fricken white picket fence. She didn't have that in her, so she was leaving.

She eased out the door and hurried to her car.

It might be a chicken way to handle it, but so be it.

The damn barge wouldn't be here until almost noon and

she had to get away before he came after her and talked her into staying. So, she'd drive over the mountains.

He'd never think of that.

Sandy drove to her mother's B&B, where she grabbed all her stuff.

Except her new blanket chest, she couldn't fit that in her car.

She'd get Terry to ship it to her.

But before she left, she ran her hands over it and thought about the sweet loving man that had given it to her.

She had to steel her heart to walk away from him. She would hurt him, if she stayed, she wasn't a homebody, she was an engineer and game developer.

Her career was in Seattle, she had to go.

She'd call her family later and say good bye.

Sandy was half way through town before she realized that tears were flowing down her cheeks.

With each mile she drove, she thought more about what she was leaving behind.

Could she do it? Maybe she could develop a new game and go independent, or she could work remotely.

No, she belonged in Seattle, she had friends there.

But really what she had was co-workers. Yes, they were friendly, but they weren't really friends.

She sniffed and grabbed another handful of tissues to wipe her face and eyes, glad she kept a full-sized box in the car. She had a tiny apartment where she might be able to find a spot for her new blanket chest, if she put pillows on top of it and made it a chair.

That was too sad to think about, having people sit on her beautiful chest.

Did she want to go back to that?

No, she really didn't.

But she had to, so she kept driving up past Kristen's house, onto the one lane road.

Did she want to leave Greg? No not at all.

But her job, her apartment, her friends… Meant nothing at all compared to Greg.

Her family was here and real friends. People she'd known all her life.

Not acquaintances, friends, real friends. And Greg.

When she finally got it through her thick head that she wanted to stay, she was on a part of the road that was too narrow to turn around.

Which made the tears flow faster.

Remembering there was a wider spot another mile or so up the road she sped up, to get to it.

As she came around what she thought, hoped, and prayed, might be the last curve before the place she could turn around, she saw a truck sideways in that wider area.

She laughed bitterly when she realized it was Greg. Parked in the middle of the road, so she couldn't get by. She stopped her car and clunked her head on the steering wheel. Greg opened the passenger side door to climb in, but first he had to put all the crap from the seat into the back. Including many tissues wet with tears.

Greg slid in and asked, "Why are you running from me?"

"I have a job and a life to get back to."

"We are—"

She shook her head. "There is no we."

Greg shouted, "There sure as hell is a we!"

Her heart squeezed painfully. "But we live in different places and—"

"That can be fixed. If you need to be in Seattle. I'll move there too."

Sandy was shocked by that statement. "But your bar."

"I'll sell it. Or hire someone to run it."

"But you love it, and you love our town, and everyone loves you."

Greg took her hands and looked into her eyes. "Yes, I do love it. But I love you more. I can work anywhere, but I need you, like I need air. I won't live without you, so just get over that right now. Do you love me?"

Sandy finally had to admit the truth. "Oh Greg, I do love you. I don't think I can live without you either. I was about to turn the car around to come back."

"So, Seattle?"

She'd made up her mind, this man was too important. "No. I can work anywhere. I can work remote on *Adventures with Tsilly* or I can resign and maybe start a new game as an independent. Steve put that idea into—"

Greg pulled her into a kiss that was hot and a bit wild. Silencing everything except her heart soaring with joy, and love for this man, that wasn't going to let her run away. Not now, not ever.

He was hers and she was his, period.

The End

Watch for the next book in this series coming in
March 2019!
Mysterious Ways

NICOLE ROMAN ARRIVES in the small town of Chedwick Washington, where there have been two recent structure fires. She's tracking her brother, Kent, whom she believes has reverted back to his pyromaniac tendencies, after the death of their parents. If the pattern she's seeing is true, her brother is in town and has started the recent fires. Nicole decides to confide her fears at the local church. Scott Davidson, the gorgeous man playing handyman, is really the pastor of the church and a volunteer firefighter.

Scott's first look at Nicole, about brings him to his knees, as lust shoots through his entire body. He's never struggled with lust, and is shocked to realize all his ideas on the subject had never been tested by someone he was truly attracted to. He forcefully pushes these thoughts aside when Nicole confides in him. She needs his help.

He must join together with her to search for her brother. Kent needs to be stopped, but Nicole and Scott have very different reasons for wanting him found.

AFTERWORD

Dear readers,

My books do not normally have such dark happenings as what Sandy's sister, Janet, has gone through with her husband. But it is unfortunately a part of life. I've known several women that have suffered at the hands of men who felt it was within their right to hurt their spouses.

Janet will heal from the abuse and rise from the ashes of her marriage and abuse. She will have her own story later in 2020. Also in 2020 we'll see Terry discover that enemies sometimes make the best lover.

The rest of the issues left open will also be addressed in future books. I didn't want to rush through them. Look for the pyromaniac closure in the next book, Mysterious Ways, coming in March.

Warmest regards,
Shirley Penick

ABOUT THE AUTHOR

About Shirley

What does a geeky math nerd know about writing romance?

That's a darn good question. As a former techy I've done everything from computer programming to international trainer. Prior to college I had lots of different jobs and activities that were so diverse, I was an anomaly.

None of that qualifies me for writing novels. But I have some darn good stories to tell and a lot of imagination.

I have lived in Colorado, Hawaii and currently reside in Washington. Going from two states with 340 days of sun to a state with 340 days of clouds, I had to do something to perk me up. And that's when I started this new adventure called author. Joining the Romance Writers of America and two local chapters, helped me learn the craft quickly and has been a ton of fun.

My family consists of two grown children, their spouses, two adorable grand-daughters, and one grand dog. My favorite activity is playing with my grand-daughters!

When the girls can't play with their amazing grandmother, my interests are reading and writing, yay! I started reading at a young age with the Nancy Drew mysteries and have continued to be an avid reader my whole life. My favorite reading material is romance, but occasionally if other stories creep into my to-be-read pile, I don't kick them out.

Some of the strange jobs I have held are a carnation grower's worker, a trap club puller, a pizza hut waitress, a software engineer, an international trainer, and a business program manager. I took welding, drafting and upholstery in high school, a long time ago, when girls didn't take those classes, so I have an eclectic bunch of knowledge and experience.

And for something really unusual… I once had a raccoon as a pet.

Join with me as I tell my stories, weaving real tidbits from my life in with imaginary ones. You'll have to guess which is which. It will be a hoot!

Made in the USA
Middletown, DE
13 March 2020